CW01638476

Rival CEO

A Shorter Novel

by:
Ainsley St Claire

Copyright 2024 Loisir Publishing

All rights reserved. No part of this publication may be reproduced, distributed or transmitted in any form or by any means, including photocopying, recording or other electronic or mechanical methods, without the prior written permission of the author, except in the case of brief quotations embodied in critical reviews and certain other noncommercial uses permitted by copyright law.

This is a work of fiction. Names, characters, places and incidents are a production of the author's imagination. Locations and public names are sometimes used for atmospheric purposes. Any resemblance to actual people, living or dead, or to businesses, companies, events, institutions or locations is completely coincidental.

Billionaire Secrets: Rival CEO/ Ainsley St Claire—1st edition

one

Justin

The Georgia Tech Hotel and Conference Center buzzes with a kinetic energy that rivals the very technology we're showcasing. Our booth is one among the two hundred that fill the expansive hall in a grid of dreams. We're all praying for good grades and maybe even the right eyes on our project, leading to a sale or the cash to make our plans a reality. Each project is a testament to sleepless nights and relentless ambition. For some students, the stakes are their futures, as their diplomas hinge on today's outcome.

I feel pretty good about my grades, but I'm also looking much farther ahead than graduation. We all are. This project has potential. We just need someone to see that. I glance around at the anxious faces but then narrow my focus back to Austin Sands, Rhys Smalls, and Theo Reed—my roommates, good friends, classmates, and comrades in arms against outdated tech and environmental ruin. We stand shoulder to shoulder beside our creation, a battery that promises revolution, not just evolution, for electric vehicles.

"Looks solid," I murmur, more to myself than my friends. It's a mantra to keep the doubts at bay, a shield against the whispers of *what if*. Our battery sits encased in a clear display, its sleek design a testament to the time it took us to create it. Inside, it has no copper and no lithium, just a sustainable answer to a world thirsty for clean energy.

"Did you see Turner's face when we slotted our battery into his engine?" Theo's voice cuts through my reverie, his grin audible even without turning to look at him. While our project is separate from the engine our friend Turner Bishop has built, we're displaying together. It just makes sense, as his contraption is a perfect demonstration for our battery, and he has to get power from somewhere. Plus, if someone happens to want to invest in both, we'll all be in this together.

"Turner's always cool as a cucumber," I reply, still scanning the crowd. His engine is called The Chess Master, and when he isn't an engineering student, he's the lead singer for a local band that just got a major record deal.

Potential investors roam the floor like sharks, their sharp suits and sharper gazes seeking the two-way street of profit. My heart hammers a rhythm of hope and fear each time someone spends any time at our booth, looking at our model or watching the demonstration video.

"Remember, guys," I say, rallying the troops with a clap on Austin's back, "it's about way more than grades today. It's about making the right connections."

"Speaking of which," Rhys interjects, tilting his chin toward a group of suited individuals working their way down the line of booths with purpose, "looks like we've got company coming. It must be nearly our turn to present on the main stage."

"Showtime," I whisper, straightening my shirt. This is our moment—the culmination of countless hours of soldering connections, programming circuitry, and dreaming bigger than we'd ever dared. We need to make sure our story captivates as much as our technology does.

"Justin," Theo mutters, drumming an anxious rhythm against the tabletop. "You think the charge will hold up when we start her?"

I glance at the video looping beside us—a sleek montage of our battery's creation story, spliced with animations of eco-friendly promises and a future painted green. But behind each frame lies our shared worry about the battery's past failures, how sometimes it still stubbornly refuses to hold a charge. I force a smile, my confidence a mask I'm afraid might crack if anything goes wrong today.

"It'll hold," I say, more prayer than promise. "We've triple-checked everything."

"Triple-checked," Austin echoes, though his eyes don't quite meet mine.

We all have the same fear, yet there's no time for doubt—not now, not with the clock ticking down to our moment in the spotlight. The problem is fixable—it has to be—but we haven't unraveled the answer yet, and things have to keep moving forward anyway.

Sure enough, when the suits arrive at our booth, they direct us to go set up for the main event.

"Hey, check out Mr. Big Shot over there," Rhys says with a nod toward Turner as we gather our things and head out.

Turner is eagerly discussing his engine design with a cluster of interested onlookers. The gleam in his eye speaks volumes; this is where he shines, balancing his mother's expectations that he find a "proper job" with his rock band's burgeoning success.

"Looks like they're into The Chess Master's layout," I comment as I begin our setup, though I stop to watch as one visitor leans in closer to examine Turner's diagrams. Turner's passion is infectious, his gestures painting pictures in the air.

"Good for him," Rhys says, genuine pride in his words. "Guy's been torn up about choosing between the band and engineering."

"He doesn't have to choose if both take off," I muse, hoping for even a single triumph for us. A successful demonstration today could be the first domino in a chain reaction leading to life as entrepreneurs, as innovators...as changemakers.

After a few minutes, Turner joins us backstage, and with careful hands, we install a freshly charged battery into his engine—a sleeping beast on the verge of awakening. The Chess Master waits, silent for now, ready to surge into motion. Will it roar to life? Or will it stutter? Today of all days, it needs to work, and honestly, it could go either way.

"Let's show them what we've got," I say.

Theo nods, determination in his features. "Let's do this," he agrees.

With a shared look, we ready ourselves to step onto the stage and into our future. "Good afternoon," I greet the crowd as the curtain parts, my voice echoing through the speakers. "We're here to introduce something that could redefine electric vehicles." My fingers dance over the tablet, cueing the video we've all but memorized. Onscreen, graphs and charts give way to vivid footage of our creation in action, showcasing our battery's potential.

"Turner Bishop," I continue, with a nod toward my friend, "has designed an engine that can propel a vehicle from zero to sixty in point-three seconds." I let the number hang in the air a moment, a testament to raw power harnessed by sheer ingenuity. "But his project is not just about speed," I add. "It's powered by a new, green sodium battery, an alternative to the conventional lithium-ion batteries that currently dominate the market and decimate the environment."

I sweep my gaze across the crowd, ensuring each attendee is included in this pivotal moment. "Sodium is vastly more abundant. Just consider the ocean's salt content. It's easier to source and gentler on our planet." The words flow, a rehearsed symphony of persuasion, as I extol the virtues of our innovation. "Instead of copper, our design utilizes aluminum, further enhancing environmental sustainability."

The audience's expressions shift from polite interest to piqued curiosity. My teammates exchange glances. We stand united on this precipice, ready to leap into the future we've dared to engineer.

"The components used in today's electric-vehicle lithium-ion battery packs are not only extremely expensive but also potentially hazardous and combustible," I explain. "These materials—lithium, nickel, cobalt, and copper—and the extraction of these scarce resources, the production methods involved, and their eventual disposal are all significant environmental obstacles. Our aim is to change that."

I click the remote, and the massive LED lights behind me flare to life, highlighting Turner's engine with our battery. The crowd leans in as the engine hums. I draw a steadying breath, ready for the climax when, suddenly, the car shudders. A collective gasp sweeps through the room.

My heart plummets. *Dammit.* But then, Turner's cool voice slices through my panic. "An excellent opportunity to demonstrate real-time diagnostics," he says, ever the showman. On the screen, a live feed from the cockpit appears, the battery's vitals pulsing.

"See here," Turner notes confidently, pointing at a graph that dances with data. "Look at The Chess Master EV engine's adaptability. It recalibrates in milliseconds." As if on cue, the car smooths out, purring once more. Relief washes over me like a warm tide. We've weathered this blip. Thanks to Turner, most of those watching won't know whether that was an engine or a battery issue.

The remainder of the presentation goes as planned, and after we return to our booth, we spend the afternoon fielding questions and chatting with people as they inspect our work.

Hours later, the hall has emptied of its crowds yet still buzzes with lingering excitement. That's when she finds me, her press badge glinting under the fluorescent lights. *Engineering Tomorrow* it reads.

Her eyes lock with mine, a hint of playfulness there. "Justin, right?" She tilts her head, her smile professional, though somehow suggestive. "My name is Diana Farley. Tell me more about this groundbreaking battery of yours."

"Of course," I say. "But it's not just mine. Rhys, Austin, and Theo—they're the gears in this machine." I gesture to where they're packing up our booth, laughing good-naturedly together. "We've had long hours and plenty of challenges, but we're driven by the same goal—to create a more sustainable future."

Her pen dances across her notepad, and she asks insightful questions, drilling down to the environmental impact of this sort of shift in the industry. In this moment, it's not about our grade or even potential investors. It's about paving a path forward, together. It would be great to get some publicity from *Engineering Tomorrow* whether our idea is funded or not. That kind of press could open job opportunities for us, in case no one is interested in our battery. But that's tomorrow's challenge.

Eventually, I've exhausted her list of questions, and she shakes my hand and turns to go. My eyes follow as she walks away, until I can no longer see her. "Guys," I start, turning to my friends with a grin that won't fade. "We actually did it."

"Killed it, more like," Austin chimes in, his usually stoic demeanor replaced by a wide smile.

"Professor Allen is waiting outside," Rhys reports, looking at his phone.

We finish packing up and spill out into the cooler evening air, and there he is, our mentor, the man who pushed us when we were ready to give up. Professor Allen approaches with a stride that signals good news.

"Stars of the show, without a doubt," he declares, clapping each of us on the back. His approval sends another wave of pride through me. "Tomorrow's filled up with back-to-back meetings, starting first thing," he continues, his eyes gleaming. "Investors are curious, and they're not just kicking tires. They're looking under the hood."

"Turner…" He turns his gaze to our engine maestro. "You've got two separate appointments for The Chess Master. They want to see what else you've got up your sleeve."

"Thanks, Professor," Turner replies, stifling a yawn.

"Tonight, you should celebrate—but not too hard. Tomorrow, we change the game." Professor Allen gives my shoulder a final pat before disappearing into the night.

Austin nudges me. "The Wicked Wolf?"

"I could use a beer or three," Theo agrees, as if there's any other way to commemorate tonight's victory.

After sending our boxes back to our lab, we find ourselves at a local dive known for its college crowd and cheap beer. The place is filled with students letting off steam after their own battles in classrooms and labs. We grab a round of beer, the plastic cups slick in our hands, a stark contrast to the high-tech equipment we've been handling all day.

"Cheers," Rhys grins, raising his cup.

"Today was an excellent conclusion to our college careers," I say, the weight of the day lifting.

"Tomorrow," Rhys adds, his eyes catching on someone at the end of the bar, "is for our future."

"Entrepreneurs," Theo agrees, the word hanging in the air like a promise.

"Damn straight," Austin confirms, tipping his cup to each of us.

Rhys exchanges a look with the brunette he's spotted, and I suspect he won't be staying long. Sure enough, with a smirk and a mock salute, he slips away from our table, his path set on a new conquest.

I lean back, absorbing the raucous laughter, scattered conversation, the sense of possibility that thrums through the room. It's a heady mix, and there's also the fact that today, we made something incredible happen.

But even that is not nearly enough. "Big day tomorrow," I remind the others, though I know it's at the forefront of their minds as well.

"Big future," Theo corrects, and we drink to that, the taste of cheap beer feeling exactly like a victory toast.

two

Crystal

The neon lights of Atlanta's nightlife blur as I weave through the throng of revelers and into The Wicked Wolf. It's a Georgia Tech hangout with a stage, and I can hear Jackie's laughter even above the noise. The weight of my failed final project is like an anchor around my neck, dragging me into murky depths where numbers and equations swirl mockingly.

"Come on, Crystal!" She tugs at my arm, her face alight with year-end relief and probably too many shots. "This is our night! Three years down, one to go!"

"Sure," I manage, forcing a smile. *Not for me.* My gaze flickers over the sea of faces, all celebrating something, anything—perhaps just life itself. But I'm mourning the death of my academic career, the cold dismissal from my professor still echoing in my skull: "*Your skills are not sufficient.*" His words, veiled in politeness, were laced with the poison of discrimination that's plagued me since I chose a path in this male-dominated field. I shake my head. I can't let that thought take hold now. Not tonight.

"Hey, what are you going to do for the summer?" Jackie's voice cuts through the din, her eyes probing. "Head back to Orlando or stick it out here in the ATL?"

I haven't told her I won't be returning to school. I don't know what to do. I sip the beer the bartender hands me, its bitterness matching my mood. "I don't know." My voice sounds hollow. "Neither option seems great right now."

"Ugh, your mom is such a pain," she says, rolling her eyes. "But you've got options, girl! You could do anything."

Can I though? My confidence has shattered along with my GPA, both casualties of an education system that never quite fit. I wasn't meant for applied mathematics, despite my stubborn attempts to prove otherwise. My heart was never in it, not like Jackie with her physics. Her passion was practically tangible as she swept through her final project. And there seems to be more room for women in physics than in math. Madame Curie, anyone?

"Maybe," I murmur, the word more wish than conviction. I look up at the sky. Atlanta holds memories now tinged with regret while Orlando… Orlando is a cage with gilded bars in the shape of my mother's expectations.

"Let's not think about it tonight," I say quickly before Jackie can press further. "Tonight, we dance, we forget, we pretend the world outside doesn't exist."

"Damn straight!" Jackie whoops, dragging me into the pulsing heart of the crowd where the bass pounds against my chest like a second heartbeat. I lose myself in the music, in the anonymity. Here, I'm not Crystal, the failed math student. Instead, I'm just another body moving to the rhythm, another soul trying to find her place in the frenzy.

But as Jackie twirls under the strobe lights, her grin wild and free, I feel another pang of envy. Her future is bright, illuminated by success and certainty, while mine is a dark road I must navigate without a map. Yet again, I push those thoughts aside and focus on dancing.

The stage is set for Velvet Anomaly, a local band whose lyrics have whispered to me through countless nights of equations and despair. *Maybe I could be a roadie for Velvet Anomaly?* The thought flits through my mind and puts a smile on my face. A butterfly daring to dream before its wings are clipped.

And then, there he is, the man of the hour. Across the bar, Justin Capriotti stands like a beacon in a sea of bodies. He's one part of today's engineering elite, radiating a success that seems wired into his DNA. He's also friends with Turner Bishop, Velvet Anomaly's lead singer, whose voice can strip you bare with a single note.

They're reveling in their glory, basking in the spotlight from today's showcase. Their tech was nothing short of miraculous, sleek and efficient, the kind of innovation that reshapes the world. And here I am, nursing my beer, wishing for that same electric charge in my brain…and the ability to turn math and science into victories instead of setbacks.

A cheer erupts from the crowd as the lights dim, signaling the imminent arrival of the band. I let myself get lost in the surge of excitement, just a fan waiting for my favorite music to take the stage. And who knows? By the end of the night, anything could happen.

After a moment, though, my gaze returns to Justin, now framed by the lights of the impending show. He catches my stare, and there it is, the upward twitch of his lips, a silent acknowledgement that sends a ripple of warmth through me. His dark hair seems to absorb the ambient glow, and those blue eyes sparkle with an intensity that feels like they're fixed solely on me. He's tall, effortlessly standing out among the crowd, and if this is going to be my last college party for a while, I'm going to make the most of it.

The opening chords of Velvet Anomaly's first song shred through the buzz of conversation, throbbing against the walls of The Wicked Wolf. It's a sound I adore—a raw fusion of Trent Reznor's edginess and Harry Styles' velvet croon—and it hooks me instantly, tugging at something primal. Jackie, beside me, matches my excitement. We're both tipsy enough to let go without a second thought, our bodies swaying to the driving beat.

And then he's there. Justin weaves toward me with a predator's grace. The air shifts, charged with electricity as he draws near. His movements are a challenge, daring me to match him beat for beat. So I do. We dance, not quite touching yet utterly entwined, every sway a wordless conversation. When he presses closer, his body against mine in a rhythm that's anything but innocent, I can't suppress the thrill that races up my spine. Dirty dancing with Justin Capriotti—it's reckless and exhilarating, and right now, there's nowhere I'd rather be.

The songs flash by, seemingly in an instant. Justin comes and goes from beside me, though Jackie never strays. We dance and sing and drink and drink, and eventually, the band's final chord resonates through the bar. I'm out of breath, a sheen of perspiration on my skin as the crowd cheers. Jackie catches my eye, her face flushed with exhilaration, and we make our way out of the crowd and to the bar.

"Hey." A voice cuts clearly through the post-concert hum, and I turn to find Justin standing next to me. He has an easy confidence, a half-smile on his face that does peculiar things to my heartbeat. "I'm Justin, and this is Austin," he says, gesturing to his friend.

"Crystal," I reply, trying to sound more composed than I feel.

Jackie offers her name with a chirpy cheerfulness. "I'm starving after all that exercise," she declares, and I agree with a nod.

Something salty and crisp is suddenly appealing. Justin suggests fried pickles, and it's unanimous. When they arrive, we all reach in, the tang of dill and crunch of batter a perfect foil to the lingering beer on my tongue. Women glance at Justin as they pass, and I can't believe he's standing with me.

Jackie and Austin dive into a conversation about their majors, and I listen with half an ear, watching animated expressions flit across their faces. They're in their element, discussing physics and sharing war stories about difficult classes and professors. A pang of regret tries to swallow me as I bite into another pickle, but I push it aside. Tonight's not about what-ifs or might-have-beens; it's about right now.

"Applied mathematics, huh?" Justin asks me, his eyes lighting up.

"Yep," I say and leave it at that. No need to tarnish the night with my failure. The lie sits heavy, but I wash it down with another sip of beer.

As the night winds down, the crowd thins. Jackie and Austin remain deep in debate, their heads bent together. I've just turned back toward him when Justin leans in, his lips finding mine in a kiss that tastes of promise and rebellion. My heart races, my senses sharpening as I kiss him back with equal fervor.

"Come back to my place?" he murmurs, blue eyes searching mine.

"Okay," I breathe, a reckless affirmation.

Jackie waves goodbye as we break away from the crowd, slipping into the cool Atlanta night. Justin laces his fingers with mine. The walk to his house is a blur of anticipation. His hand is warm and certain, and I squeeze, anchoring myself to the moment.

"Here we are," Justin says, pushing open the front door with a flourish. The house is a typical one close to campus. It would be condemned in any other neighborhood in the city.

The door closes behind us with a thud that punctuates the sudden urgency in our movements. I fumble for the hem of his T-shirt. His hands are more skilled, deftly peeling my blouse away, sending it fluttering to the floor.

"Wow," I giggle, breathless, but there's no pause in our frenzied disrobing. I kick off my shoes, and they clatter against the wall. His belt hits the ground. Our pants follow, a trail of crumpled denim carcasses in our wake.

We navigate the hallway, leaving a trail of clothing—a sock here, a shirt there as we make our way to his room.

Inside, we're bathed in the dim glow of a single lamp. The sight of Justin naked sends a jolt through me. He stands before me as if carved from stone, hard planes that are difficult not to run my hands over.

"Justin…" I drink in the sight of him, but words are lost when he pulls me close. I jump up, legs wrapping around his waist.

He lays me down on the bed. "You're so beautiful."

His fingers trace delicate lines of fire along my skin, igniting a hunger deep within me. I arch my back, wordlessly urging him to continue, to explore every inch of me. His touch is electric, sending shivers down my spine and leaving me breathless with anticipation.

A moan slips past my lips as he teases. His fingers slide between my folds and bring me to the edge before retreating. "Please," I whimper, begging him to take me higher, to push me over the precipice.

He gives me what I crave, thrusting his fingers deep inside, stretching me wide as our eyes lock. I gasp, writhing beneath him, lost in the pure pleasure of his touch.

As my climax washes over me, his kiss is warm and hungry, our tongues dueling with a fiery passion. I grip his shoulders, pulling him closer, desperate for the connection.

With a low growl, he pulls away, leaving me panting and wanting more.

The night air from the open window brushes over my heated skin as Justin reaches for the side table, procuring a foil packet with a practiced flick of his fingers. I let out a half-nervous, half-delighted chuckle. "I'm not convinced that's gonna fit," I tease, eyeing him with a mix of jest and genuine concern.

He meets my gaze, a twinkle of humor in his eyes. "Trust me," he replies. "I'll take it slow. We'll be more than fine." His assurance calms me, and I nod, sighing.

Justin slips the condom over his erection and looks at me with a hunger that matches my furious desire. I hardly recognize myself.

"Is this okay?"

I nod. "Yes." You've got to adore a man who asks for consent.

He positions himself at my entrance, his tip pressing gently against my wet, aching core. I whimper as he enters me, inch by slow inch. My body screams for more, craving the sensation of being completely filled. Finally, with a deep, guttural groan, he thrusts forward, burying himself inside me. My back arches, my nails digging into his shoulders as our bodies become one.

Our rhythm builds, and I cling to him, my legs wrapping tighter around his waist, attempting to pull him even deeper. Our movements grow rough and primal, our kisses turning frantic as we lose ourselves in the all-consuming passion between us.

It won't be long before I reach the edge once more. Justin's eyes lock with mine, and he pounds into me harder, faster, my entire body humming with need.

As I teeter on the brink, he thrusts one last time, sending me over the edge. My body convulses around him as I climax, moaning his name like a prayer. He grips my hips, steady and strong, pulling me closer with each surge of his body. The pleasure washes over me, a tidal wave of pure ecstasy that leaves me breathless and spent. His eyes never leave mine as he pants, riding out his own release.

As our bodies still, our hearts pound in sync, our breaths mingling with the scent of sweat and desire that fills the room. He pulls out slowly and helps me to rest on my side, our bodies still entwined. I stroke his cheek with my fingers, and he smiles softly, seeming content.

"That was…incredible," I whisper.

He nods, his eyes soft. "I've never felt anything like that before. You… You're incredible."

Despite the day's turmoil, the world outside fades away, replaced by the warmth of his touch and the afterglow of our shared passion. In this moment, there is nothing else that matters.

I sigh contentedly. Lying here, spent and panting, I'm smitten beyond reason.

three

Justin

Pounding on my bedroom door rips me from sleep, and I'm disoriented, the memory of last night at The Wicked Wolf still clouding my mind.

"We need to go," Rhys yells through the door. The room spins slightly as I sit up. The girl—Crissy? Christa? Crystal?—is still snuggled against me, her breathing deep and even in the quiet of the morning light.

"Hey," I mutter, nudging her gently. Her eyelashes flutter, but she doesn't wake. "I've gotta go meet with some people this morning." I watch her for a second longer, her features soft and unfamiliar in the daylight. "Stay as long as you want."

Slipping from the warm tangle of sheets, I steady myself and make my way to the shower. The cold splash of water sharpens my senses, washing away the remnants of last night's overindulgence. I dress quickly, pulling on khaki pants and a blue and white striped Polo button down, the fabric crisp against my skin. Ready—or as ready as I'll ever be—I grab my phone and wallet, stepping out into the fresh promise of the day.

The spring sun is just beginning to climb higher in the sky. My friends are waiting for me downstairs, bleary-eyed and grinning despite their hangovers. Theo claps me on the back, his chuckle low and knowing as he looks over at Rhys, who has reappeared after his early departure last night. "Looks like someone had a good time."

Rhys smirks. "She was a very happy woman. I lost count at five." He elbows Austin, who rolls his eyes but can't suppress a smile. It seems Austin got lucky with his friend at the bar last night. I wonder if he realizes the girl she was with is still upstairs in my bed. I'm not about to bring that up now. It's all good.

"Guess we all have our talents," Austin quips, and there's a round of laughter that shakes off the last of our sleepiness.

We shuffle down the street to McDonald's, the familiar smell of coffee and fast food the solution to our aching heads. I order an Egg McMuffin and the biggest coffee they have, and as we eat, the conversation turns to today's agenda. Our shared anticipation crackles in the air.

"Six venture capital companies," Rhys says, shaking his head. "Can you believe it?"

"Today could change everything," Theo adds, his gaze meeting mine.

"Let's show them what we've got," I agree.

We finish our breakfast, and the caffeine is beginning to clear the fog in my brain. We toss our trash and head out, our strides syncing up as we walk toward the future, whatever it may hold.

"First thing I'm doing," I announce, "is getting my mom something nice. Maybe a vacation. She's never really traveled." My mom raised my brother and sister and me with more love than resources.

"House for my mom." Theo nods. "She deserves that much."

"Man, I'm going straight for a Ferrari." Rhys chuckles.

"I'll take one of everything," Austin declares, and laughter bubbles up among us.

We sober quickly, though, as the weight of the day presses down. When we arrive back at the convention center, we sit down on some benches outside to get our act together. The business plan sprawls across our laps, my copy riddled with annotations and dog-eared corners.

"Okay, let's get our story straight on the charge issue," I suggest, and we huddle closer, heads bowed over the diagrams and charts like generals over a battlefield map. "We've buried the inconsistent-charging detail here, so let's try to leave it that way. I'm hoping it will go unnoticed until we have a more solid solution." I look up to get their feeling on that, and they all nod.

"Makes sense, but temperature regulation has to be the crux." Of course, Rhys can't let this go. He taps a finger on the graph that shows overheating metrics.

"Right." I nod. "But we're going to have a solid workaround with the new cooling-system design. We'll just need to communicate how it's scalable—eventually. Not today."

"Scalability's fine, but what about charging speed?" Austin interjects, always the one to poke holes, ensuring we're airtight.

"Working on that," I say, undeterred. "If we can integrate the supercapacitor tech, we're golden."

"But let's set that aside for now," Theo adds, the strategist among us, looking at the bigger picture. "Today, we need to help them see the vision, feel the potential."

"Exactly," I affirm. "It's not just about solving the problem. It's about revolutionizing the game."

We run through possible questions until the remaining challenges ahead seem smooth enough that our future funder may not even notice.

"All right, we're ready," I declare.

"Let's do this," Theo says as we rise from the bench and collect our things.

We're silent, and my nerves crackle as we step into the lobby. Purpose propels us through the familiar space and back to the convention center. What was an open hall full of displays yesterday has now been sectioned into rooms, each one numbered and with a series of chairs outside the doors. Inside the rooms, sound machines whirr and fans buzz, a cacophony of white noise designed to keep prying ears at bay. The corridors are filled with classmates, who are all here to do the same thing—to make tomorrow brighter.

"Looks pretty serious," Theo murmurs beside me, his gaze sweeping across the area.

"Like they're guarding state secrets," Rhys adds with a wry grin.

"Only their futures," I reply, trying to keep my tone light.

Before we can speculate further, we reach the table with a giant banner that says *Check In*. "Gentlemen, welcome." Dr. Allen greets us with a smile. "It's good to see you. You have quite the busy day. Congratulations."

My chest is bursting with pride.

"Your hostess today is Kimberly Davis," he continues. "She'll move you from one appointment to the next. Anything you need, she's here to assist."

A shapely brunette steps forward. "Nice to meet you."

Austin stuffs his hands in his pockets, his shy charm turned up to full wattage. "Well, if all our needs are met with such grace, we're in excellent hands," he quips, earning a polite laugh from Kimberly and collective eye rolls from the rest of us.

"Ever the ladies' man," Theo teases under his breath.

Kimberly, seeming unfazed, leads us ahead and opens the door to our first meeting. "This is Indria Singh," she says as we enter the makeshift room.

A woman in a sharp business suit rises to shake our hands. "Welcome," she says, her voice firm yet inviting. "Let's talk about your vision."

I extend our business plan to her. "Thank you, Ms. Singh," I say as she takes it.

She looks it over for just a few moments. "Your battery technology—" she begins.

"—is groundbreaking," I finish, conviction bolstered by the nods of my partners. "And we have solutions for the challenges we face."

"Excellent," she responds, jotting a note. Then her questions begin in earnest, but our carefully rehearsed answers seem up to the task.

Our time with Indria Singh concludes with a firm handshake and a promise of consideration, with the caveat that it would require a move to India. That's a big move. We exit, with only a moment to exchange hopeful glances before we meet the next venture capitalist. Kimberly has us hustling down the hall to our next designated room.

"Good job, guys," Rhys whispers, a hint of excitement breaking through his usually nonchalant demeanor.

"Stay focused," I remind them. "We've got more ground to cover."

Then we're filing into the next space and doing our song and dance all over again. Mostly with similar results. Our answers are ready for the questions we receive, and the potential investors seem largely convinced. And so, the day unfolds. One by one, Kimberly guides us to our appointments. We share our vision, distribute our plans, and field their questions. Some investors nod along, clearly seeing the potential; others probe deeper, challenging us to defend every aspect of our proposal. With each encounter, my confidence rises. I know we're going to see success today.

"Five down, one to go," Theo says as we exit the second-to-last compartment.

"Still standing," I affirm, the image of my mother's proud face spurring me onward. Her unwavering support steadies my resolve. This isn't just for us. It's for those who believed when there was nothing to see.

"Next one's going to be even better," Austin declares, already angling toward the next door, the next chance to make our mark.

Kimberly leads us into the final room for our last pitch of the day. "I'd like to introduce you to Mason Sullivan and Dillon Healy, two of the founders of SHN in San Francisco. They've successfully launched over five hundred startups, including

Lancaster Holdings, Firefly, Honeycomb Games, and PayFriend."

We settle around the table and face these men in their bespoke casual wear, the embodiment of venture-capital prestige.

"Mr. Sullivan, Mr. Healy," I begin, extending my hand in greeting. They return the gesture, their handshakes firm.

Dillon, his gaze sharp, flips through our business plan with an analytical precision that sets my nerves on edge. "Tell me," he says without looking up, "how do you plan to address the battery-charging issue?"

His question stops me cold. He's the first to ask this. We'd done so well today with having it go unnoticed. My pulse quickens as I exchange a look with the team. We've rehearsed for everything—except this.

Mason leans back in his chair, the ghost of a smile on his lips. "We noticed the time of day changes quite drastically during your looped demo," he adds, his tone casual yet loaded with implications.

Austin clears his throat. "Our current plan involves—" But before he can outline our strategy, Mason raises a hand, stopping him.

"We're not sure your current plan will work," Mason says, his voice calm but authoritative. "It's likely been tried before. What else could you come up with?" There's no malice in his smile, just the confidence of a man who has seen many come and go in this industry.

A momentary silence falls over the room as the weight of his statement sinks in. It's a blow, but not a knockout. I'm working to regroup mentally when Mason continues, redirecting the conversation.

"However," he says, making eye contact with each of us, "if we choose to invest and reach a mutual agreement, our involvement would extend beyond funding." He then lays out a future in which SHN would put our project in their incubator, paying us small salaries as we work toward finalizing our battery. They would shoulder the administrative burdens—

recruiting, handling accounts receivable and payables—freeing us to focus solely on perfecting our product.

It's very different from what I know we envisioned, yet it echoes the collaborative spirit we've fostered within our own team. But at the same time, they're not giving us money outright. I'm not sure what to think.

"We want innovators like you to do what they do best—innovate," Mason concludes.

We exchange looks, and I can see a silent consensus forming between us. The guys are open to this, just as I think I am. This is an opportunity, and SHN seems truly invested in our success.

"Thank you, Mr. Sullivan, Mr. Healy," I say with a nod. "Your feedback is invaluable, and we hope to have the chance to work together."

We shake hands once more, and I can feel excitement and anticipation brewing within me. When the door closes behind us, Professor Allen is waiting. "Well?"

I shrug. "It's hard to say. We think we did well, and I think there's some real potential, but no one has fully committed yet. It will all come down to whether someone actually wants to invest."

He nods. "My team will collect the offers and go through each of them with your IP attorney. Let's meet tomorrow morning and see where things lie. Then we can figure out your plan."

"Thanks, Professor," Rhys says.

The heavy door of the convention center swings shut behind us, and a wave of relief washes over me as we step into the bright Atlanta sunlight.

"Who's hungry?" Austin asks.

"Those box lunches were not enough," I declare. "Beer and burgers on me." I lead the way back across the street to The Wicked Wolf, where the scent of hops and grilled meat greets us like an old friend, promising a brief respite before tomorrow's verdict.

We slide into a booth after a quick stop at the bar and look at each other with wondering eyes, finally able to speak freely. "Cheers to hopefully not having our dreams crushed," Rhys quips, raising his glass with a wry smile. We all touch glasses, the clink resonating.

"I think we did well," I assure them. "Something is bound to work out, right?"

"Staying in Atlanta would be perfect," Theo muses, taking a swig of his beer. And we did meet with a locally based funder. "But Austin, Texas, showed a lot of interest."

"True, and that might be workable, but India feels too far out there," I add, shaking my head. I'm not sure it's even on the table for us. Our roots are here, our lives, our vision.

A little while later, as we tear into our burgers, the conversation pivots to SHN. "They zeroed in on the battery issue like they knew it before we opened our mouths," I say, still impressed by Mason Sullivan and Dillon Healy's acumen.

"Working with them would be next level. They've navigated these waters before," Theo agrees, ketchup smearing at the corner of his mouth.

Austin, usually the most buoyant among us, wears a frown that starts unease brewing in my gut. "I'm just worried," he confesses, pushing fries around with his fork. "Like they said, what if my plan's already been done? What if I'm out of ideas?"

"Hey," I interject. "You're the ideas guy. You'll think of something new. You always do. That's what they'll be paying us for. We'll work together." But despite my encouraging words, he doesn't seem convinced.

And maybe the others aren't either. "SHN seemed like they'd be willing to problem solve," Rhys says, leaning back with a sigh. "But let's face it, guys, they might not bite. They've seen it all before."

We nod, and the table falls silent. There's nothing we can say to that.

Once our bellies are full, the exhaustion of the day creeps in, and soon, we're all a little brain dead. We call it an early night and walk back to our house, though I wonder how well any of us will sleep as we anticipate the news of tomorrow.

I shuffle up to the house and open the front door. The others trail in behind me, but I'm drawn to my bed. Last night was what I needed, but after the adrenaline rush of today, I'm worn out.

Yet when I reach my room, I find my companion from last evening still there. My eyes widen, even as I do my best to hide my shock. "Hey," I whisper, and she stirs, a sleepy smile curving her lips.

"You said I was free to go when I was ready, but I thought maybe we could enjoy another night."

My heart beats faster as my mind whirs. I can't make sense of this, but I also can't resist it. "I'm cool with that," I say as I join her in bed.

Morning light creeps in, too soon, too bright. A phone is ringing relentlessly. *My phone,* I realize as my brain comes back online. Reluctantly, I disentangle from my Wicked Wolf friend's embrace and grab the insistent device. "Hello?"

"Justin, it's Professor Allen." His voice is a crackle of energy over the line.

"Let me get the guys."

I pull on my boxers and walk out to the living room. They guys are all there, in various states of dress and eating breakfast. "We're all here." I stretch the sleep from my limbs and place my phone on the coffee table, hitting the speaker button.

"You boys better sit down for this," our professor says.

Heart hammering, I look around at each of them. They've all come to attention.

"Four of the six companies have come forward with offers," Professor Allen says, and the room erupts. "That's more than anyone else received."

Fists pump the air, and we're a tangle of back-slapping euphoria. But even as we revel, I know the real work is just beginning. Soon, we'll be poring over details with Professor Allen and the IP lawyer he insisted we hire—our futures distilled into legalese and percentages.

"I'll be here in my office when you can get here," our professor says when we've quieted enough to hear him. "We have a lot to go over."

Rhys jumps up. "We're on our way."

"We'll get dressed and be right over," Theo says.

Austin turns and points at Theo. "Yes. I'll get dressed first," he says.

Seems like we were loud enough that my bed companion should be awake, but her eyes remained closed when I slip back into my room. I change quickly and leave a note for her, letting her know I'm not sure when I'll be back. I really need to get her name. Does she not have any other place to go?

I can't think about that now, though, and I return to the living room to meet the guys. We race over to campus and the engineering department.

Professor Allen is in his office when we arrive, and he leads us down the hall to a conference room. There, I shift in my chair, the leather creaking. Professor Allen stands at the head of the table, papers fanned out like a hand of cards he's about to reveal. His eyes meet mine, and then he lays it all out.

"Three million for forty-percent equity from the VC in Austin, Texas," he begins, his voice even, betraying none of his opinions on the matter. "And they'd be potentially open to more later."

My stomach tightens. That's a hefty slice of the company pie—far heftier than we were aiming to give away. The "*open to more later*" dangles in the air like a double-edged promise.

Beside me, I can sense Theo's uneasiness, his foot tapping a silent but frantic rhythm against the floor. Rhys runs a hand through his hair, a telltale sign of his stress, while Austin sits stone-faced, analysis flickering behind his eyes.

Our lawyer, a woman with sharp features and sharper intellect, leans forward. "Keep in mind that *more* implies further dilution of your ownership. They'll want an even bigger piece of the pie if they inject additional capital."

My fingers drum on the tabletop, reality settling around

us like a cold fog. This offer is a gamble, one that could pay off or leave us choked out of our own vision. We've dreamed big, but here we are, facing the stark numbers that could tether us.

"Let's move on," Allen suggests, flipping to the next page. "Eight million for thirty percent from the local VC."

A collective breath is sucked in by four sets of lungs. This is more money, less equity. On paper, it shines brighter, but the gleam doesn't reach our guts.

The lawyer stands. "However, you need to be wary of the poison-pill clause embedded in their contract. It's been making headlines—and none of them good. There was a case in San Francisco not long ago where the founders of Quick Reels were pushed out under false pretenses. It took them a decade to get justice, and they never got the money. You'd be wise to consider this path only as a last resort."

I can feel myself nodding. *Poison pill.* The term alone sends a shiver down my spine. We're not just playing with numbers; we're dancing with control, with the future of what we've built. I know the case. She doesn't have to push me hard to look past this one. "Let's weigh our options carefully," I tell my friends. "We knew it wouldn't be easy to let go of part of what we've created, but we need these investments to grow. We can do this. We just have to be smart."

The air in the room is static, charged with anticipation as we wait for the next offer. This one has an AV component, and a Silicon Valley investor appears on the screen. "We're prepared to offer two million for five percent of your business," he says. "Angel funding," he adds, with a hint of pride. "But there will be more if you hit the steep deliverables we set." The possibility dangles before us like a carrot—more money, more growth, a brighter future.

Our lawyer, ever the voice of reason, pauses the video and interjects with a note of caution. "If you walk away from the work, they hold the right to take it elsewhere. You could end up with nothing." Her words land like a punch to the gut. I look around at my friends, seeing my fear reflected in their eyes.

We thought we knew the stakes, but this… This is a whole

new level of risk. Yet isn't that what we signed up for? We're in the business of innovation, betting on the edge of tomorrow.

Then comes the final offer, and with it, a surge of relief so strong I feel it in my bones. *SHN. San Francisco. Incubator*. These words spell out an entirely different kind of future, one where we're not just scrappy entrepreneurs but part of something bigger.

"SHN will start you off with minimal paychecks for three-percent equity," our lawyer reads from the contract. "They'll support your work as you resolve your battery's charge-retention issue, and they will fund your payroll and costs at the office. It's like a line of credit. And as your company grows, so will your expenses and their equity. Right now, they're offering up to $120 million for forty-nine percent." Her eyes meet mine, serious and unflinching. "But hopefully you won't need them that much."

When we nod, she continues. "Also, this deal demands exclusivity. Accept their money, and you're shutting the door on any other venture capital."

I absorb her words, their weight settling in my chest. This isn't just another step; it's a leap into a vast unknown. We'll have to relocate across the country.

San Francisco. A city of dreamers, of innovators, where our idea might just find the legs to run. SHN is offering us not just a chance to succeed, but to soar. The risks are monumental, but so are the rewards.

"Thank you," I say to the lawyer, my voice steady despite the turmoil inside. I look around at my partners, at these brilliant minds who've become my family. Now, it's time to choose our next horizon.

She packs up her things, and we thank Professor Allen. He urges us to think about how we plan to divide the company among ourselves and to consider any other stakeholders who might be entitled to a portion as well as what a funder might want. I nod, but at this point, it all just feels overwhelming. I can't absorb any more information. The guys and I need to discuss our options privately. It seems obvious to me what we should do, but I'm not sure everyone feels the same way.

We walk single file out of the room, agreeing that we'll let Professor Allen and the intellectual property attorney know our decision as soon as possible.

We walk outside into the late-morning sunshine.

"SHN's offer is massive," Austin says, his voice tinged with awe, "but they're going to be all up in our tech, man."

Theo's brow is furrowed. "And what if they play us off each other? Divide and conquer?"

Rhys joins in, and their words spiral toward fever pitch. The group teeters on the edge of despair, ready to tumble into the pit of fear that entrepreneurship often disguises as caution.

"Guys, hold up," I interject, halting mid-stride. They turn to me, their faces mirroring my internal conflict. "We're spinning out. Let's just…look at something."

I fish out my phone, fingers tapping with purpose until SHN's website gleams from the screen. We huddle close as I navigate to a page boldly titled *Success Stories*. A list of companies unfolds before us, names synonymous with achievement and innovation, legends of Silicon Valley that once stood where we are now. Today, they're some of the largest companies in the Bay Area.

"Look at this," I breathe. They fall silent as they take in the logos, the testimonials, the undeniable proof of SHN's influence.

"Damn," Rhys murmurs.

The lawyer's words echo in my mind. Her approval of SHN is a solid anchor amidst the storm of options. It's more than just money. It's mentorship. It's networking. It's a fast-track to becoming a name that others will one day read on this very page.

"Right?" I say, locking eyes with each of the guys in turn. "They know what they're doing. They've built empires."

Our initial rush of panic gradually subsides, replaced by a dawning realization that with SHN, our vision has it's best chance of becoming a reality. It's a leap of faith, but isn't that what brought us together in the first place?

"San Francisco," Theo says, almost dreamily, putting his hands in his pockets and turning toward the horizon. "That could be us."

four

Justin

I adjust the collar of my shirt, a nervous habit that's become more pronounced today. Crystal hovers by the apartment door, fidgeting with the strap of her purse. We've been together nearly nonstop the last two weeks. Thankfully, when Theo introduced himself a couple days in, I got her name. And she's been great through the mess of the investors and the final days of school. She's a calming, steady force, and somehow just what I needed. Evidently, her roommate situation isn't great, so she's just as happy to hang at my place as anywhere else.

Now, it's graduation day eve at Georgia Tech, and I'm practically giddy with anticipation of all that lies ahead. Last night, after a marathon sex session, I suggested Crystal join us when we move to San Francisco. She shocked me by saying she'd love to come. I'm not sure how I'm going to tell the guys, but it's not like she's going to live with us. She'll find a job out there and a place to live.

"Will your dad and stepmom make it to dinner tonight? Or just your mom?" Crystal's voice trembles slightly, betraying her anxiety.

Crystal is aware of my family dynamics. My mother is amazing, always showing love and support, while my father is a narcissist. In middle school, my mom left my dad and moved down to Denver to make a new life for herself. She took my brother and sister with her, but I opted to stay behind. Not long ago, she remarried a great guy. She's happy.

On the other hand, my dad is the complete opposite. He's a highly respected professor at Colorado State University who puts his students and work above everything else. It seems to me that his work, his students, his research, and even his golf game come before his own family. He's now had two more failed marriages with former students and is currently on his fourth wife. I can understand why Crystal is apprehensive.

I shake my head. "No, they're flying out first thing in the morning. Dad's got graduation duties as chair of the political science department at Colorado State, but he'll be here in time for graduation." She nods, but I'm not sure if that information has made her feel better or worse. "Hey," I say, stepping closer and cupping her cheek. "They're going to love you. Just be yourself and don't stress, okay?"

She offers a tentative smile, and I nod, hoping my confidence is contagious.

The drive to the restaurant is quiet, save for the hum of tires on asphalt and the evening traffic. When we arrive, my mother spots us first.

"Justin!" She opens her arms wide, and I step into her embrace, smelling the familiar scent of jasmine on her scarf. Her smile is broad, genuine, and I mirror it.

"Mom…" I greet her warmly, then turn to introduce Crystal. "This is Crystal Brown."

"It's so lovely to meet you," my mom says, pulling Crystal into a hug. "I'm Gina Aldo-Capriotti."

Crystal's initial stiffness melts away in the warmth of my mother's welcome. Beside her, Graham Hitchcock, my stepfather, extends his hand with a cordial grin he reserves for moments of true joy.

"Crystal, so glad to meet you," he says.

She shakes his hand. "Likewise, Mr. Hitchcock."

"Please, call me Graham."

My brother, Brandon, pops over, his eighteen-year-old energy barely contained. "Hey, Justin. Hey, you must be Crystal." He gives her a playful nudge, and I see her mouth twitch.

"Nice to meet you, Brandon."

"Call me Bran. Everyone does."

My sister, Patrice, ever the observant sixteen-year-old, hangs back slightly before approaching. Her gaze flits between Crystal and me. Then, as if making up her mind, she steps forward, offering a shy smile. "Remember, you picked Justin, and we're a package deal," she teases.

Crystal laughs, the sound light and airy. "Thanks, Patrice. I think I'm ready for it."

We settle into our seats, laughter and conversation flowing easily around the table. Crystal's smiles grow more frequent, her laughter more heartfelt. As I watch her with my family, embraced by their acceptance and cheer, a deep contentment settles within me. I'm taking a lot of risks right now, and everything is about to be totally new. But I'm excited that she's coming with us to San Francisco, as that will be something that stays the same. We'll already know each other when we get there. And hanging out with Crystal is just easy. She's fun, but also steady, and I need more of that in my life, right?

The server appears nearby, ready to take our orders. Graham, with the authority of a seasoned lawyer, waves his hand grandly, setting the tone for the evening. "Order whatever you'd like, folks," he announces with a generous smile. "Tonight's on me."

With those instructions, I order a ribeye, medium-rare, just how I like it, and Crystal asks for a petite filet mignon.

As we wait for our food, Graham dives into tales of his law firm's latest cases in Denver. His words are a steady stream, punctuated by the occasional emphatic gesture. Meanwhile, Mom shares updates about her consulting company, her voice ringing with pride and ambition.

It's Brandon who finally shifts gears, tossing a bombshell into the mix like a teenager dropping his backpack at the door. "Anyway, I've decided on CU for fall," he says, eyes glinting with mischief.

There's a beat of silence before Graham chuckles and shakes his head.

"Enzo's going to love that," I quip, referring to our dad. "Paying tuition when you could have gone to CSU for free."

"Freedom has its price," Brandon retorts, grinning.

Patrice rolls her eyes, clearly unimpressed with our brotherly banter. "Lucky you," she mutters. "At least you get to leave the house. I'm stuck being the last Capriotti kid at home."

After the laughter settles, I choose the moment to drop my own news. "Speaking of leaving," I start, "Crystal will be joining me in San Francisco."

Surprise flickers across my family's faces, quickly replaced by smiles and congratulatory cheers. Glasses clink and Crystal beams, swept up again in their warmth.

Gina leans forward to address Crystal directly. "Do you have a job lined up in San Francisco?"

"I've put my resume out to a few companies already," Crystal replies coolly, tucking a stray lock of golden hair behind her ear.

"And what's your degree in?" my mother follows up.

"Applied mathematics," Crystal says. There's a slight hitch in her voice, but nobody else seems to notice. It's subtle, but it speaks volumes to me. She's stepping away from her studies to be with me.

The table erupts into another round of cheers and well-wishes, the air buzzing with the excitement of what lies ahead.

"Here's to new beginnings," Graham toasts, lifting his glass high.

"New beginnings," we echo, and as the glass touches my lips, I know this is more than a toast. It's a promise of the future, one that Crystal and I are about to embark on together.

The next morning, the sun shines through the grand windows of McCamish Pavilion, casting long shadows across rows of seats that buzz with the gathering crowd. Crystal's hand finds mine, her grip reassuring as we navigate the throngs of graduates and guests congregated for Georgia Tech's commencement ceremony.

"Ready to meet my dad and Thea?" I ask, feeling her tension in the slight tremble of her fingers. She did great last night, but that doesn't seem to have made her feel any more confident about today.

She gives me an apprehensive smile, nodding. "As ready as I'll ever be," she says, but there's a spark of determination in her eyes that tells me she's braver than she lets on.

We find Enzo Capriotti, my father, and his wife, Thea Sheridan, seated practically as far as possible from where my mother and Graham will be, an ocean of unfamiliar faces between them. Dad's expression is unreadable as he stands to greet us, his eyes flickering to Crystal before settling on me. Thea, ever the peacemaker, wears a warm smile that eases some of the tension.

"Congratulations, Justin," Dad says, his voice lacking the enthusiasm one might expect.

"Thank you, Dad. This is Crystal."

She extends her hand with practiced grace. "It's a pleasure to meet you both," she says.

"Likewise," Thea responds, her kindness genuine as she pulls Crystal into a light hug.

I look around, and suddenly, it's time. "Looks like I need to line up."

Crystal squeezes my hand, and Dad nods. "We'll meet you following the ceremony."

Thea invites Crystal to remain with them, and I leave her as Thea urges Dad to take notes on how they might improve the graduation ceremonies at his university.

I find my place in line, and we enter to "Pomp and Circumstance."

We take our seats, and I exchange a quick glance with Theo, who sits beside Austin, Rhys, and Turner. But there's no time for words as the chatter around us fades and the ceremony begins.

Midway through the event, the lights dim, and a slideshow appears on the screen, illuminating the pavilion with images of hard work and innovation. When our project appears, the funding we've secured highlighted, a ripple of applause and backslapping ensues. It's surreal—our success projected for everyone to see, validating years of dedication.

There's a tap on my shoulder, and I turn to see my friends grinning broadly. "Couldn't have done it without you," I tell them, acknowledging the truth we all know. Our bond is as strong as the project we've built.

Amidst all the clapping and congratulations, I exhale, only then realizing I've been holding my breath. Today isn't just about diplomas and accolades and family interactions; it's about our future, ripe with possibility, and the friends who will be in my life forever.

As the ceremony draws to a close, I think of Crystal in the crowd. No matter where life takes us, we're in it together now. I feel ready to face the challenges and triumphs.

With diplomas in hand, we stride across the stage to a crescendo of cheers. Flashbulbs pop and cameras click, capturing our grins. Then we're herded for group photos, five guys bonded by late nights and relentless ambition and projects that complement one another perfectly.

"Justin!" I hear Crystal's voice before I see her, and then she's there, her arms flung around me. I spin her, and her laughter mingles with the applause still ringing in my ears.

"Congrats, genius," she says, her eyes sparkling.

"Thanks so much for your support," I reply, my heart swelling with gratitude.

Mom appears, camera in hand, and ushers us into position for yet another picture. "Big smiles, everyone!"

We comply, Crystal fitting into the group as if she's always been part of it. After a few more snaps and poses, Mom pulls me aside, her expression softening.

"Justin, I really like Crystal," she murmurs, brushing a stray lock of hair from my face. "But remember, life is going to change rapidly now. You're young, and the path you're on. It's going to be demanding."

I nod. She speaks from experience, from a place of love and perhaps a tinge of regret.

"Make sure you invest time in your relationship, too," she continues. "Balancing everything won't be easy."

"I know. I will," I promise, though the enormity of what lies ahead is just beginning to dawn on me.

Later, at our house, the graduation celebration unfolds. The backyard teems with guests, laughter floats through the air, and the tap of the keg hisses rhythmically as cup after cup is filled with frothy beer. Tables overflow with food, a feast fit for the hungry horde of celebrants.

Our families began the afternoon with us, but as the evening crept on and more of our friends arrived, they've headed back to their hotels.

"Here's to new beginnings!" I raise my cup.

"New beginnings!" the crowd choruses back.

The night unfolds in a blur of congratulations, shared stories, and raucous toasts. I steal glances at Crystal, her presence a grounding force. Mom's words echo in my mind; I need to make time for her and for us.

I weave through the clusters of people, each step taking me closer to Turner, who's practically holding court near the keg. His charisma is magnetic, drawing in admirers like moths to a flame.

"Turner, you superstar!" a girl from our mechanics class giggles, fluttering her eyelashes as she hands him a Sharpie. "Can I have your autograph?"

"Only if you promise not to sell it on eBay," he jokes, scrawling his name with a flourish across the back of her graduation program.

I chuckle. Turner always did know how to command an audience. "Seems like you've got quite the fan club," I say, bumping his shoulder as I join the circle.

"Justin, my man," he replies. "It's all in good fun. Who knew being nerds would make us this popular? Why am I wasting my time with music?"

"Guess it comes with being brilliant," I tease, and we share a laugh that's more like a victory cry.

Eventually, the last guests trickle away, and Crystal and I slip quietly into the sanctuary of my room. The soft rustle of fabric against fabric fills the space as we crawl into bed.

"Any second thoughts about heading to San Francisco with me?" I ask, watching her face for any hint of hesitation.

"None," Crystal murmurs, her eyes meeting mine. She nestles close, and I wrap my arms around her. Her breathing slows, and soon, she's asleep.

And that settles it. Whatever we are, whatever we become, we'll discover it together in San Francisco.

five

Crystal

I grip the zipper, a final tug sealing away the last remnants of my life here as my suitcase zips closed. The last two days have been a whirl of packing up my life and helping Justin do the same. I look over the barren walls of my room, once plastered with posters and Polaroids. I'm ready—or at least I tell myself I am.

"Crystal," Jackie's voice cuts through the silence. "You're really going to do this? Throw it all away for some guy?" Her accusation hangs heavy between us.

I can't meet her eyes. Not when they reflect a truth I'm not ready to face. "Jackie, it's not just about him," I lie smoothly, more for myself than for her. The words come out rehearsed; I've been convincing myself of them for weeks. "I hate it here. School's been wrong for me…for so long." I avoid mentioning the notice from the school that I'm no longer welcome.

She scoffs, arms crossed, her disappointment a living

thing in the room with us. "So, you're just going to run off to California? Do you even know this guy?"

"Enough to know I need this change," I counter, steadying my voice. It includes a quiet plea for her to understand. This is my escape hatch, and I'm jumping through it with or without Justin.

"Fine." Her voice cracks, and she turns on her heel, storming out of the room. I hear the front door slam, leaving me alone in what's left of our apartment.

I don't have much time to dwell. The rumble of the Goodwill truck vibrates through the windowpane, and I shuffle downstairs, dragging my suitcase behind me. The driver and I exchange a few curt nods as he starts clearing out my bedroom furniture. Piece by piece, my life here is carted off, stripped bare until nothing remains.

Then, as if on cue, Jackie reappears. Her eyes are red-rimmed, her anger dissolved into something softer, sadder. I drop my facade, and suddenly, we're just two friends standing amidst the echo of goodbye.

"Jackie..." I start, but words fail me.

"Shut up, Crystal," she says, but there's no heat in it, only the quivering of unshed tears. We fall into each other, our hug a tangle of limbs and heartache. We cry because it's ending, because it's beginning, and because neither of us knows what comes next.

"I can't believe with only one year left of school, you'd just drop out. And for a guy no less! Take care of yourself, okay?" she murmurs into my shoulder, her voice muffled.

"I will," I promise, squeezing her tighter. And I mean it. Whatever lies ahead in California, with or without Justin, I'll find my way.

I cross campus with my bag trailing behind me, heading for Justin's house. I haven't brought much, just enough to start anew in a different city, putting this rundown town and university behind me for good. A few minutes later, my suitcase thuds against the steps leading up to Justin's place, and my heart pounds. I pause at the door, taking a steadying breath before I raise my hand and knock.

"Hey, Crystal!" Rhys pulls open the door. His smile falters when he sees my suitcase. "You're here."

"Surprise?" My attempt at lightness falls flat as Justin and his other roommates emerge from the depths of the house. Justin ushers me in and rolls my suitcase to the corner.

"Whoa, she's coming with us?" Theo asks, eyebrows shooting to his hairline. Austin and Rhys exchange a look I can't quite decipher.

"Justin, man, you didn't say anything about this." Austin's tone isn't angry, but it's far from welcoming.

"Can we talk? Outside?" Justin gestures to the others, and they step onto the porch. The door closes behind them, leaving me to my thoughts. *Is this a mistake? Why didn't he tell them?*

They're going to tell me no. I'm going to be stranded here with nowhere to go. My hands twist together, knuckles whitening as I wait for them to return.

After what seems like an eternity, the door swings open again, and the guys are all smiling—relieved smiles, amused smiles, but smiles nonetheless.

"All right, you're in." Rhys chuckles. "But you owe us a turn behind the wheel."

"Thanks, guys," I manage, relief flooding through me like sunshine after a storm. "Not a problem."

"Let's get this show on the road!" Theo claps his hands, and we dive into the turmoil of moving. One by one, we schlep things out to the van—boxes stacked precariously, duffel bags wedged into every available nook. The small moving van groans under the weight of our collective lives, but eventually, everything finds its place. We stand back, a ragtag crew. This is either going to be great, or it's a giant mistake. *San Francisco, here we come.*

"Finally," Justin says, wiping his brow. He tosses me the keys to the moving van. "You ready to take the first shift?"

"Born ready," I lie. But I take the keys and climb into the driver's seat, Justin hopping in beside me.

The moving van leads the two other cars in our caravan,

and we're connected by shortwave walkie-talkie radios. *I can do this* is my mantra on repeat as we navigate downtown. The Atlanta streets are writhing with traffic, but as we merge onto the interstate, the city gives way to open road, and I exhale. It's real. I'm doing this. I'm moving to California with my boyfriend.

Well, we haven't actually said what we are, but we're moving across the country together so…

"We need some tunes," Justin notes. He connects his phone to Spotify and the truck speakers, then tunes in some sort of indie rock with a beat that demands movement. He grins and starts a clumsy dance in his seat, his motion exaggerated by the rocking of the van.

I laugh, letting the rhythm take me, my hips swaying as much as the drive allows. "Look at us go," I say, eyes on the road but spirit soaring.

"Best road trip ever," Justin declares, and I want to believe him.

I grip the steering wheel tighter. This is the start of my great new adventure.

We work our way west, the traffic thinning, and our speed as fast as the van will allow. In a few hours, we're deep in Alabama. The sun is high, and I've needed to use the bathroom for the last hundred miles.

The radio that connects our ragtag caravan squawks. "Breaker one-nine, this is Bumblebee. We're in need of comfort station."

My brow furrows as I look at Justin.

"He needs to go to the bathroom." Justin picks up the radio laughing. "This is a closed radio, you dork."

"Just adding levity," Rhys says. "I'm dying here, listening to nonstop Kiss and Metallica. Help me!"

"There's a stop up here, and we can get food and gas," Justin says.

"Roger, one-nine," Rhys replies.

I nod. "Good. I also need to go, and the van is getting below the three-quarter mark in gas."

A few minutes later, we pull into a gas station, and Justin

jumps out to fill the tank. I rub at the knots in my neck, trying to coax them into relaxation. At the fast food restaurant adjoining the gas station, Austin orders enough burgers and fries to sustain an army—or at least a couple carloads of hungry twenty-somethings.

"Hey," Justin says when he returns from the convenience store. There's a mischievous glint in his eye that I can't resist. He hands me a small, wrapped item, his fingers brushing mine. "For you."

I unwrap it to find a refrigerator magnet—a cartoonish depiction of Alabama's landmarks. "It's the first of many firsts for us," he says, his voice warm with promise.

I lean in, pressing my lips to his in a kiss that tastes like adventure. From the next car, Theo lets out an exaggerated groan, but I barely hear it.

"Come on, lovebirds, let's eat and hit the road again!" Theo calls.

We switch spots after dinner; Justin takes the wheel of the moving van while I navigate. Once we're back on the road, we reconnect his phone to Spotify, and the game of name that tune begins. Laughter fills the cab, intermingling with the melodies of old hits and new chart-toppers. The night settles over us like a blanket, stars twinkling.

Hours later, the neon vacancy sign of a roadside motel beckons like a lighthouse to weary sailors. We pile out of the cars, stretching limbs and stifling yawns, and shuffle toward two rooms with two double beds that smell faintly of pine cleaner.

"Shotgun—not sharing with Rhys," Justin jokes as he, Rhys, and I enter the first room. He tosses his duffel onto the closer bed, but then he winks at me, and I know exactly what's on his mind. He pulls me close under the guise of a goodnight hug, yet his hands wander with familiar intent.

"Justin," I whisper against his ear, "not with Rhys here."

He pauses, then laughs softly. "Yeah, bad idea."

With each state line we cross, Justin hands me a new magnet, a quirky, colorful token that I accept with a smile that mirrors his own. Tennessee's magnet is a salute to Elvis, Arkansas boasts a cartoon chicken, Oklahoma's a miniature red wagon, and Texas a lone star that glitters faintly in the late-afternoon sun.

"Collecting memories," he says, each time our fingers brush, and I'm smitten all over again.

New Mexico surprises me with its stark beauty; the magnet, a chili pepper wreath, is fiery against my palm, and Arizona's cactus stands tall on its magnetic backing in my growing collection. With every stop, with every night spent in yet another motel room, I fall deeper into this journey, into the life I'm weaving with Justin.

Finally, California greets us with a golden bear magnet, symbolizing the end of our road trip but the beginning of everything else.

We navigate north and eventually reach the crowded streets of San Francisco. Austin's found them an apartment in the heart of it all, and I can barely process how much city there is until we're standing in front of their new apartment.

"Here we are," Justin says. And this does appear to be the right place, but it's nothing like the pictures he holds in his hands. There's a gritty realness to it—homeless people huddle in doorways and the ground littered with trash. The buildings up and down the block press close together, no gap between them, no grass—only stretches of concrete and steep hills dressed in asphalt.

"Cozy," Rhys quips behind me, and I catch a shared look between the guys.

Justin has explained that the smaller their salaries, the less money they take from SHN, and that limits SHN's stake in EnergiFusion. The guys want to keep it theirs as much as possible. They're living together to save money, thinking practically about this new venture, and I respect that.

"Definitely…different," I manage. The city is alive with an energy that's foreign yet thrilling, and I know it's going to take some getting used to.

"Come on," Justin urges, taking my hand and leading me inside. "This is just the start."

I nod, the magnets in my pocket a reminder of the journey behind us—and the adventure that lies ahead.

A few hours later, the boxes are unloaded, and the moving van has been returned. Austin and Rhys have one room and for now Justin and I will share the other with Theo. But Theo declared pretty much right away that he'll be sleeping on the couch. It's not a perfect solution, but until I have a job, I can't afford anything else.

Living with the guys is going to be tough—five of us in a small, two-bedroom apartment. The only way I can do this is to remind myself it's only temporary. Once I have a job, I'll move out.

Now, we're ready to explore. We call a rideshare, and the five of us squeeze inside. Soon enough, the familiar scent of ocean salt hits me. My heart flutters with anticipation—this is the first time I've seen the Pacific Ocean.

"Look!" Theo points out the window, his excitement evident.

I crane my neck and catch my first glimpse of the Golden Gate Bridge. Clad in its iconic orange paint, it stands out against the crisp blue sky.

"Wow," is all I manage to say, my breath catching at the sight that has symbolized this city for me.

"Welcome to the Pacific, Crystal," Justin murmurs, his hand finding mine.

The rideshare drops us off at Pier 39, and instantly, the vibrancy of Fisherman's Wharf envelops us. Tourists bustle past. There is so much to take in. We wander around, snapping photos of each other with the bridge as our backdrop. Justin presses a kiss to my forehead as he takes a selfie of us and saves it to the home screen on his phone.

Justin grabs my hand and pulls me away from the guys, flagging down a taxi. He whispers something to the driver, and we speed through the city, passing skyscrapers and crowded streets. The cab stops at a busy corner, and Justin leads me down a street lined with designer storefronts. We window shop, admiring shoes that cost more than our rent and clothing we could only dream of affording.

"We'll have this someday," Justin says, squeezing my hand.

We continue walking until we reach Alta Vista Park. We climb up a steep set of stairs to the top where we're greeted with an incredible view of the city. The sun is setting over the Golden Gate Bridge, casting a warm glow over the entire landscape. I can't believe I'm here, experiencing this moment with Justin by my side. I take in every detail—the elegant homes surrounding the park, the sparkling bay in the distance, and Justin's beaming smile. This is a memory I'll treasure forever.

We spend the next three days drinking in every bit of San Francisco. We explore Golden Gate Park, where I marvel at the acres of green grass and trees—a contrast to the urban landscape of our new neighborhood. We ride the cable cars, clinging to the sides as they clatter up steep hills, offering panoramic views of the city. We visit Chinatown with the rich aroma of spices and dim sum floating through the air.

"Feels like we've stepped into another country," Justin comments, a wide smile spreading across his face.

"It's a part of San Francisco's charm," Theo replies, snagging a pork bun from a street vendor.

Oracle Park beckons us next, its stadium by the bay a field of dreams. We take turns standing in front of a green screen with a batting helmet on, pretending we're hitting home runs over the right-field wall, splashing into McCovey Cove.

"Giants game, anyone?" Austin suggests, but we're too caught up in the whirlwind of firsts to commit to anything yet.

Our final adventure takes us on a boat tour to Alcatraz. As the island looms closer, an eerie chill brushes over me despite the sun's warmth. We step onto the rock and roam the cells, the dining hall, the recreation yard. It's haunting and fascinating at the same time.

"I can't imagine being cooped up here," Justin whispers as

we peer into the cramped confines of a solitary cell.

"Freedom's just across the water, yet worlds away," I muse, squeezing his hand.

When it's time to return, the city sprawls out before us beyond the water, and it no longer feels quite so foreign. No matter what happens with Justin, I feel like these last several days have bonded us together for life.

"San Francisco suits you," Justin says, nudging me as the wind whips through my hair.

"It suits us," I reply.

six

Justin

The first light of dawn is barely creeping through the blinds when I roll out of bed, careful not to jostle Crystal. She's a tangle of sheets and determination. Even in sleep, her brow is furrowed with purpose. We've had a couple weeks to acclimate, and today, she dives into the job hunt. I know nothing will stop her until she lands on her feet. And, after meeting with lawyers and the team at SHN last week to finalize everything, today is the guys' and my first day of work for EnergiFusion.

I dress quietly, pulling my jacket from the back of a chair. The soft shuffle of fabric doesn't wake her, and I lean over, press a kiss to her temple, and whisper a soft wish for success. "See you tonight," I murmur, though she still doesn't stir. With one last look, I slip out the door.

The morning air chills my lungs as I stride out to Theo's car, which is idling at the curb with Austin and Rhys in the backseat. He's already behind the wheel, a half-smile on his face that doesn't quite reach his eyes. There's a tension here, an unspoken question hanging between us.

"How much longer do you think Crystal will be crashing with us?" Theo asks as soon as I buckle in, pulling away from the curb. He navigates the early traffic with ease, but his eyes flicker to me.

I chew on the inside of my cheek, considering. "Not long," I say with more certainty than I feel. "She's got a stack of resumes and enough fire to fuel a small sun. She just needs to land a job, save up a bit. She won't be underfoot for long."

Theo nods, but his silence is loaded, heavy with thoughts he doesn't voice. I get it; our place isn't exactly a palace, and space is at a premium—only two bedrooms for the five of us. But Crystal's no freeloader. She'll pull her weight. We just need to give her a minute.

"Knowing Crystal, she'll probably have interviews lined up by the end of the day." A grin breaks across my face. She's walked me through pages of companies she's going to apply with. I know she's motivated.

Theo chuckles, and the tension dissipates like fog in sunlight. "That's Crystal, all right."

When we arrive, Theo parks in the garage, and as we approach the front, the glass doors of SHN glide open with a whisper. The incubator is on the first three floors, and SHN offices are above.

In that moment, I step into a future I've only dreamed about.

Austin's eyes are wide, Rhys lets out a low whistle, and even Theo's usual smirk is something more like childlike wonder. Emerson Healy strides toward us, her presence commanding and a smile on her lips as if she holds the keys to the kingdom.

"Welcome, EnergiFusion," she says, her voice echoing slightly in the expansive lobby. "I'm Emerson, as you may recall, and I'll be your guide to everything SHN."

She starts off toward the interior of the building, and we trail behind her like ducklings. She leads us through a maze of halls, past windows revealing glimpses of other startups in their various stages, their occupants a blur of ambition and caffeine.

"Here it is," Emerson announces, swinging open a door to reveal an office space empty except for four desks, some cubicle dividers, and a stunning view of the Bay Bridge.

This is where we'll create something revolutionary.

"Your lab is just next door," she continues, gesturing down the hall. "Fully equipped for all your R&D needs."

Rhys's grin widens. I'm sure he's already mentally assembling circuits and soldering connections.

"And let's not forget the essentials," Emerson adds, guiding us to a large break room where a fridge stands like a monolith, its contents promising uninterrupted work hours, fueled by cold drinks and quick bites.

"With the addition of EnergiFusion, we now have twenty-five companies in the incubator. SHN is here to support you with HR, reception, accounts payable, and admin until you grow enough to manage it yourself. For now, you focus on the battery; we'll help you handle the rest." She looks around and waits for each of us to nod our understanding. "Classes in finance, management, marketing…" She ticks them off on her fingers. "All coming up. And when you're ready to grow beyond these walls, we'll help find you a new space. Consider this your launchpad."

"Thank you," I manage, feeling entirely overwhelmed.

With that, we shake hands, and she leaves us to our new domain.

After unloading and unpacking the boxes we brought with us, we just continue our work from where we left off back in Atlanta. The pressure of fixing our charging problem weighs heavy, and there's no time for wandering around the city anymore. We need to get down to business.

Hours later, as shadows lengthen and screens glow, we decide to call it a day. My phone buzzes with a reminder of life outside these walls, and without hesitation, I text Crystal, hoping she'll join us in celebration of our first day of EnergiFusion over beers and food.

Me: Drinks and dinner. You should come.

I send her the address.

Crystal: Be there soon.

A smile spreads across my face. I'm anxious to see how many interviews she's lined up. In the meantime, the guys and I head out, and when we arrive, the bar is loud, laughter and clinking glasses filling the air.

We find drinks and a table—in that order—and Austin raises a toast to EnergiFusion, to dreams made real. With that, the weight of the day lifts.

A few minutes later, Crystal slides into the booth beside me. "How'd the job hunt go?" I ask, tucking a loose strand of hair behind her ear.

"Set up a few interviews," she says, triumph in her eyes.

"Knew you would," I say.

She turns her smile toward the guys, who nod in greeting as they lift their beers and continue their conversation about the overheating issue on the battery.

She cuddles closer, and I drape an arm around her, feeling the pieces of today lock into place. We order, eat, and laugh, the night a celebration. *This is it.* We're really doing this. We're building more than batteries.

The night air is cooler when Crystal and I escape the bar alone some hours later, leaving the others to have one more round. Crystal's hand finds mine as we weave through the streets. The apartment is quiet when we arrive, and I lock the door to our bedroom with a soft click, sealing us inside our private sanctuary.

"Finally alone," I whisper, my breath warm on her ear, and she tilts her head back, offering her lips for a kiss. I find the zipper at the back of her dress, and her skin under my fingertips sparks a longing that's been smoldering since Atlanta.

I trail kisses down her neck, each one a testament of

gratitude for her presence here with me. Her shoulders are soft beneath my lips, curves of strength and resilience that have carried us both to this moment, and the moonlight dances across her skin as her dress disappears. My mouth finds her breasts, suckling gently, reverently.

Her soft moans are the sweetest melody, and I sink lower, adoration guiding my movements. With tender precision, I coax pleasure from her depths, my fingers and tongue working in harmony until the shudders of her release ripple through her like a wave crashing onto a shore.

As her breath slows, she pulls me up to face her, her eyes dark with desire. I stand, and she watches as I undress, the intensity in her gaze stoking the fire within me. Each piece of clothing discarded is like a layer of the world falling away, leaving only raw truth, only us.

The rustle of the condom wrapper is a whisper against the silence. I roll it on. Then, with a shared breath of anticipation, I join with her. It's a perfect fit, the warmth of her enveloping me completely, and I lose myself in the sensation. We move together in hurried urgency, mindful of the time. Our roommates will be home any minute. We hold nothing back, giving everything in this fleeting moment.

And then, together, we crest, reaching the pinnacle of connection where only we exist. For now, in the darkness of our locked room, we are united as one.

In the quiet afterglow, I trace lazy circles on Crystal's back, feeling the rise and fall of her breath against my chest. The room is dim, light seeping in only from beneath the door.

"Today was… It was hard," she murmurs, her voice a fragile thread in the hush that surrounds us. "I got an interview in Palo Alto."

"That's great, Crystal!" I reply, trying to infuse some hope into her outlook.

She shifts, propping herself up on an elbow to look at me. "It's just… When I looked it up, it would take nearly three hours to get there by bus." A shadow crosses her face. "It feels so overwhelming."

"Hey, don't worry about that," I say, my thumb caressing her cheek. "The important thing is that you have an opportunity. We'll figure out the logistics, okay?"

She nods, but her eyes remain clouded. "I just… I'm scared the others, especially Theo, might want me out if I can't contribute soon."

"Crystal, listen to me…" My hands frame her face, forcing her to meet my gaze. "You're not going anywhere. You've got all the time you need to find the right job. And I promise, Theo, Austin, Rhys—they're not going to kick you out. We're all in this together." I can't lose her. She believes in me, and I need that right now. I've never had someone in my life who could understand what I need so clearly, and then she makes sure I get it. We all need that. I'll get the guys to understand.

"Thank you, Justin," she whispers, and relief seems to uncoil within her.

"Always." My lips find hers in a reassuring kiss, gentle and lingering.

We stay like that for a moment longer, savoring the closeness before the practicalities of life nudge at us. With a soft sigh, I untangle from her embrace and slip out of bed, moving quietly to unlock the door.

Sliding back under the covers, I open my arms, and Crystal curls into me. Our bodies fit together as naturally as breathing, the rhythm of our hearts syncing once more.

seven

Crystal

The warmth of the bed holds me hostage, but I'm only faking sleep when Justin's alarm sounds at an ungodly hour. His side of the bed dips as he rolls out, the faintest hint of daylight peeking through the blinds. I hear the rustle of his clothes, the soft pat of his socked feet against the hardwood floor as he leaves the room. He's heading into the office again. I keep my eyes shut, my breathing even, feigning the peace of slumber I haven't truly felt in weeks.

It's been three months now since we landed in this fog-wrapped city, and I'm more alone than ever. The guys leave each morning before dawn and return to fall into bed at night. I'm by myself all day every day. I've had fifteen interviews, resulting in fifteen rejections. Each "we'll be in touch" stings a little sharper, each polite decline is like a twist of the knife. No degree to flash, sure, but it's not like all I'm good for is flipping burgers.

My phone pings from the nightstand, a sharp note in the

morning silence. I can't ignore that like I can the mess I'm sure has been made all over again in the rest of the apartment. I crack one eye open and read the message without lifting my head from the pillow.

Mom: Why drop out of school to follow some guy to California?

Jackie. It had to be Jackie who told her. My old roommate, confidante, and supposed friend. Anger flares, hot and quick. I trusted her. I click the button to lock the screen, leaving the message unanswered. I'm not ready for the conversation Mom wants to have.

I stew in silence, the bed emptier without Justin's presence, and the apartment now quiet since everyone has gone. Mom's question looms large. *Why did I do this?*

I sit up in bed and toss back my meds with a gulp of water from the glass that's been sitting on the nightstand since last night. Scanning the job postings on my laptop, hope flickers feebly with each click. Barista, receptionist, retail—it's all the same dance, just different tunes. Nothing bites; nothing even nibbles. I slam the laptop shut, the finality echoing off the bare walls.

I go out to the living area and survey the mess left by Justin and his friends—empty pizza boxes, soda cans ringed with sticky residue. It looks like they've ransacked the place, not lived in it. I'll clean it up, eventually. But right now, I can't deal with the reminders of my current life as part-time ghost, full-time maid.

With a sigh, I grab the remote and flick on the TV. Morning shows beam at me with plastic cheerfulness, hosts chatting about celebrity scandals and the latest weight-loss fads. It's background noise, white static to drown out the silence and simmering frustration. I sink into the couch, letting the mindless chatter wash over me.

Then my phone pings—a message from Theo. Unlike Austin and Rhys, who treat me as part of the furniture, Theo actually sees me. He and Justin are all that's keeping me together right now.

Theo: Good morning. How are you holding up?

Me: Fine. Just another quiet morning.

Quiet morning doesn't begin to cover the loneliness that stretches out like an endless road before me or the way I'm haunting my own life, unseen and unheard.

Theo: When was the last time you got out?

I look at the ceiling. His question seems like an interrogation under a spotlight.

I pause, the TV's laugh track suddenly sounding grotesque. When did I last step outside and feel the sun on my skin? Days blend together. I don't bother to count them. But it's probably been over a week since I put on something other than pajamas or laughed over drinks with Justin and the guys.

Me: It's been a while.

Theo: Meet us for lunch today?

Theo doesn't miss much. He and Justin have probably been comparing notes about me. I hesitate but then realize I have no real reason to say no. My schedule is as empty as the apartment feels.

Me: Sure, sounds good.

It's a reason to dress, to get outside, to breathe fresh air. *Right*?

Theo: Great. We'll see you at the incubator around 12:30.

I set my phone down and stand, stretching limbs stiff from

too little use. I'm meeting them for lunch. At least it's something. A small step, maybe, but in a direction that isn't confined by these four walls.

We're not meeting for a few hours, but the invitation invigorates me. I shower and dry my hair and apply makeup. I think I'm excited to have something to do that won't end in rejection.

I slip into jeans, the fabric alien after days of loungewear, and my sweater is a soft embrace. I glance outside; the San Francisco breeze carries the promise of lunch outdoors.

When it's time, I step out of the apartment, letting the door click shut behind me and already feeling better than I've felt in days.

The walk does additional wonders, clearing the cobwebs of isolation as the city bustles around me. By the time I reach the familiar office building, my pulse has quickened—not from the walk, but with the anticipation of human contact.

"Crystal!" Emerson's voice is a warm welcome as I enter. Emerson Healy is one of the partners at SHN, and she pretty much runs the incubator. I've met her a few times when I've brought things to the office. She engulfs me in a hug. "How you holding up?"

"I'm doing just fine," I lie smoothly, a smile hiding the storm beneath.

When I walk back to the EnergiFusion offices, Theo hugs me as well. "I'm so glad you came."

"I'm glad you asked."

He smiles. "Give me just a minute, and we'll be ready."

Theo grabs the team as I go to greet Justin, and in a few minutes, we all walk over to the sandwich shop across the street.

Justin laces his fingers with mine. "I'm so glad you're here. I feel like we never see each other anymore."

We find a table outdoors and dig into our sandwiches, but Austin and Rhys are like dark clouds ready to burst. They pick at their food, grumbling about something techy before standing abruptly and leaving without so much as a backward glance. I watch them go, wondering what I did this time to upset them.

Justin catches my eye. "Don't mind them," he says, his voice low and reassuring. "Just another bug they can't figure out."

I nod, unsure how to fill the silence that follows.

Then Theo turns to me. "So, what's the job hunt looking like?"

I sigh, letting my guard down just a fraction. "Right now, it's a choice between flipping burgers or…well, flipping burgers." I laugh bitterly. "For my sanity, I need to do something. But minimum wage isn't going to cut it for moving out."

There's a beat of silence as they digest my words, and I wonder if I've shared too much. But I might as well be honest.

Justin's hand comes to rest on my shoulder, drawing me back from the edge of my spiraling thoughts. "Crystal," he says, a hint of something like hope in his tone, "we think we might have another option for you. Would you be willing to come work with us? We're swamped and could really use an extra pair of hands."

I tilt my head, caught off guard. "Work? At EnergiFusion?"

"Yeah," Justin continues, a smile spreading across his face as he looks over at Theo. "We need someone to handle some administrative tasks and keep things organized, and Emerson's team is busy with the other startups in the incubator. They can't get to all we'd need them to do."

"To put it simply," Theo adds, "we're drowning. Between the classes they want us to take and our work, too much isn't getting done."

"It was Emerson's idea to hire someone, and we immediately thought of you," Justin explains.

"What would you need me to do?"

"Order supplies for the lab, fetch things we need, answer calls—you know, office-manager stuff." Justin shrugs as if it's no big deal, but his eyes search mine. "The SHN team is always here to back you up."

Office manager echoes through my mind, sounding infinitely more substantial than *burger flipper*. I straighten my back, interest piqued. “What does it pay?” I ask, trying to sound nonchalant.

“Your salary is like ours, it comes out of SHN’s investment in EnergiFusion, so we’ll need your help keeping costs down. That means it’s minimum wage to start,” Theo answers. “But we’ve got healthcare benefits, and hey, it’s experience you can leverage later on.”

Healthcare. That resonates with me, heavy with the weight of necessity. My medication bottles are getting closer to empty, whispering warnings with every rattle. “I’m in,” I say with a nod before doubt can creep in and choke out the words. Excitement flutters in my chest. “When do I start?”

eight

Justin

The soft clicking of Crystal's keyboard is a soothing counterpoint to the sizzle and pop of ideas that fizz out just as fast as we conceive them. It's been a month since she joined us, and she's definitely been a positive addition to the team. She's the voice that greets callers with a warmth we can't muster, buried as we are in schematics and simulations.

"Can I grab anyone coffee?" Crystal's voice cuts through the tension that's settled over the workspace.

"Make mine a double," Austin grumbles from his perch by the whiteboard, marker in hand, eyes bloodshot from too many nights chasing solutions.

"Same here," Rhys chimes in without looking up, fingers flying over his laptop, while Theo just nods, lost in a sea of circuit boards.

I'm on the brink, teetering between gratitude and something akin to envy at how Crystal seems to be flourishing, her earlier job woes dissolved into a distant memory. It was hard to convince SHN to let her join us, but Theo and I did it. And the office is better for it, all those niggling tasks that used to loom over us now dispatched with a quiet efficiency that's almost magical. And Crystal seems much better emotionally too.

"Hey, Justin, you too?" She catches my eye.

"Uh, yeah. Thanks."

She smiles, and I let myself bask in the simple normalcy she's brought to our startup's madness. We have a consultation with Mason Sullivan and Dillon Healy coming up, and we've not made very much progress. The problem still eating us alive? Battery duration. The charge still refuses to hold reliably.

"Guys, we're so close," I say, trying to inject optimism into the room. "We've got the charge, and we're able to convert electrical energy into mechanical energy. We just need to marry the two without the battery dying."

"Seems like a shotgun wedding at this point," Theo mutters, and there's a collective sigh.

We've been at this for hours, days, weeks—long enough for any semblance of work-life balance to have become a punchline. It's like we're stuck in a loop, each breakthrough causing yet another thing we thought we'd fixed to not work.

"Let's take five," I suggest, rubbing the bridge of my nose, the onset of a headache blooming that has nothing to do with caffeine withdrawal.

"Five minutes or five hours?" Rhys asks.

"Let's aim for minutes and see where we land." I attempt a smile.

As the guys stretch and groan, standing up from their respective battle stations, I watch Crystal return, arms laden with cups emanating steam and the promise of productivity.

"Your lifesaver has arrived," she announces, distributing the cups with a flourish that lifts the mood just a fraction.

"Thanks, you're a star," I tell her, accepting my cup and taking a tentative sip.

"Any progress?" she asks.

"Progress and regression seem to be in a dance-off right

now," I admit, forcing a chuckle.

"Keep at it. You'll find the rhythm," she says with a conviction I wish I could bottle and pour over our battery cells.

"Here's hoping it's not a tango," Austin adds dryly.

We agree to a thirty-minute break. I want to see the sunshine, so I go for a walk around the block and get a Rice Krispies Treat for an afternoon pick-me-up. Now, I'm ready. I know we're close to getting this right.

"Back to it," I announce when I return. I roll my shoulders and settle in.

Later that evening, the sun dips below the horizon as I push through a set of swinging doors, the familiar clank and squeal mixing with the chatter of Vinny's Restaurant. My shoulders are hunched from the day's labor, muscles aching for reprieve.

Theo pats my back with a knowing smirk, "Groundhog Day, huh?"

I nod, too tired to conjure up a proper response.

The group of us claims our usual booth, the worn leather groaning under our weight. It's become a routine, as predictable as the challenges we wrestle with all day.

"Be right back," Crystal says, sliding out of the booth almost as soon as we've all slid in.

Her departure stirs something in Austin. He leans forward, elbows on the table, voice low. "So, Justin, when do you suppose Crystal's moving out?"

"What? Why would she move out?"

"Come on, man," Rhys cuts in. "Theo's paying a quarter of the rent and living on the couch."

I set the fork down, the clatter louder than intended. "We're paying her next to nothing, and she takes care of everything." I hear myself. I sound defensive. But she brings order to our mayhem.

"Sure, but I think it might help all of us to have

some…space," Austin suggests, tapping his fingers against the table. "Either we find a new place, or you two should."

A chill races down my spine. They were surprised she came with us to begin with, but they've seemed happy with her work. It hasn't been so bad living together, has it? I do feel bad that Theo's on the couch, but I don't think there's any way Crystal and I could afford a place of our own.

"Look, you know I asked her to come with us in the moment," I add hastily. "I didn't expect her to quit school and join us, but it's been working out. For everyone."

Before they can counter, Crystal slides back into her spot, her presence instantly ending the conversation. After a moment, our server arrives with menus, and we resume our evening. But the aftertaste of confrontation lingers... *What do they expect her to do? What do they want me to do?*

The guys have been better with Crystal since Monday, even though we never really finished our conversation. Hopefully, I convinced them we just don't have any other options right now. We're all making sacrifices to get this to work. Anyway, right now, it's Friday night, and the noise of the modern city fades behind me as the guys and I step into the Moscone Center, which SHN has transformed into a cathedral to nostalgia tonight. SHN is famous for their parties. Each year, they celebrate with the Silicon Valley elite, and this time, EnergiFusion was invited.

Tonight, the eighties are back with a vengeance, clawing their way out of memory's vault with neon claws and synthesized beats. Crystal has been flitting around all week, her excitement ramping up as she assisted Emerson's team at SHN with the setup.

"Look at this place," I murmur, taking in the retro decorations that have made the hall a time machine. My gaze wanders, seeking Crystal, who should stand out as a beacon of eighties fashion. She spent an hour earlier wrestling her hair into gravity-defying shapes, the scent of AquaNet so pervasive that it lingered long after she left.

Now, as I crane my neck, scanning the sea of leg warmers and acid-wash jeans, I catch sight of her. The big hair, the dramatic makeup—she's a walking tribute to the decade of excess. Her clothes scream confidence—bright colors and shoulder pads that rival any linebacker's protection gear.

"Man, she nailed it," Austin says with a chuckle.

I nod, feeling a twinge of pride. "She's going to love tonight."

The four of us are dressed *Miami Vice* style—pastel shades and rolled sleeves. It's a costume, but isn't that the point? I'll slip into another skin for the evening and forget the relentless pursuit of solving EnergiFusion's battery dilemma.

"Ready to party like it's nineteen *eighty*-nine?" Rhys asks, quirking an eyebrow as he adjusts his faux Ray-Bans.

"Let's just hope our dance moves haven't aged as badly as some of these tunes," Theo chimes in.

"Tonight, we're undercover police trying to flip the bad drug dealers," I declare. "We have no time for dancing."

"Let's make it legendary," Austin agrees, clapping me on the back as we merge with the crowd.

Crystal waves us over, a clipboard in her hand. "You guys look totally rad," she says.

"Wow, Crystal, you really nailed the look," Theo tells her, seeming a bit mesmerized by her transformation from meticulous office manager to vibrant, shoulder-padded powerhouse.

"Thanks, Theo!" She beams. "Don't miss Depeche Mode on the center stage at ten thirty. And if you're feeling adventurous, there's roller skating in the main room." She glances down at her list. "And keep an eye out for the servers with hors d'oeuvres. They'll be making the rounds all night."

"Thanks for the heads up," I reply, already scheduling our evening around the promised performance. Depeche Mode is not to be missed.

As we venture deeper into the neon-lit room, all moving

in different directions, Mason Sullivan strolls over to me, his attire screaming *preppy* louder than any John Hughes film. He takes a drink and grimaces at the brightly colored beverage in his hand. "Can you believe this?" he grumbles, shaking his head. "Nearly a million dollars sunk into this event, and not a drop of scotch or bourbon in sight. These frozen daiquiris are giving me a headache."

"Here…" I offer my can of light beer with a chuckle. "It's not top shelf, but at least, it won't make your brain freeze."

Mason waves it off. "Thanks, but no thanks. I'm going to be a team player. I just can't complain to my wife. You've met her, right? She planned the drinks, so you get my complaints instead."

Before he can continue his rant, his wife, Caroline, glides over, looking every inch the epitome of eighties glamour—tall, statuesque, and absolutely dazzling. She slips her arm through Mason's, her gaze soft but firm.

"Come on," she urges with a smile that could melt hearts—or at least defrost Mason's icy demeanor. "Let's not spend the night picking apart the menu. Let's enjoy the party."

With a sigh that borders on melodramatic, Mason nods for me to follow as he makes his way into the throng of partygoers. Rhys materializes by my side and shrugs. Where our funder goes, so shall we.

Mason navigates us through clusters of Silicon Valley elites until he sees something he likes. "Justin and Rhys, you've got to meet Nate Lancaster," he says.

A tall man turns as we approach, his presence commanding even without the eighties-tailored, high-waisted trousers and oversized jacket over an attention-grabbing, frilly shirt. He extends a hand, his grip firm, his gaze sharp but not unkind. "Good to meet you both," he says with a nod.

Mason doesn't waste a moment. "Nate, this is half of the brain behind EnergiFusion. They're on the cusp of revolutionizing EV batteries."

I swallow hard, the weight of expectation heavy on my chest. But before I can articulate our vision, Nate produces a bottle of Woodford Reserve, seemingly from thin air, a feat more magical at this moment than any tech innovation.

"Let's talk over something decent," he suggests, pouring the amber liquid into glasses he's pilfered from a nearby bar.

We toast and sip, the warmth of the bourbon cutting through my nerves. Nate listens intently as I outline our hurdles and breakthroughs. He's unnervingly focused. I've read about this guy. He built an empire from nothing after getting out of the military, and he's weathered personal tragedy and still persevered.

"Sounds promising," he murmurs when I pause to catch my breath.

Before I can delve deeper, the crowd parts like the Red Sea, and Grayson Blackstone steps through, his charisma filling the space around us. This is the head of Firefly, the behemoth shopping service that has reshaped retail. Rhys shifts closer, bumping my shoulder with his. I don't dare look his way for fear I'll lose it.

"Caught wind there was real liquor floating around," Grayson quips with a smile.

"Join us," Mason urges, refilling glasses with a flourish. "This is Justin Capriotti and Rhys Smalls from EnergiFusion. Here come Austin Sands and Theo Reed."

Austin slides up beside me, and we exchange pleasantries with these men who have scaled heights we've only dreamed of. Through the buzz of alcohol and conversation, one thought anchors me. *Tonight, we are not just dreamers. We are contenders.*

We talk a short while longer, until someone calls Mason and Nate away.

Crystal joins us and laces her fingers with mine. Everything is coming together, better than I ever dreamed of.

"Can you believe this?" Austin murmurs as they go.

"Never in my wildest dreams," I reply, turning toward Theo and Rhys, who are propped against a sleek, faux arcade cabinet, their expressions mirroring our own awe.

"Look at them all," I say, gesturing subtly to the sea of wealth and power around us. The titans of tech mingle effortlessly here, their conversations likely shaping the future even in their leisure. I catch snippets of dialogue about market trends and mergers.

"Feels surreal, doesn't it?" Theo chuckles. Rhys nods, his gaze tracking a particularly influential CEO I can't name as he passes by. There's respect there, and a quiet yearning.

"We're standing on the precipice," Austin says, clinking his glass against mine. "One foot in our old world, one in theirs."

"Here's to chasing what's next," Rhys declares, raising his glass.

"To building the future," Theo adds.

"Together," Crystal says as she gives my hand a squeeze.

Their words resonate, anchoring the moment. We toast to ambition, to the pioneers around us, to EnergiFusion, and to the unknown adventures waiting beyond the horizon. Tonight, we have arrived.

nine

Crystal

The smudge of coffee grounds on the crumpled napkin is like a slap in the face. Austin just drops it on my desk without a glance up from his phone, the list of office supplies scrawled in his hurried handwriting.

"Need these by tomorrow," he mumbles, already heading back to the sanctuary of his cluttered cubicle.

I stare at the napkin, the very embodiment of disregard. No "please" dances at the edge of the paper, no "thank you" lingers in the air behind him. I'm invisible, a ghost in the machine of this startup while they play at being visionaries.

A part of me wants to stand up, gather my things, and walk out the door—let them learn the hard way how much weight I pull around here. How valuable I am. But I'm also grateful for the experience this job is giving me, and I know no one is raking in the cash at this point. I just wish they'd value what I do for them and be more appreciative. I believe in their work, though, so regardless, I'll probably stick around. It's not like I haven't tried to find other jobs already.

The familiar ping from my cell phone draws me back to reality.

Teagan: Free for lunch?

Her message beams with the warmth we shared at that wild SHN party, where I met her as we worked together, checking in guests. Teagan Kohl, with her brilliant mind, is the head of IntelliThread Innovations, another company here in the incubator. She's an entrepreneur, a creator, and someone who knows the value of collaboration.

Me: Yes! Save me from the Mexican fiesta in the lunchroom. Meet you at the ladies room in 5.

The prospect of lunch, of escaping this thankless place even for an hour, is a breath of fresh air. Justin believes every problem can be solved by talking, but it doesn't work with these guys. They remain the same inconsiderate jerks they've always been. I am unable to afford moving out and when Justin and I looked at our combined income, I couldn't find anything even close to what we could afford, so staying here is my only option. However, I am saving money, so eventually, I'll have the means to leave this situation—my job and the shared apartment—behind. I push Austin's napkin to the side, a problem for future Crystal. Right now, I've got a date with a friend. And that's what I most urgently need.

A few minutes later, I'm walking with Teagan outside, the sun a rare companion in our trek to Connie's Bistro. We order sandwiches, the kind with artisan bread and layers of fresh ingredients that offer a small escape in every bite. As we settle on the grass in the park across the way, the warmth seeps through my jeans, comforting against the coolness of the earth beneath us.

"Seriously," I begin, unwrapping the sandwich as if peeling back the layers of my frustration, "they've got no clue how much I do for them." I take a hefty bite, letting the flavors mingle before I continue. "And Austin acts like he's king of the world. A dirty napkin for a shopping list? Really?"

Teagan chuckles, but her eyes are sympathetic. "Why do you stay then?" she asks, plucking a blade of grass and twirling it between her fingers.

I sigh, my gaze drifting across the park to where other office escapees savor their lunches. There are a lot of reasons, not all of which I'm ready to share. But I do think Teagan is someone I can trust. "Health insurance," I confess, the words more bitter than my rye bread. "Got diagnosed with bipolar disorder two years back. And the cocktail of meds I'm on? Not cheap without a decent plan."

"Ah, the indispensable coverage." Teagan nods knowingly. Her voice softens. "Anxiety disorder here. I get it. Without my meds, I'd be a ship without a sail."

"Chemicals." I smile wryly, lifting my sandwich in toast. "Our unsung heroes."

We laugh together, a moment of shared understanding.

"Speaking of unsung," I venture, feeling bold. "How's your dating life?" She alluded to some frustration in this area the other night, and she was at the event without a date.

Teagan scoffs. "Oh, please. The guys around here think they're God's gift. But they're more like yesterday's fish market haul, reeking of arrogance and stale pick-up lines. They brag about funding like it equates to the size of their dicks."

"Yikes," I reply. "Guess it's not just the workplace that can leave a bad taste in your mouth."

"Exactly," she says, taking another bite of her sandwich. "But enough about the dating cesspool. This sunshine is too good to waste."

"Agreed," I say, leaning back on my hands, face tilted towards the sky. The simple joy of the moment washes over me.

The sun winks at us between the leaves as Teagan stretches out on the grass, looking content. "So what's the story with you and Justin?" she asks after a moment.

I smile. "Justin? He's…different." I pluck at the grass. "I

met him back in Atlanta, where we were at school. He's the reason I'm here in California."

"Sounds like he's made quite an impression," Teagan teases, her eyes sparkling with interest.

"More than I expected," I admit, warmth bubbling inside me. But I've said about all I'm ready to say. "I'm happy, Teagan. Truly. He's a good guy. The rest is just details, right?"

She gives me an encouraging nod, and when I don't add anything further, she lets the conversation drift away with the breeze, replaced by comfortable silence as we turn back to the business of eating our lunch.

Back at the office, the work is waiting, right where I left it. Austin's list of office supplies still needs to be managed. I wade through, dispatching orders while taming the wilds of office logistics.

As the printer whirs in protest with a paper jam, Theo pops his head over the cubicle wall, desperation in his eyes. "Crystal, the copy machine's doing that thing again."

"All right, give me five minutes," I say, without looking up.

Before I can fulfill my promise to fix the ink issue no one seems able to manage but me, Justin gently grabs my elbow, pulling me into the seclusion of a quiet hallway. Then his lips are on mine, firm and insistent. The world falls away, leaving only his touch, his taste.

"I've missed you," he whispers against my mouth.

"Missed me?" I tease, breathless. "You saw me this morning."

"Still too long," he says. "We need a break. Let's escape for a weekend. Just us, Napa Valley, wine, and nothing else."

The idea blooms in my chest like spring flowers, vibrant and promising. "I love it," I tell him. "Just what we need. Are you sure you can take the time away? You've been working nonstop since you started."

"Yep. I told the guys we all needed to get away. We have to recharge somehow, so we're all going to do it, just not at the same time."

I nod. "Smart. I think that makes sense. Maybe the time away will spark a breakthrough."

He gives me another kiss before stepping back. "I'll make the arrangements."

I watch him head off down the hall, a flutter in my stomach. A weekend away sounds like a dream, one I'm eager to fall into. But first, I have a battle to win—with a rebellious printer and a needy copy machine.

When I return and open the door to our office space, there's something unexpected inside—two officers in uniform. My heart hammers as they turn toward me. They stride over, and every pair of eyes in the room follows their movement.

"Crystal Brown?" one of them asks, her voice firm but not unkind.

"Y-yes, that's me." My voice trembles.

"Could we speak in private for a moment?" the other officer says, gesturing back out to the hallway.

"Of course," I reply. I lead them to one of the small conference rooms, which feels like a march to the gallows, each step heavy with dread. *What could this possibly be about?* Once inside, the walls seem to close in around us.

"I'm Officer Montgomery," the woman says, her partner standing a little behind her. "Your mother requested a wellness check."

The words hit me like a gust of cold air.

Justin appears in the doorway, about to join us, but I raise my hand, stopping him mid-step. He hesitates, then nods. *"Is everything okay?"* he mouths.

I manage a half-nod, even though nothing is okay. He retreats back down the hall.

I return my attention to the officers. "Look, I work at a startup. Downtime isn't a luxury we get often," I explain. "I haven't been able to call my mom as much as she'd like."

"Understandable," Officer Montgomery says, softening

slightly. "But given your medical history…"

My cheeks flush with heat as she unceremoniously drops the words *bipolar disorder* into the conversation. How dare my mother betray my privacy like this?

"Please just let her know you're okay," the officer suggests. "A quick call might ease her worries."

"Fine," I agree, even though nothing about this is fine. "I'll call her."

After they leave, I push the door to the office suite open, stepping into a room that suddenly seems too bright, too full of prying eyes.

Justin is immediately at my side, his face etched with concern. "Are you all right? What happened?" he presses.

My mind spirals for a moment. Should I be honest? Teagan was great when I told her the truth. But this is too big a risk—my job, my living situation, my heart, it all hinges on this one person. I'm not ready yet. "Nothing serious," I lie as smoothly as I can, my heart pounding against my ribs. "I witnessed an accident a while back but didn't think much of it. They just wanted more information."

"An accident?" His eyes search mine, looking for the truth I'm not ready to give him.

"Yeah, a guy pulled out in traffic and got hit." I grimace, as if remembering the incident.

"Okay…" he says, though his hesitation speaks volumes. "If you need anything—"

"Thanks, Justin," I cut him off gently. "I appreciate it."

He watches me another moment before finally gathering something from his desk and heading back to the lab. As I stand there, surrounded by the hum of the office, I feel more disconnected than ever.

I sit at my desk and press the cool glass of my phone against my forehead, taking a moment to collect myself. The office has returned to its usual rhythm, with the guys all in the lab, but adrenaline still courses through me. Slowly, I dial Mom's number, and wouldn't you know, she sends me to voicemail. *Figures.*

The beep sounds. "Mom…" I push back the anger and betrayal. "If you ever send the police to check on me again, that's it. We're done. Don't expect me to answer your calls or texts."

It's not just about her overstepping; it's about protecting the fragile barrier between my disorder and the reality I've fought so hard to maintain. With a deep breath, I disconnect. It feels good to stand my ground. In fact…

I navigate to her contact, press down until options emerge, and select *Block this Caller*. It's a digital amputation, swift and clean, yet somewhere beneath the numbness of my anger, I sense the phantom ache of what I'm losing. *I can't do it.* I navigate away from the screen before completing the task.

But if she does this to me again, I will sever all ties to her and my father.

Now, for the hardest part. I lift my head, sliding the mask of professionalism back into place and painting a smile across my features. It should be enough to fool anyone who doesn't look too closely.

"Hey, Crystal, everything cool?" Theo asks, coming in from the lab.

"Totally," I say, my voice light, almost airy. "Just another day at the office, right?"

He nods, seeming reassured, and rummages through a box of parts for a moment before going back down the hall to his work. "Are we still good for drinks after work tonight?"

"I'm counting on it." I take a deep breath and move forward, my feet carrying me through familiar motions, my mind whirring with tasks and timelines. For now, I still have a handle on this semblance of normalcy, even as I wonder how many more cracks I can plaster over before everything comes tumbling down.

ten

Crystal

Ever since the police showed up with their questions last week, Justin's been like a shadow to me, my personal guardian angel, hovering so close I can feel the warmth of his concern. It's sweet, it's suffocating, but right now, it's what's keeping me from falling apart. The embarrassment still stings. I keep imagining my mother's voice on the phone, shrill with worry, when she called the police because I missed one too many calls. She doesn't get it. Her pressure about school, my mental health, is like a weight on my chest, and I've been dodging that conversation like bullets.

"Ready for an adventure?" Justin's voice pulls me out of my spiraling thoughts.

I look up from where I'm sitting on the bed and nod, forcing a smile. I keep that smile firmly in place as we pack his car, throwing our overnight bags in the backseat. This is a first for us, a weekend away, just the two of us, no work or drama. And wine. Lots of wine. I catch a glimpse of his profile, eyes set on the road but a smile on his face. How did I get so lucky? After a minute, it's not so hard to keep my smile.

The early-morning fog lifts as we approach the Golden Gate Bridge, which stretches out before us like a gateway to another world—a world where mothers don't call the police on their daughters and where the word *school* isn't synonymous with failure. "Wow, look at that," I murmur, my breath fogging up the window as I lean closer. The bridge looms larger than life, its cables reaching skyward like the strings of some celestial instrument.

Justin chuckles beside me. "Pictures don't do it justice."

We share a moment of awe, my troubles momentarily forgotten. San Francisco shrinks behind us, and I look down at the water. I never realized how high up we would be. The boats below look like toys in a bathtub.

"Scared?" he asks, his hand finding mine for a reassuring squeeze.

"Thrilled," I correct him, and it's true. With the wind in my hair and Justin by my side, I can do anything. I make a silent promise to myself. I'll enjoy this weekend. I'll let go of the guilt, the embarrassment, and the fear. At least for now. Because sometimes, you need to cross a bridge to see the path ahead. And if the timing is right, I'll even tell Justin about my bipolar diagnosis.

"Look at that," he murmurs sometime later. The landscape has shifted as he navigates the winding road.

"Everything feels so…organized," I reply, looking at the rows of grapevines that must cover acres in Napa Valley.

We stop in downtown Yountville around lunchtime and order sandwiches at a small café.

"Are you having fun?" Justin asks.

"Yes." I nod vigorously. "I wonder what would have happened if you'd never come to me at that Velvet Anomaly show."

He grins. "You were a siren calling me from across the crowded room."

"That seems like a long time ago," I tell him. "Do you

regret inviting me out to California?"

He stops mid-bite. "Never. Do you regret coming? Not finishing your degree? Because I'm sure you can transfer to Berkeley."

I lean back in my seat and look out at the majestic view. "No. I mean, eventually I want to go back to school, but I don't want to study applied mathematics. It's a misogynistic field. When I figure out what I want to be when I grow up, I'll go back."

After lunch, we drive a little farther and pull up at the quaint house we'll call home for the night. It's wrapped in a shawl of ivy, aged wood whispering stories of countless sunsets. We barely have time to admire our room before we're off again, leaving the car behind to meet the tour that will shepherd us through the afternoon's wine tastings.

The van is small, intimate. There are just eight of us in the group. Our first stop is a boutique winery, and their merlot is rich velvet against my tongue. I catch Justin watching me with eyes that say he savors my reaction more than the wine.

"Good?" he asks, his smile easy, and I nod, not trusting myself to speak without betraying the flutter in my chest.

Each winery has its own story, its own flavor. We sip cabernet sauvignon that dances bold and spicy on our palates, and zinfandels that blush with the memory of summer berries. Laughter bubbles up around us, and I join in, the freedom intoxicating.

"Never knew wine could be this much fun," Justin says, and I agree. There's joy in the simple process of discovery. I can feel it binding us closer than any grapevine could.

As the van carries us back, the day's warmth lingers on my skin. Justin's hand settles on my back. "Should we grab some dinner?"

"I'm still full from lunch," I tell him. But really, I'm just looking forward to a night in, without the usual roommates.

After a short walk, we re-enter our temporary haven, the room now cast in the rosy glow of dusk. Justin's touch is gentle as he guides me to the bed, a silent question in his eyes that I answer with a nod, surrendering to his care.

He worships me with mouth and fingers. "You're the most beautiful woman I've ever seen."

Every nerve is on fire, and I arch my back, inviting him closer. He obliges without hesitation. His lips claim mine in a kiss that's as urgent as it is tender, our tongues dancing and exploring. I run my hands through his hair, pulling him closer as I revel in his body pressed against mine.

Desire makes the room spin as he continues to explore every inch of my body. His heart races in sync with mine, and I know this moment will be forever etched in my memory. This man, this beautiful, passionate creature, is worshipping me in a way I never thought possible.

As his lips trail down my stomach, and he looks up at me. "Tell me what you want."

"I want to come," I pant.

His tongue dances along the inside of my thigh, tracing an invisible path to the center of my desire. I gasp, my hips arching as a wave of need crashes over me.

He presses his mouth against me, his tongue delving inside as he coaxes my climax closer. I grab his head, guiding him as my breath hitches and deepens. The first quiver of pleasure spreads through me like wildfire.

"Oh…yes…" I cry, every nerve ending singing with his touch. He sucks and licks, coaxing me closer to that elusive edge. And then, with a final jolt of ecstasy, I shatter into pieces, my release tearing through me like a freight train.

When I finally open my eyes, I find him looking up at me, a satisfied smile on his face. He kisses me gently, his lips still damp from my desire.

"You're so good at that," I whisper. "It should be illegal." I reach for his hardness. "How can I make you happy?"

He chuckles softly, his eyes never leaving mine. "How about a little lick?"

I crawl down his body, licking, kissing, and exploring his hard planes. His cock is weeping, and his breath catches as I lick the tip. His taste is sweet, and the scent of him fills my nostrils. I run my tongue around the ridge of his cock, teasing him gently before moving down, tracing the line of his shaft with my mouth. He shudders beneath me, his hands gripping the sheets.

I take him into my mouth, closing my lips around the head and sucking lightly as his muted moans fill the room. I slide my mouth farther down, my tongue probing the crevices as my hands hold him steady.

He gasps, his hips bucking slightly as he tries to push deeper into my mouth. I pull away, kissing the tip of his shaft before starting again, my rhythm steady and sure.

His breaths come faster, his body arching off the bed as he grows harder, reaching for that elusive release. "Oh, God," he breathes, his voice barely a whisper. "You're going to make me come."

"I want you to come inside me," I tell him.

He nods. "I want that too."

Positioning himself between my legs, he pushes in deep. The sound of flesh slapping against flesh echoes through the room. I moan, my hands gripping his hips as he pounds into me. Each thrust drives me closer to the precipice. The surge builds inside me, a wave of ecstasy gathering as he continues to thrust.

"Oh fuck," he groans, his arms shaking. "I'm not gonna last much longer."

"Neither am I," I pant, my body trembling with the force of my impending release.

His hips move faster, harder, and my climax builds, the pleasure coursing through me. I scream his name, my body arching up to meet his as I'm swept away by pleasure.

My muscles clench around him as I ride the waves. He groans, his eyes rolling back in his head, as he nears the peak of his release.

"I'm gonna come," he growls, his voice hoarse.

His cock pulses inside me, releasing his seed. The sensation is overwhelming, and I scream his name again as the last shudders of my orgasm wash over me.

We collapse onto the bed, our bodies slick with sweat. "This is so much better here than at the apartment," he marvels.

I snuggle in closely. "I agree. I wish we could afford to

move into our own place."

"Once we get this battery figured out, we're going to get a great place together."

Justin's arms are a fortress around me. I bury my face in the warmth of his neck, breathing the scent of earth and wine that clings to his skin. I'm safe here, secure in his embrace, the anxieties that so often crowd my mind banished to the shadows for now.

I should tell him about the tempests in my head, about the disorder that colors my world in shades of mania and depression. But the words stick in my throat, clinging to a fear of tarnishing this perfect moment, of burdening our weekend with my reality.

"Everything okay?" he murmurs. He must sense my tension.

"Perfect," I whisper because it is. For these fleeting hours, everything is just as it should be. The confession can wait. Tonight, I choose to savor the serenity of being simply, unequivocally with Justin.

We slept in this morning and wandered around the quaint little town before we began our drive back to San Francisco this afternoon. The sun casts a golden glow over the vineyards as we leave the enchantment of Napa behind, and soon our car is humming along the roads that cut through the East Bay into Vallejo. The landscape changes, urban edges creeping in.

"Look, there's Berkeley," Justin says, pointing toward clusters of buildings crowning the hills ahead.

Something stirs in my chest, a mix of nostalgia and a yearning I can't quite name. "Let's stop," I suggest.

We park near the university and step out to stretch our legs. We wander aimlessly, our footsteps echoing on the campus paths. Justin's hand finds mine, his fingers a comforting pressure.

"You know, if you ever want to get back into school, I'm behind you," he says, his gaze fixed on the iconic Campanile bell tower cutting into the sky.

A lump forms in my throat, heavy with things unsaid. I squeeze his hand, grateful for his support but weighed down by the reality of what that would entail. Starting again seems like stepping backward, and I'm not ready to face that yet.

"Thanks, Justin. That means a lot," I manage.

What I don't tell him is how deeply I'm falling for him or how his faith in me both uplifts and terrifies me.

We return to the car, the cityscape of San Francisco welcoming us back as we cross the Bay Bridge. The skyline is jagged against the horizon, familiar and foreboding all at once. Soon, we'll be back at EnergiFusion again.

eleven

Justin

I return from the lab to my desk after another wrong path with our battery. The cooler air in here offers silent solace as I settle into my cluttered space. I instinctively reach for my phone, thumb-scrolling through notifications until I pause at a missed call from Dad. Odd. He never calls.

I search for a reason he'd call me and decide he and Thea are most likely getting a divorce. She's closer in age to me than him, and I know from experience he's difficult to live with.

"Hey," Crystal's voice slices through my thoughts as sudden and arresting as lightning. She closes the office door with a decisive click. Our private world seals shut. "Theo told me it didn't work."

"Unfortunately." I sigh, running a hand through my hair. "We can't figure this out. We make one minor change and then something that has always worked fine goes haywire."

"Are you going to work late?"

I look around my desk at all the piles. "I have so much to do."

She pouts, eyes glinting with a disappointment she doesn't voice, and I'm struck by how well she understands the demands of my world. "Maybe I'll see if Teagan's up for some trouble," she muses.

"That sounds better than going through the financial report for my meeting with SHN." I try to smile. "Have fun for the both of us, okay?"

"Always do." She winks and slips out of the office, closing the door behind her.

My phone vibrates, slicing through the silence Crystal's departure left behind. I hesitate for a fraction of a second before I swipe to answer.

"Justin?" The voice on the other end is my father's, but it sounds like it's been dragged over gravel. It's raw, almost unrecognizable. My spine stiffens; this isn't about a divorce.

"Hey, Dad. What's going on?" My voice is steady, betraying none of the concern that's starting to claw at my insides.

"Justin," he starts, and there's a tremor in his voice. "I've got bad news. It's cancer, colon cancer. You need to come home."

The world tilts slightly, as if those words have knocked something out of alignment. Crystal, who is walking back by with Teagan, pauses, her hand on the doorknob. She must read the shift in my body language. I feel like I'm made of stone. She comes back in and stands close, her touch light on my arm.

"Have you told Brandon or Patrice yet?" I ask, though I'm not sure I want the answer.

"They don't know," he says, bitterness seeping into his tone. "They're traitors, living in their own worlds. I... I don't want them here."

There's a pause, and then another voice filters through, warm and female. "Justin, it's Thea. Please, honey, come back to Colorado. Your father needs you."

"Okay," I say because what else can I say? "I'll come."

Crystal squeezes my arm, a silent vow of support, and I

realize she hasn't left my side.

After ending the call, I pull up my banking app. The numbers stare back at me, accusingly low after the indulgence of our Napa getaway. There's no wiggle room for another plane ticket, especially not with the gouging prices of last-minute flights.

"Damn," I mutter under my breath.

"Justin." Crystal's voice is soft but firm. "You need to go. Don't worry about the cost."

I look up at her, and it's like she's infusing me with strength, with clarity. "Yeah, I do."

I go next door to the lab, where Austin, Rhys, and Theo are gathered. Their chatter fades as they take in my grim expression.

"My dad just called," I explain. "He's sick—in the hospital. I need to head back to Colorado for a few days."

"Of course, man," Austin says, putting a hand on my shoulder. "Take all the time you need."

"Let us know if there's anything we can do," Rhys adds.

"Thanks," I say, gratitude mingling with the anxiety in my stomach.

Back at my desk, I navigate the airline website, fingers a little numb as I click through the reservation process. A flight leaving in three hours stares back at me from the screen. It's now or never.

"Booked," I announce, more to myself than anyone else, as I shut down my computer and stand. There are calls to make, bags to pack, and goodbyes—however temporary—to say.

Crystal's hand is at my back, propelling me forward and into the rideshare. Once we're inside, it darts through the congested streets. We're a tangle of urgency and frayed nerves, racing against the clock, against the weight of my father's diagnosis. Every red light seems like an eternity, every honk and brake screech a discordant soundtrack to my mounting anxiety.

"Come on," I mutter under my breath. We finally skid to a stop outside our place, and I'm out the door before the driver can fully brake.

"Pack light," Crystal reminds me, her voice steady as she follows me inside. "Only essentials."

In a flurry of motion, I stuff clothing into a duffel bag, my movements mechanical. Toothbrush. Charger. The bare minimum for an unknown number of days at my childhood home.

"Call your mom," Crystal says, handing me my phone as I zip up the bag. She stands with me, Theo's car keys in hand.

"Hey, Mom," I say, the second ring barely complete before she answers.

Her voice is soothing, but I can hear concern in every word. I quickly relay what little I know. She promises that either Patrice or Brandon will be at the airport to pick me up when I land.

"Thanks," I say, the lump in my throat making it hard to swallow. "I'll see you soon."

We climb into Theo's car, the city seems to conspire against us, trapping us in its snarled veins of traffic. I watch precious minutes slip away on the dashboard clock, despite Crystal's best efforts to navigate the traffic.

"Maybe… maybe I should've taken a later flight," I murmur, second-guessing myself for the hundredth time.

But Crystal shakes her head. "We'll be fine. Let's just get you there."

We pull up to the airport drop-off zone with no time to spare. I lean across the seat and press a quick, hard kiss to Crystal's lips. "Thank you," I whisper, shouldering my bag and bolting toward the terminal.

"Call when you arrive," she yells after me.

Security is a blur of bins and conveyor belts. I half-jog, half-stumble to my gate, arriving just as they're announcing last boarding call. The attendant gives me a tight smile as she scans my boarding pass, and I duck into the jet bridge, heart pounding.

The plane is packed, the air heavy with too many travelers crammed into a small space. My seat, 35E, is exactly where I don't want to be—in the middle of the last row, wedged between a snoring man and a restless toddler, the omnipresent stench of the lavatory hanging like a foul cloud.

I buckle in and close my eyes. This is the longest flight I've ever faced, not in hours or miles but in the weight of what awaits me at the end. I'm sandwiched between realities, the past and the present pushing against me from either side.

My thoughts tunnel back through the years, to when my mother packed her bags and walked out, taking far more than just the contents of her closet. She left with my younger brother and sister. She begged me to come with her, but I couldn't. I stayed with Dad, not out of loyalty or love, but out of fear of leaving him alone. I'd wanted us to be a family, but I soon realized the man who could command a lecture hall with his booming voice couldn't navigate the silence of an empty house. My presence wasn't enough to make him happy, yet I couldn't muster the strength to leave. He mostly ignored me or criticized me, and I came to hate him for holding me back, for making me feel small, and now…cancer. The word is a stone in my stomach, heavy and cold. *What am I supposed to feel?*

I try to sleep, but slumber evades me, slipping through the cracks of my restlessness. Finally, the captain announces our descent, and relief washes over me. The landing gear hits the tarmac with a jolt that travels up my spine, grounding me back to reality.

I'm nearly the last person off the plane. The cleaning crew is already working their way down the aisles as I pass. But I move quickly once I've exited, as I can navigate this airport on autopilot. *My family awaits.* The thought should comfort me, but it only tightens the knot in my gut.

I take the escalator up from the train to the main terminal, and there they are. Brandon and Patrice stand waiting, looking more than a little anxious.

"Justin!" Patrice waves, her smile warm. Brandon just nods, but his eyes brighten as I approach.

"Hey," I manage, my voice hoarse from the dry cabin air. "Thanks for the last-minute pick up."

We exchange quick hugs, and they lead me to the car. We set off toward my mother's house, and the cityscape blurs past, a smear of lights against the evening sky.

Our conversation is sparse, tiptoeing around the elephant in the room—Dad's illness. We'll have time for that later. Now, it's about reconnection, about the strange comfort of being among those who share your blood, if not always your opinions.

We pull into Mom and Graham's driveway, and the scent of home-cooked food wafts out to greet us as we enter the house. She's laid out a spread of tacos, my favorite since childhood. It's a simple gesture, but it anchors me, reminds me of better times.

"Justin…" She wraps me in a hug that smells of spices and warmth.

"Thanks, Mom," I say, my throat tight.

Graham also hugs me, and then we settle around the table, plates piled high, and for a moment, I can pretend we're just a family sharing a meal. Stories and laughter fill the spaces between bites, and the weight on my shoulders lightens, if only for the night.

After we've finished, I linger at the table, the tangy bite of salsa still on my tongue, and Mom leans forward, her eyes curious. "So, how are things with Crystal?" she asks.

"Actually, it's going great," I reply, feeling myself smile. "We just got back from a weekend up in Napa. It's a balancing act, you know? Working and living together with Austin, Rhys, and Theo. It gets crowded."

"Sounds like you needed the getaway," Graham chimes in as he reaches for Mom's hand.

"How is the battery working out?" Brandon asks. "I have a science fair project coming up if you want to throw it over for that."

"You'd fail." I chuckle, shaking my head. "But we'll get it figured out."

Later, I stand in the doorway of my childhood room. It's unchanged from the summer I lived here between high school graduation and starting at Georgia Tech. I worked at Elitches, the local amusement park. I enter and drop my bag on the floor by the bed.

Graham appears, his figure framed by the hallway light.

"Justin, if you need anything—anything at all—just let us know, okay?" His voice is gruff but kind.

Graham was the person who stepped in and took care of my mother, brother, sister, and me, even though I lived with my dad. He's always treated the three of us as his own kids. And when my dad was putting pressure on me to stay in Fort Collins and go to Colorado State where the tuition would be free, Graham encouraged me to accept my spot at Georgia Tech.

"Thanks, Graham," I say, the words thick in my throat. "I appreciate it."

"We're lending you the car to go up to your father's tomorrow," he adds before he turns away. "Be sure to give him our best and let him know we'll come up at a moment's notice if he needs us." Graham is not a fan of my father, so this is an unexpected kindness.

"Will do," I assure him.

The bed beckons, and I give in, sinking into sheets that smell faintly of fabric softener and something else, something like safety.

I thumb the screen of my phone, which casts a blue glow over the darkened room. The message I type to Thea is short, devoid of the emotion churning within me.

Me: Got to Mom's safely. Heading up to see Dad in the morning.

My thumb hovers before I press send, the digital words a flimsy bridge across the expanding distance between here and what awaits.

The reply comes more quickly than I expect.

Thea: Looking forward to seeing you. He's at Poudre Valley Memorial, Room 307.

With a heavy sigh, I switch apps and hit Crystal's name, bringing the phone to my ear. I texted her when the plane touched down, but I did promise to call. The line rings twice before her voice, bright and clear, spills through. "Hey, you made it."

"Hey, yeah, I'm at my mom's." I sink into the pillows, the tension of the day unfurling slightly at the sound of her voice.

"Everything okay?" There's concern woven through her words, a tightness that tells me she's still holding her breath, waiting for the other shoe to drop.

"As okay as it can be, considering," I admit. "It's just…a lot to take in."

There's a pause, and I picture her nodding on the other end. "I can imagine. I miss you already."

"Miss you too." I close my eyes for a moment. "How are you holding up?"

"Ah, Theo and I are going out for drinks," she says, a forced lightness to her tone. "You know, trying to keep busy while you're away. But don't worry about us, just focus on your family, okay?"

"Okay." Just saying the word seems like a promise, one that's heavier to carry than I expected. "Take care, all right? And give Theo a hard time for me."

"Always do." She chuckles, and the familiar sound warms me. "Call me when you can, Justin. We're all here for you."

"Will do." I hang up, placing the phone on the nightstand, where its screen fades to black. With a weary exhale, I shut my eyes, letting sleep claim me, if only to escape all that's going wrong in my life.

twelve

Crystal

We had pizza at the office today, and after work, Rhys and Austin were heading out to meet women, so Theo and I are taking ourselves out for a drink, as we do on occasion when everyone else is occupied. I give the nightly password and push through the heavy, unmarked door of Bourbon and Branch. The dim lighting casts shadows across our path, bouncing off bottles that line the wall like silent sentinels of a bygone era. I inhale the scent of aged whiskey and leather. The ambiance of the speakeasy bar envelops me, a stark contrast to the crisp vineyard air that filled my weekend.

"Tell me everything," Theo urges as he slides into the booth across from me. "How was Napa with Justin?"

I smile at the memory, the intimacy of being alone and away from the commotion of city life. "It was wonderful," I confess. "We toured a couple of vineyards, bought some wine, but honestly…" I lower my voice, leaning in. "We mostly enjoyed the quiet. Just us."

"Sounds perfect," he says, seeming happy for me.

I nod and sip the cocktail our server brings over from the bar, its complex flavors a welcome distraction from the gnawing concern that always seems to bubble beneath the surface—all the lies and secrets about my health, money, Justin, the guys at work, my job. In an instant, it comes rushing to the forefront.

As if sensing my shift in mood, Theo's brow furrows. "Why are you two still crammed in our tiny apartment, anyway?" His question is casual, but I hear the underlying point that he'd like to not be sleeping on the couch.

I let out a dry laugh, tracing the rim of my glass with my finger. "I should move out, but with what you pay me…" My voice trails off.

He studies me. "What do you want, Crystal?" he asks, not just as a friend, I suspect, but as someone who holds weight in the decision-making at work.

I take a deep breath, gathering my scattered thoughts. "A measure of respect would be nice," I say firmly. "And that comes with a share of the company, doesn't it? If you can't give me a pay increase, then at least some stake in the company. But ideally…both."

I look up into Theo's eyes, searching for a sign of what he's going to say next. He leans back in the booth, his gaze distant as if sorting through an invisible spreadsheet of possibilities and outcomes.

"Your salary…it's not something we can adjust on a whim," he finally says, his voice measured. "SHN gave us a specific amount of money, and it's taking us longer to figure this out than everyone hoped, and right now, dividing the company further is off the table."

There is a twist in my gut, the familiar sting of disappointment. But I stay quiet, waiting for him to elaborate.

"See, there's a divide at the top—whether to remain private or go public." He swirls the remnants of his drink. "We're close to really nailing this thing, Crystal. Sales alone could make us billions without having to share a slice of the pie with stockholders."

I pause, taking in the weight of his words. This is news to me. Justin, despite all our time together, hasn't breathed a word about these developments. But then again, we've been trying to build a relationship beyond the confines of work, seeking common ground elsewhere.

"Justin didn't mention any of this," I confess. I recall the scraps of paper and napkin from Austin with hastily scrawled lists of demands—no *please*, no *thank you*. A sour taste builds in my mouth. "Sometimes, I feel like just the hired help."

"Sorry about that," Theo says with a nod. "It's disrespectful, I know. I'll have a word with the guys. We need to do better. You're an important part of the team these days."

"Thanks, Theo." I manage a half-smile, appreciating his understanding. Though I suppose if any of them are going to get this, it's him. He's shown the most interest in getting to know me these past months, rather than just tolerating my presence. I consider him a friend. I suppose that makes this a small victory, but it means something that he acknowledges the issue. The promise of change, even if it's just in how we communicate, seems like a step in the right direction. I take another sip of my cocktail.

"Anyway…" Theo starts with a wry smile. "I think it's time I admit defeat in the love department."

"Defeat?" I arch an eyebrow, intrigued by the sudden change in conversation.

"Yup. How am I supposed to bring someone back to our place? It's like a clown-car situation with you and Justin hogging the double bed and me squeezed on the couch." He chuckles, but again, I feel the jab. I just don't know what I can do about it.

I laugh along, imagining the cramped quarters of our shared room. "I see your point. Though if you found someone, maybe you could spend nights at her place instead?"

"Or I'll keep crashing in your bed while you're off on romantic getaways to Napa," he teases.

"Maybe." I smirk. "The Napa trip was…really something. It's a great retreat that's so close."

"Any news on Justin's dad?" Theo leans back, seeming to study me for a moment.

"I spoke to him briefly earlier. He's staying with his mom tonight, and he'll drive up to the hospital in the morning. All I know is their relationship seems tense, from what little I picked up at graduation."

"Sounds complicated." Theo's face softens with empathy. "You'll probably be the first to know more. Can you keep me posted?"

"Of course," I promise. After all, Theo's more than just a roommate. Justin and all the guys are close friends, not just work partners, and I know they'd do anything for one another.

After a little while, we drain what's left in our glasses and wrap up the remnants of our conversation, ready to step out into the fall night. The cool air nips at my cheeks as we walk back to the house. I draw my jacket tighter around me, comforted by Theo's presence beside me.

"My mom was always in and out of hospitals," I say, breaking the silence that had cocooned us. "She was just kind of fragile, you know? Dad worked two jobs, but it was never quite enough."

Theo nods, his gaze thoughtful under the streetlights. He knows snippets of this story, the edges that have frayed over time and conversations, but I've never laid it all out like this before.

"College was their dream for me," I continue with a wistful smile. "Their beacon of hope amidst the endless medical bills and worry. But now, with everything… I'm just…" I trail off, struggling to articulate the sense of being adrift on an open sea without a compass.

"Lost?" Theo offers the word gently, almost as if he's plucking it from the tangled thoughts in my head.

"Exactly."

"Ever think about going back to school?" he asks as we turn the corner onto our street, the familiar outline of our apartment building coming into view.

"Back to school?"

"Yeah, there are plenty of great places around here. And

hey, if applied mathematics isn't your jam anymore, you could always try something new."

I nod. "Justin says the same thing. We stopped at Berkeley on our way back from Napa. I just don't know what I'd study." I roll the idea around in my mind like a smooth pebble.

"Think about it," Theo says as we reach our door. "You'll find something that ignites your passion."

"Thanks, Theo," I say, offering him a smile. "I can sleep on the couch tonight. You can have the bedroom to yourself."

"No. You sleep in the bedroom. I want to play some video games to wind down anyway.

"Goodnight then."

"Goodnight."

Later, lying in bed with the soft glow of the moon filtering through the window, I let my mind wander to the possibilities Theo's words have unearthed. When Justin suggested school, I thought it was just his way of being supportive. Now that Theo has mentioned it, too, I realize maybe that's what's missing.

The ceiling above becomes a blank screen where I project images of lecture halls and textbooks, each subject a potential key to unlocking a part of myself that's remained dormant for too long.

"Marketing?" I muse silently, picturing vibrant campaigns and the psychology behind them. "Creative writing?" My heart flutters at the thought of penning stories, of characters coming to life under my fingertips. "Art history?" I've always enjoyed the allure of past cultures and the evolution of beauty across ages.

Each option is a doorway to a different future, and I lie here, caught in the gravity of choice. UC Berkeley isn't far, and after our short visit this weekend, it seems more appealing.

"Maybe it's time," I whisper to the quiet room.

thirteen

Justin

The ribbon of cars stretches endlessly before me, a sluggish train that winds its way from Denver to my father. Fifty miles shouldn't take two hours, but the universe seems indifferent to urgency or the torment of my thoughts. I'm trapped in this automotive purgatory, inching forward while my mind races back through every terse conversation, every missed opportunity with my father. I'm not even sure how I feel about the fact that he's dying.

When I finally pull into the hospital parking lot, it seems less like an arrival and more like a surrender. I kill the engine, though my hands still grip the wheel as if it might anchor me against the tidal wave of anxiety threatening to sweep me away. Thea's text message glows on my phone. *Room 307.* I commit it to memory and shove the phone into my pocket, steeling myself for what awaits.

I stride into the hospital, the antiseptic smell engulfing me, and head straight for the elevators. As I draw nearer to Dad's room, I realize there's a crowd in the hallway, bodies huddled in quiet conversation. There's an unmistakable air of reverence among them, and I know without asking that they are here for him.

Dad's charm has always been an enigma to me. To his students, he's a mentor, a guiding light, and their respect for him is palpable in their somber vigil. But I remember the man who came home each night, a silent shadow drained by his own brilliance, having reserved none of his energy for us, his family.

As I approach, there's a subtle shift in the atmosphere, a collective tightening as eyes flick toward me, wondering who I am and why I have the right to push past them. I offer no greeting, just a nod as I slip into the room where my father lies.

"Justin," he breathes. "You made it."

Somehow, his simple acknowledgment seems like an accusation. I've come all this way, less than twenty-four hours after he called, but I wonder if it will ever be far enough.

Thea wraps me in a hug, and before I can formulate a response, the door swings open again. A tall woman enters, *Dr. Keller* embroidered on her white coat, her presence commanding enough to get the students sitting near the bed on their feet with a simple gesture. "Okay, everyone, visiting hours are over for now. Dr. Capriotti needs his rest," she declares. "Only family in the room now."

The students shuffle out, leaving just the four of us enclosed within the sterile walls of the hospital room. The doctor introduces herself briskly to me, then turns to my father. "Dr. Capriotti, as we've discussed, your cancer was caught early, and I'm optimistic about the surgery tomorrow. Recovery should be swift."

Dad nods, his face firming with a resilience that borders on defiance. "I'll be lecturing in no time," he says with a confidence that irks me.

Swift recovery? He let me worry that this visit could be the last. Did he think our relationship was so strained I wouldn't come if he told the truth? *No. He adores the attention.*

I stand before them—credit card maxed out, travel weary, and emotionally spent—prepared for a final farewell that now seems premature. The irony isn't lost on me; how typical of Dad to turn the tables, making his recovery another hurdle for me to navigate.

Thea's hand comes to rest on Dad's arm. "You should try to get some rest," she says.

Dad's eyes flash with that familiar stubborn spark as he looks up at her, irritation in his features. "I don't need babysitting, Thea," he snaps. Then, without missing a beat, he turns his sharp gaze to me. "And you," he growls, "you could show a little gratitude for once."

I bite back my retort, the sting of his words clashing with the concern that pulled me across states. *I'm here, aren't I?* What, exactly, am I supposed to be grateful for? But I swallow the words; arguing would only exhaust us both.

Seeming unfazed, Dr. Keller gives us the rundown on what to expect tomorrow. Thea and I nod and don't ask many questions. Then when *she* suggests Dad rest, he nods and shuts his eyes.

Thea and I exit Dad's room, and the hallway outside remains crowded with eager faces, young students who hang on the periphery of Dad's influence like satellites. They murmur among themselves, casting glances toward his door, toward us.

"Dr. Capriotti needs his rest," Thea announces, her voice carrying a note of authority. It's a practiced tone, no doubt honed from years of managing classrooms and unruly undergrads.

As we wait for the elevator, Thea turns to me. "Lunch?" she asks, a tentative offer extended like an olive branch.

"Sure," I reply, more out of need to escape the hospital's oppressive atmosphere than actual hunger.

Then, something catches my eye. I nod toward Dad's room, where the door has swung open again, revealing a swarm of students filtering back in. Thea follows my gaze, her surprise evident. "I thought they'd give him space," she murmurs.

"Looks like Dad's gravitational pull is stronger than we thought," I say, but there's no humor in my voice, just resignation. Dad always did have a way of bending situations—and people—to his will.

The elevator dings its arrival, and we step inside, leaving sickbed politics and quiet family battles behind.

A few minutes later, the bell above the door jingles as we enter Avogadro's Number sandwich shop, a refuge from the hospital's antiseptic chill. Here the air is rich with the scent of baked bread and cured meats.

"Still know your order by heart?" Thea asks, likely trying to keep the conversation light.

"Like it was tattooed on my brain," I reply, stepping up to the counter. The man behind it greets us with a nod that seems to say *the usual?* though I haven't been here in years. My order rolls off my tongue—a pastrami sandwich with Havarti, extra spicy mustard, and a tangle of pickled peppers. On impulse, I grab a bag of salt and vinegar chips. Thea opts for simplicity, a basic BLT, and adds a similar bag of chips to our tray.

We settle in a corner booth, away from the lunchtime bustle, where the sunlight filters through a checkerboard of smudges on the window. There's a moment of silence as we unwrap our sandwiches, the paper crinkling loudly in the quiet between us.

"How are you holding up?" I ask, breaking the stillness.

The smile Thea offers is practiced. "I've been better," she confesses, picking at the edge of her sandwich. "I filed for divorce just before… Well, before the diagnosis."

Understanding floods through me, mingling with a twinge of guilt for not being there when she might have needed support. "I'm sorry, Thea." My words are genuine, but they seem inadequate against the backdrop of everything else crumbling down.

She waves off my apology, a flick of her wrist that sends a piece of lettuce skittering across the table. "It's life, right? We roll with it." She takes a bite of her BLT, a punctuation mark to her statement.

We fall into a rhythm of eating and small talk, the crunch of our chips filling the spaces where deeper conversations might loom. Eventually, Thea looks up from her plate, her expression softening. "You know, your dad—despite everything—he's incredibly proud of you."

I pause mid-chew, the sharp tang of mustard suddenly overwhelming. "He never says so."

"But he does, Justin. In his lectures, among his colleagues, your success is his favorite topic." Her eyes hold mine, earnest and revealing.

Surprise crashes through me without warning. *Dad talks about me? Boasts about what I've done?* It's a thread of connection in a tapestry that often seems frayed beyond repair.

"Thanks for telling me," I manage, the words thick around a lump in my throat.

I focus on the remaining half of my sandwich, and eventually, I shuffle back to the hospital, the hum of Thea's car fading behind me. The sterile smell again greets me as I push back through the sliding doors.

Outside Dad's room, I'm a statue among the bustle, phone pressed to my ear. My team's voices crackle with static and urgency from San Francisco. We're going around again about the EV battery that's become my daily puzzle. "No, we can't just recalibrate the thermal management system," I tell them, pinching the bridge of my nose. "It's more complex than that."

"Justin, we've tried everything," Austin insists, his voice tight with frustration.

"Keep at it," I say, though doubt is a heavy stone in my stomach. "I'll review the schematics tonight. We'll figure this out." I end the call, exhaling a long breath.

Slipping into Dad's room, I find him holding court from his bed, a thin blanket draped over him like royal robes. Students cluster around, hanging on every word. I slide into a corner, seemingly unnoticed, my gaze flickering between my father's animated gestures and the relentless inbox on my phone screen.

Hours trickle by, and Dad's audience thins as visiting hours wane, their reluctant goodbyes echoing softly. Finally, a nurse ushers the last of them out with a polite finality that brooks no argument.

"Looks like it's closing time for the fan club," I muse, approaching the bedside.

"Ah, but the star has arrived," Dad quips. Yet there's a tinge of reproach in his smile. "Glad you could make it."

"Wouldn't miss it," I reply, though guilt gnaws at me. "But I have to head back tomorrow. I'll stay for your surgery, but I need to get back to my work. It's not going smoothly."

"Always something with you," he says, a hint of disappointment coloring his words. "But you're a troubleshooter. You'll get it sorted."

"Hope so," I murmur, looking away. There's comfort in his confidence, even if it seems misplaced right now. "Anyway, get some rest, Dad. Big day tomorrow."

"Will do," he replies, settling back against his pillows. His eyes, though tired, hold mine for a moment longer before he closes them.

"See you in the morning," I add, though it's more to the silence than to him. I leave the room, the click of the door behind me sealing the end of a day that stretched too long and cut too deep.

Back at his house a little while later, I lie in my childhood bed, the springs creaking under my weight as if in complaint at my return. The glow-in-the-dark stars on the ceiling have long lost their luminescence, but I can still make them out in the moonlight sneaking through the blinds. It's ironic how a room so full of boyhood dreams now seems like a mausoleum for happiness that was never truly there.

Why did I stay? The question dances around the edges of my thoughts, elusive yet persistent. Mom had offered to take me with her, but there was Dad, hollowed out by her departure, a shell of the vibrant teacher everyone adored. I'd thought, foolishly, that I could fill that void, be the solution to his solitude. But some things are beyond repair, and my presence was just another reminder of what he'd lost.

The digital clock on the nightstand flicks to midnight, and I still can't shake the restlessness churning within me. I reach for my phone and dial Crystal's number; she answers on the second ring, her voice sleepy yet concerned.

"Hey, it's me," I murmur, sitting up and running a hand through my hair. "Sorry, did I wake you?"

"No, it's okay. How's your dad?" Crystal's always good like that, putting others' needs before her own.

I sigh heavily. That's a hard question for me to answer. "He's…the same. Full of bravado for his audience, but there's an edge to it, you know? Like he's performing even when it's just us."

Crystal doesn't rush to fill the silence that follows. She seems to know I'm not finished.

"I've been thinking about it all—my childhood, growing up with him. I stayed because he was hurt, and I thought I could fix things, make him happy again. But I couldn't, and I won't ever be able to." My voice is steady, but the truth of the words is like a punch to the gut.

"Justin, you were just a kid," she says softly. "You can't blame yourself for trying to help your dad."

"Maybe. But I've realized I never want to be like him. Not the way he let his pain consume him or how he pushed everyone else away when they needed him. And especially not the way he makes everything about him, even in his weakest moments."

"Then you won't be," she replies. "You're aware, and that's more than half the battle. You care, Justin. That's what sets you apart."

"Thanks, Crystal," I whisper. "I needed to hear that."

"Anytime. Now, get some sleep, okay? You've got a lot to handle when you get back."

"Will do. Goodnight," I say, ending the call and returning the phone to the nightstand. The room seems less suffocating now, the shadows not as menacing. Maybe that's what facing the truth of my father's imperfections does, or maybe it's the result of assurance from someone who believes in me.

I ease back onto the pillow, closing my eyes, and once again, I resolve… *I won't be like my father.*

I push through the hospital doors, the morning light casting long, angular shadows across the hallway. The scent of antiseptic hangs heavy, a stark contrast to the crisp Colorado air outside. As I round the corner to enter my father's room, I'm again greeted by a small congregation of eager young faces. His teaching assistant and several grad students are clustered around his bed, hanging on his every word.

"Thank you all for coming," I say, my voice steady but devoid of the warmth expected in such reunions. Their murmurs of acknowledgment feel distant. "He appreciates it more than you know."

Dr. Keller arrives, this time in her scrubs and with her hair tucked away in a net. "Okay, everyone who is not family needs to leave."

The students slowly disappear, with promises that they'll be there waiting for his return.

Thea and I wish Dad well, and then he's rolled away, leaving us alone for a few moments. The surgery should go relatively quickly, so we wait down in the cafeteria, choosing a table far away from the students clustered to one side. We drink burned coffee and make small talk.

When the time is up, we return upstairs, and the nurses take us to a private area. Dad's surgery has been successful, they tell us, and he'll be out of recovery shortly and wheeled back to his room.

Thea tells me about the new condo she's found, close to Horsetooth Reservoir. "I hope we can keep in touch and be friends after this is all over," she says. "I'm so proud of your success."

"I'd like that," I tell her, and I mean it.

They roll Dad in, and he seems alert, already chatting. I smile and stand to approach him, but he waves his students in. I catch my father's eye, searching for some sign of connection, but it's as if we're looking at each other across an insurmountable chasm. No words pass between us; what is there left to say? There's no real reason for me to be here, so with a curt nod, I turn and leave the room, the absence of any emotion from my father as telling as a shout in the silence.

The drive back to my mother's house is uneventful, the car now just another vessel carrying me from one point of unresolved history to another. I pull into the driveway, and she's already at the door, her smile wide and welcoming.

"How is he doing?" she asks before I can even unbuckle my seatbelt.

"Stable," I reply, handing her the keys. "His surgery went well, and he's doing great. He was back to holding court when I left."

Mom nods, likely understanding the subtext of that statement. She's going to drive me to the airport, and after I've gone inside to gather the rest of my things, we stop for lunch on the way not far from her house. We slide into a booth at a little Mexican restaurant we used to frequent, the smell of spices and sizzling meats flooding my senses.

"Try the carnitas," Mom suggests. "They've added a new salsa verde that's incredible."

"Sounds great." I nod, allowing myself a moment of indulgence in the comfort food of my past.

Throughout the meal, Mom fusses over me, refilling my water glass before it's half empty, asking about work and my life in San Francisco, anything to reaffirm the connection she's always tried to maintain. It's a stark contrast to the emotional void of my father's hospital room.

As we finish our food, she reaches across the table, squeezing my hand. "Graham and I are planning a trip out to see you soon," she says, her tone hopeful but tentative, as if bracing for rejection.

"Good," I manage, the word catching slightly in my throat. "That would be nice."

After that, the ride out to the airport goes way too fast. I miss her so much, wish I had more of her in my life.

We linger at the curb, the goodbye stretching as she clings to our hug, my arms patting her back in a rhythm. Then, with a final wave, I watch her drive away, and I head to security and on to my flight.

I shuffle down the narrow aisle of the plane, trying not to bump into every person as I make my way to the back. I reach the last row and slump into the middle seat, with the persistent odor of the nearby bathroom again invading my space.

As the plane taxis to the runway, my phone buzzes with unread emails and missed calls, a digital tether to my life in San Francisco. I ignore them, choosing instead to watch the world outside shrink away. The engines roar, and we lift off, the city below becoming a patchwork of memories I'm not sure I want to keep.

For the duration of the flight, I remain in my cramped quarters, the middle seat like a metaphor for my life—stuck between where I've come from and where I'm going. But then I think about Crystal. She's something good that's part of my future, and I can't wait to see her.

fourteen

Crystal

Justin left for the office before dawn, and it's a couple hours later when my day gets started. I'm so glad he's back, as I feel much steadier with him around. He reminds me of my purpose here. His father's diagnosis weighs on him, but despite that, he's focused on getting the battery issue figured out. That's the key to everything, it seems.

I throw the blankets back and head for the bathroom. The cool tile of the floor sends a shiver up my spine as I unscrew the cap from the next amber bottle. I shake the prescribed morning mix into my palm and swallow them down, chasing the pills with a gulp of tap water straight from my cupped hand. The bottles go back into hiding in my makeup bag, nestled between a mascara wand and a compact mirror, their presence a reminder of the invisible thread tethering me to routine and stability.

I shake the bag and the few pills that remain rattle like distant thunder. Lithium, risperidone, an antidepressant I can never remember the name of—they form a chemical chorus that has become my daily hymn. Now, I need someone who can see me and grant me new scripts.

I zip up the bag and stare at my reflection for a moment too long, my mind churning with the task ahead. My doctor in Atlanta, with her stern but caring gaze, stressed the importance of continuity in my treatment before I left. "*One final ninety-day script*," she had said, her voice firm when I begged for the last renewal. "*You'll need to find someone in San Francisco*." She's renewed me once since then, after a phone consult, but I know I can't ask a second time. So, I need to find someone who will prescribe and, hopefully, not make me sit on a couch and tell them about my feelings for my mother or Justin or anything. I don't have time for that. But the alternative, a life unmedicated and untethered, is a risk I can't afford to take.

I get to work an hour later, just in time to learn Dr. Shayne McKay has had a cancellation today. I seize it before it can slip away. Her office is close enough to work to be convenient, yet far enough to not be recognized or seen coming and going. The trick is that I have to leave *now*, but it's really not even a choice. I have to.

So, I steal back out of the office, without saying a thing. The guys won't even notice I'm gone. I return to the sidewalk, and after a few blocks' walk, I push open the door to an office washed in soothing shades of green, punctuated by splashes of yellow. It seems less like a clinical space and more like a tranquil retreat. I explain who I am to the receptionist, and in just a few moments, Dr. McKay appears, her attire mirroring the room's casual elegance. Her clothes flow with a boho chic that suggests comfort in one's own skin—a state I envy.

"Dr. McKay?" I stand as she approaches.

"Please, call me Shayne," she says with a smile. "And you're Crystal?"

"Yes." I extend a hand, then remember the bottles. With a slight fumble, I pull them from my bag and pass them over instead. I wonder if they're all she'll see when she looks at me—an aggregate of diagnoses and milligrams.

"Thank you," she says. She leads me down a hall to her office, setting the bottles aside with care as we both take our seats, the ritual introduction bridging the gap between stranger and confidant.

"Where are you from, Crystal?" she asks, her voice soft in a way that encourages honesty without demanding it.

"The Miami area," I reply, my words floating out like hesitant butterflies. It's a simple answer, but behind it lies a mosaic of sun-drenched memories and shadowed corners I'm not ready to explore.

"Quite the change from there to here. And Atlanta, I see from your records. What took you there?"

"Georgia Tech." The pride that should accompany those two words is muted, dulled by the circumstances of my departure.

"Ah, that's impressive," she says with a nod. "You must be very smart."

A laugh, short and devoid of humor, escapes me before I can catch it. "Not really," I mutter, feeling the familiar tug of inadequacy. The office seems to shrink, and I'm left clutching at the remnants of a self-esteem fractured long ago.

"Tell me about that," Dr. McKay prompts, likely sensing the fault lines in my response.

"School was…challenging," I begin, the words clumsy and insufficient. "It wasn't just the academics. It was everything." I draw in a breath, try to steady myself on the precipice of confession. "I was failing some of my classes, so I withdrew at the end of last year. My relationship with my parents is strained because of that. And my mom has bipolar disorder, too, so it's complicated."

"Complicated," she repeats with a nod. "And does that concern you, in light of your own health?"

"More than concern," I admit, the truth spilling out like water breaching a dam. "It terrifies me. And I'm ashamed of failing, and there's Justin—" My throat tightens around his name, around the fear that clings to it.

"Justin?" She prompts, her pen poised but her attention

fully on me.

"He's my boyfriend. The person I came out here with. He doesn't know about my diagnosis. I don't want him to see how difficult I can be," I confess, staring down at my fidgeting hands. "If he finds out I'm sick, he'll realize what he's gotten into, and he won't want to be with me."

"Crystal," Dr. McKay says, her voice a lighthouse beam cutting through fog, "it's brave to share these fears. Let's work through them together."

As I nod, the first real thread of connection and understanding blooms since I moved to San Francisco. Our time wraps up, and Dr. McKay's pen dances across her notepad as she scribbles out prescriptions for all my medications, her movements deliberate and methodical.

"Here you go," she says, extending the scripts to me. "This is for thirty days."

"Only thirty?" My voice betrays a flicker of panic, a contrast to the calm I've been feigning. I hold the papers tight in my hands, but they're weightless compared to the anchor of dread settling in my stomach.

Dr. McKay leans back, folding her arms. "Yes, Crystal. It's important that we establish a proper understanding of your needs."

"But I…" The protest dies on my lips, words collapsing under the earnestness in her gaze.

"Your health is my priority," she explains. "And I need to know you better to ensure that we're on the right path. That's why I'll be seeing you again next week."

I nod, recognizing the wisdom in her approach even as frustration simmers beneath my skin. "I understand."

"Good. Shall we pencil you in at the same day and time next week?"

"Sure," I respond, still clutching the thirty-day lifeline.

When I step out of the office, the world outside hasn't changed; it moves with the same indifference of routine. The walk back to the office is a blur, my mind preoccupied, replaying the session, dissecting every exchange for hidden meanings.

I push through the doors of the building, bracing myself for questions or curious glances about where I've been for the last hour and a half, but none come. The receptionist barely lifts her head from the screen, and the people from other startups I pass on the way to our office space are absorbed in their own bubbles of activity. When I reach the EnergiFusion space, the guys are still in the lab. It's as if I never left.

Though I'm grateful to avoid their questions as I return to my desk, the reality of isolation in plain sight settles over me like dust. I boot up the computer, the screen flickering to life, demanding my focus. The project awaits. Aluminum prices won't research themselves. Fingers poised over the keyboard, I dive into the numbers, letting the familiarity of data analysis shroud the residual unease from the session, from the limited prescription, from the fear of being truly seen.

Thirty days of meds. A required weekly confessional. Thirty days to find my footing in this new rhythm of therapy and truth. The guys will never notice that I'm out of the office, but sharing in therapy is a waste of my time. Telling some doctor why I struggle with my mother or the guys at work isn't going to change anything about my life. Have to play the game, though, I suppose.

After a few minutes at my desk, I feel myself settle in. The graphs and figures are a welcome distraction from the worries of the rest of my life and the press of telling Justin who I really am.

fifteen

Justin

We're coming up on being here in the incubator for a year, and today, we're meeting with the partners at SHN—at their request. I'm not sure what that means. We've come close a few times, but we haven't had any lasting movement forward with the charging issue. We fix one thing and then something else doesn't work. I hope our time hasn't run out. If they boot us, we're screwed in so many ways.

I'm fussing with the stack of coasters on the table in one of the incubator's conference rooms when Mason Sullivan strides in. Cameron Newhouse trails behind him like an ominous shadow, his reputation as SHN's chief of technology preceding him.

"Justin, good to see you," Mason says, clasping my hand firmly. His gaze is piercing yet not unkind. "How's your father doing?"

"Better," I reply, managing a half-smile. "We think they

caught the cancer in time when they operated last fall, and his recovery seems nearly complete, so…all fingers are crossed."

Austin, Rhys, and Theo file into the room, and we all take seats at the table.

"Good, good to hear that," Mason nods, settling into one of the leather chairs.

Cameron remains standing. There's a beat of silence before he lays a roll of plans on the table. The schematics spread out like a map to our collective dreams, instantly recognizable down to the last capacitor. It's our EV battery, our brainchild. Confusion knots my stomach. Why would he have this?

"Guys…" Cameron says, and something about his tone sends a chill down my spine. "This is posted on the dark web."

The words hit like a physical blow. Panic flares, a wildfire in dry grass. I exchange frantic looks with Austin, Rhys, and Theo. Our life's work, just out there for any tech pirate to plunder? The consequences could derail everything we've built.

"Are you certain?" Theo's voice cuts through the thick air, demanding proof.

"Unfortunately, yes." Cameron's expression is grim. "And this leak poses a significant threat to EnergiFusion's future."

My mind races, trying to piece together how our tightly guarded secret slipped through our fingers. This isn't just a setback; it's a disaster. The room seems suddenly claustrophobic as the weight of our predicament settles on my shoulders.

The air in the room crackles with unsaid accusations and suspicion. I scan each face, my friends, co-conspirators in this dream turned nightmare. I know it's not them. We've fortified our company against corporate espionage, every line of code encrypted, every prototype locked away. How then? How has our blueprint found its way into the digital shadows?

"Justin," Austin's voice cuts through my thoughts. "Could Crystal—?"

"No." The word is out before he finishes, fierce and reflexive. The mere suggestion that Crystal, with her quiet determination and endless support, could stab us in the back stings like a hornet. It's absurd, unthinkable. Yet, the seed of doubt once planted is not so easily uprooted. I suppose she's as close to us as anyone. She could have gotten access…

"She's asked for a raise, and we've not given it," Austin presses, eyes searching mine for the lie he thinks he'll find.

"Stop it," I snap, anger boiling over. "She wouldn't. Not ever."

Across from me, Theo shifts uncomfortably, his gaze fixed on some invisible point between us. "She did ask about having a stake in the company…" His words hang awkwardly, a half-hearted attempt to rationalize the mistrust.

"Enough!" My fist hammers the table, the sound echoing off the walls.

Quiet descends once more, broken only by the shuffle of paper as Rhys leans over the schematics sprawled across the table. His finger traces the lines, pausing here and there, his brow furrowed in thought. The tension lingers like a bad aftertaste, but I watch him, hoping for a distraction, any lifeline.

"Guys," he finally says, "these… These are old." He points to a trio of modifications on the battery design. "Look, we improved this section, reduced the sodium cells, remember?" There's a hopeful note in his voice that seizes my attention.

"Are you sure?" I lean in, examining the areas he indicates. Recognition dawns; he's right. These plans are ancient history, relics of our early trials and original design.

"We made changes here and here not long after we got here almost a year ago," Rhys continues, a touch of relief smoothing the lines of worry on his face.

A collective exhale fills the room, the pressure easing slightly. These outdated plans, while valuable, don't hold the key to our current innovations. We're vulnerable, yes, but not fatally wounded.

"Okay, so it's a setback, not a death sentence," I concede, allowing myself a sliver of hope. We have a chance to tighten our defenses, protect what's truly important—the future we've yet to build.

"Who would have a copy of these plans?" Mason asks. "The fact that your intellectual property is out there is a concern."

"We showed these plans to all the venture capitalists we presented to, as well as some of our professors and their teaching assistants in addition to the five of us," I report, thinking carefully. "Oh, and Turner Bishop too."

"Can you put the list together and send that over to us?" Mason says. "I'd like to send it to Clear Security to have them do some checking on anyone who had access."

"Sure." I nod. "Not a problem." I don't know that we have all that information. I feel ready to vomit.

I slump into my chair, fuming silently as the murmurs of suspicion still buzz around us like persistent flies. Crystal's name has been unfairly dragged through the mud, a scapegoat for our collective paranoia. It's ludicrous; she's the backbone of this operation in ways none of us can quantify. I glance toward the office, picturing her empty desk, cluttered with invoices and quotes she's meticulously compiled to save us a fortune. She's probably running errands for us right now. If we had to cough up her true worth in wages, EnergiFusion would bleed out.

"Look, guys," Mason says, fixing each of us with a stern gaze. "You've done well as a team, but it's time to specialize. You need structure, to be better organized. You can continue to make decisions together and equally, but we need to identify roles."

The room falls silent. We've prided ourselves on having equal footing, making decisions as a unit. But Mason's right—our ship needs clear captains, not just a crew shouting directions.

"Let's hash it out, then," I say. We all have our strengths and areas of expertise, but the idea of singling out responsibilities is alien.

We debate, argue, and finally, begrudgingly, agree. Each of us wants the top spot. But it comes together. Theo, whose organizational skills have always kept us afloat, will manage operations. Austin, with his knack for tech, becomes head of technology.

Rhys clears his throat, drawing our attention. "I'm not sure about handling finances," he admits, rubbing the back of his neck. "I mean, I can keep my bank accounts from overdrafting, but…"

"Rhys, you're sharp," I assure him, though my confidence in his financial acumen is as wobbly as his own. "We'll figure it out together."

So that leaves me. I take on the mantle of CEO, a title that seems both empowering and terrifying.

At the end of our discussion, Mason nods, seeming satisfied with our makeshift division of labor. This new way of working settles on my shoulders like a lead cloak. This is uncharted territory for all of us, but we have to navigate it if we want to keep our dream—and our control of it—alive.

The office is silent now, save for the hum of our prototype battery in the corner. Mason's gaze sweeps over us, expectant. "So…" He folds his hands on the conference table. "How soon can we resolve the charge-retention issue? It's been a year. You've used more money than we expected by this point. Yes, you've worked hard to keep your salary expenses low, but there have been lab costs and a whole lot of supplies. SHN now owns about fifteen percent of EnergiFusion, and we've let you retain full control, but maybe it's time for a different approach. What are you thinking?"

We exchange glances, each of us likely hoping someone else has a timeline to offer. None of us does. It's like admitting to a room full of doctors that you can't find the heartbeat.

"Still working on it," I mutter, but it seems like I'm confessing a sin.

Cameron leans forward, the light catching on his glasses. "Have you guys heard of Fraser Lamb?" At the mention of this Silicon Valley electrical engineering legend, a spark of recognition lights up the room. "He might be interested in helping…for a price."

A piece of the business, a slice of our dream, in exchange for a solution. The words hang heavy, and a ripple of tension passes through my partners.

"Let's talk this over," Theo suggests, eyeing the plans scattered across the table. "Offsite."

Mason nods and stands. "Talk it over. But you've been dealing with this same issue for over a year. We'll either need to figure it out or shut you down."

Austin gasps. The pressure has been mostly on him as the expert in chemical and electrical engineering. But there's no shame in needing some help…right?

We all shake hands, and Mason and Cameron head out, leaving us with a big decision to make.

We return to our office to gather our things, and Crystal returns just as we're headed out. "Where did you go?" I ask her.

She holds up a ream of paper. "We need it for the marketing materials."

"We're heading over to Bourbon and Branch to talk after our meeting with SHN."

"Do you want me to join you?"

I lean in and kiss her forehead. "I know you have plans, and we're just going to talk. SHN found a copy of our early plans on the dark web, so we need to sort that out." I pause, but there's no need to worry her with the ultimatum SHN has given us. "Can you compile a list of people who would have had access to the plans before we graduated? I'm thinking the TAs, the venture capitalists we met, and anyone else you can think of?"

"Sure." She gives me a quick kiss. "See you back at the apartment."

The four of us take a rideshare the ten blocks to Bourbon and Branch, and after giving the password, we enter. The speakeasy is dimly lit, a stark contrast to the brightness of our incubator. An hour later, we're huddled into a high-backed booth, drinks in hand, the weight of potential failure pressing us into the leather seats.

"Fraser's good," Austin says, sipping his whiskey. "But are we ready to cut him in?"

"Only if he delivers," Rhys adds, his brow furrowed. He's already calculating the risks, I can tell.

I turn my beer bottle in my hands, watching the condensation trail down the glass. "If he solves the problem, it'll be worth it." I know that to be true. "SHN's money is no good to us if we can't finish what we've started. And they'll own everything outright if we have to walk away."

"Agreed." Theo nods decisively. "We pay him for his time, but a share of the company comes only with success."

"Success…" I echo, tasting the word. It's bittersweet, lined with compromise but laced with hope. "It's been a year, so maybe another perspective is what we need."

We lift our glasses in toast. We need Fraser Lamb to bridge the gap between vision and reality, even if it means sharing a piece of our future.

"Here's to solving the unsolvable." I salute them with my bottle, meeting each of their eyes. They nod.

"Here's to EnergiFusion," they chorus back.

For a moment, the burden is lighter among us, diluted by camaraderie and alcohol. But as the night deepens, I know the real work is just beginning.

A little while later, I've traded my beer for whiskey, which leaves a warm trail down my throat as I set down my glass. The conversation takes a turn, the weight of business decisions giving way to the personal.

"Speaking of hard work," Theo muses, swirling his drink, "what's Crystal up to tonight?"

I smile at the mention of her name. It comes so naturally. "She's out with Teagan. Some much-needed girl time." Leaning back, I feel a mix of pride and guilt. "You know, she got us fifteen quotes on aluminum providers earlier today. She's grinding for barely more than minimum wage."

Across the table, the guys exchange glances. "That's dedication," Austin acknowledges, tipping his glass to her efforts. "But she still doesn't contribute to rent, and Theo is still sleeping on the couch. Not to mention, when was the last time she paid for her own drinks? She's compensated out of our pockets."

"Yeah," Rhys agrees, his voice softer than usual. "We owe her our appreciation, but she's paid well."

Paid well? Hardly. Maybe by Atlanta numbers, but she can't even afford to move out. We've talked about this. Why can't they understand? I guess everyone is caught up in how little money we have and how meager our salaries are, compared to so many in Silicon Valley. But those others have made it, and we haven't yet, and Crystal is helping us get there. She deserves more.

A contemplative silence settles over our booth, but then Theo, ever the instigator, nudges the conversation forward. "So, Mr. CEO," he says with an impish glint, "you and Crystal have almost hit the one-year mark. Got any plans?"

There's an anticipatory pause, as if the very walls are leaning in to listen. I take a deep breath. "I've been thinking about it," I tell them, my heartbeat accelerating at the confession. "I'm considering proposing, actually."

"Proposing?" Rhys chortles, his skepticism thinly veiled. "That's one way to shut down her share-of-the-company spiel."

"Rhys…" I warn, the edge in my voice sharper than I intended. But what he's said holds a kernel of truth. Crystal has been vocal about her concerns, her ambitions—and if I'm honest with myself, it complicates things.

"Easy, man. Just poking fun," Rhys says, raising his hands in a gesture of peace. But his words linger.

I shake my head, trying to dislodge the doubt. "Let's have another round," I suggest, signaling the bartender. "And here's to taking risks—for EnergiFusion, for love, for everything in between."

Glasses clink, and a new resolve settles in my chest. We're going to find a way forward for EnergiFusion, and I'll talk to Crystal soon, lay bare my hopes and fears once and for all.

After our walk home, the click of the lock echoes through the hollow space as I step into the apartment first. It's quiet—too quiet—and I can tell immediately that Crystal's not here, leaving me with a blend of longing and concern. She's rarely out without me—or maybe Theo—and though I know she's with Teagan, the emptiness remains striking.

"Hey, you okay?" Theo asks.

I turn to find the guys behind me, their forms just shadows

against the backdrop of the night. "Yeah," I reply. I toss my keys on the small table by the door and shrug off my jacket, hanging it over the back of a chair. My gaze drifts to the couch, to the spot where Crystal usually curls up with her laptop, chasing down leads or comparing prices for whatever we need.

I can almost picture her there, her focus absolute, her brow furrowed in concentration. The urge to call her, to have her tell me about her night, surges within me. But I force it down, knowing she deserves her time with Teagan, her momentary escape from the relentless pace we've all been keeping.

"Let's fire up the gaming console," suggests Austin, patting me on the shoulder. He knows, they all know, how much I miss her when she's not around.

"Sure," I say, allowing myself to be led toward the entertainment center. Rhys is already scrolling through the game library. I settle on the couch, grabbing a controller. The familiar weight of it in my hands grounds me, brings me back to countless nights spent like this. We choose a game, something cooperative, something that demands less of our frayed nerves and more of our ability to function as a unit.

But as the game loads, I can't shake the image of Crystal from my mind—the way her eyes light up when she talks about finding a better deal, the pride in her voice when she saves the company money. It stings, knowing that earlier I let suspicion tarnish my trust in her, even if only for a moment. And it stings more to know my partners are the source of that suspicion.

"First round's on Justin," Rhys declares, breaking into my thoughts with a lopsided grin.

"Deal," I agree because, despite everything, these moments with the guys are important too. They're the fabric of EnergiFusion, of this life we're building. I pull my phone from my pocket and order some Scofflaw IPA—a beer from Atlanta—for delivery.

We play, we laugh, and we lose track of time. But through it all, I hold on to the warmth of Crystal's smile, the unwavering support she's given me, given all of us.

I resolve all over again to make things right, to show her

in no uncertain terms how much she means to me, and to all of us.

sixteen

Crystal

The following Monday, my cluttered desk is buried in an avalanche of reports as I try to sculpt them into something palatable for the public eye. It's not just about selling the idea; it's about making the science digestible. Rick Newman, the marketing lead at SHN, watches over my shoulder as I type out the last sentences that break down our electric vehicle battery's complicated science into bite-sized pieces for potential buyers at the Automotive Showcase we have coming up.

Anyone who sells anything to the automotive industry—air bags, seatbelts, carpeting, equipment, robots—has a chance at this four-day convention to show off what's new to carmakers. SHN has brokered this opportunity for us to show the industry what we have. We won't have batteries to sell just yet, but if we can spark interest in the technology, EnergiFusion could get a cash injection from interested parties who will reserve the right to buy from us in the future. It's a huge chance to make a big leap forward without having to get more funding from SHN.

"Crystal, this is impressive," Rick says, his voice tinged with surprise. "You've managed to make quantum chemistry sound like a high school science project."

I give him a half-smile, brushing off the compliment as I scan the document for errors. "Thanks, I guess eventually the tech talk kind of becomes your second language."

He shakes his head. "No, it's more than familiarity. You have a genuine talent for technical writing. You should recognize that."

That brings a more genuine smile. It's not often I get praise for work like this, which mostly goes unnoticed.

I check the time, and I need to get to the weekly staff meeting. I usually try to avoid them. I'd rather watch paint dry than listen to the guys talk during my workday about everything they already talk about at the apartment, when we go out for drinks and meals, and over coffee. But today I have to present my findings on a request from Mason Sullivan. He asked me to streamline costs, starting with our mobile phone package, and after doing some research, I have options for us to consider.

I excuse myself and approach the conference room, where Justin waves me in. When it's my turn, I stand before the weary eyes of the team and lay out options for the new cell phone plan. "—and with this transition, we'll not only cut costs but also streamline our communication," I conclude, hopeful for some semblance of approval. Instead, the air hangs thick with silence. The guys just seem tired and disinterested.

"Any questions?" I ask.

"Yeah, I'm not moving my cell phone over to a company plan." Rhys crosses his arms and stares me down.

Heat floods my cheeks as I reel from the sting. "I'm doing my job," I snap.

"Whatever," Austin says with a dismissive shrug. "I'm not moving my number either."

My frustration boils over into defiance. Why do they have to argue with everything I do or suggest? I'm not a second-class citizen just because I have a vagina and breasts. Or because I wasn't with them in the very beginning, back when we were at school.

"I think it's a great idea," Justin says. "I'm in if it saves us money."

I throw my hands up. "I did this research at Mason's request. You can take it up with him." My voice is a blade, sharp and cold, severing the last thread of my patience. I spin on my heel and storm out, abandoning the battle. They are not worth my energy or time.

The door slams behind me, echoing my inner turmoil. Back at my desk I snatch a sticky note and scrawl *out for the day* on it. Even that is more than they deserve.

I'm so upset that I don't stop until the waterfront greets me with its briny kiss, a welcome reprieve from the bitter taste of the morning's events.

I pause, leaning against the railing, watching the cars cross the Bay Bridge. Treasure Island rests like a jewel amidst the waters. I need a break.

Berkeley also lies out there, a beacon of possibility. An urge, magnetic and sudden, propels me toward the BART station. The train settles me with its soothing motion as I leave San Francisco behind and head toward a new opportunity.

When I arrive, the Berkeley campus unfolds before me like a promise. I let the thrum of student life wash over me, each step lighter than the last. The shadow of the office fades. It's been a year since I spent time with the frenetic and carefree pace of campus life. As eager as I was to get out of Georgia Tech, I find I miss this.

After a moment I gravitate toward the library, an edifice of quiet grandeur nestled among the trees. I smell the books, and my heart calms as I walk up to the desk. "Do you have a course catalog?" I ask the librarian.

"Of course," she replies, her smile soft as she hands me a thick booklet. "You can keep it."

I sink into a chair by the window, light filtering through stained glass, casting mosaics of color across the open pages. The technical-writing course description beckons, the words aligning with my newfound interest. It's more than interesting, actually; it resonates, vibrating with the possibility of what I could become.

The ride back on the BART is a blur, the catalog resting on my lap like a treasure map. Marketing classes leap from the page, stirring something within me. Applied mathematics was a path chosen, not discovered, but this? This ignites a fire that math never did.

Later, Justin takes me out for dinner, leaving the guys to what they usually do—go to a bar and drink a beer and eat pub food. All of the day's frustrations bubble to the surface as we eat. Justin listens, his expression revealing the tension he feels, bearing both the role of CEO and confidant. I pour out the indignities I suffer and the weight of the constant burden of proving myself.

"Crystal, just ignore them," Justin says, reaching across the table, his touch meant to soothe. "You're incredible at what you do. If you want to stay, stay. If you want to go, maybe it's time they learn just how much you do for us."

He wants to be supportive, but his words leave me caught between loyalty and the desire to forge my own path. Does he really mean that? What would happen if I left? Stay or go—each option opens a different battlefield, filled with its own landmines.

"Maybe," I murmur. I'm not sure what to do, but I like the idea of classes that could lead to a life where I am seen, acknowledged, and valued.

When we return to the apartment, it's empty, and Justin gets that look in his eyes. He reaches for my hand and pulls me close. His lips seal over mine, and I nearly float away. When we break, he pulls me to our bedroom.

The click of the bedroom door shutting behind us resonates through the quiet of our apartment. Justin turns the lock, and his hands find their way to my shoulders, the warmth of his touch chasing away the chill of the outside. "Let me take care of you," he says, eyes brimming with an empathy that tugs at the tension knotted within me.

He eases me out of my jacket, and it falls forgotten to the

floor. He deftly unbuttons my blouse. I allow the fabric to slip from my skin, baring myself to his gaze. He whispers words that weave around me like a spell. *Beautiful, smart, amazing*—each one soothes the bruises of the day.

With a gentleness that masks his excitement, he undresses me fully, guiding me to the bed. The sheets are cool as I lie on my stomach, waiting, exposed but unafraid. I close my eyes, surrendering to the sensation of his hands gliding over me.

Justin's touch is firm yet tender as he massages my shoulders, kneading the knots to bring relaxation. I let out a sigh, sinking deeper into the mattress.

His hands travel down my spine, igniting trails of fire that flicker along my nerves. And then, his touch becomes teasing, dancing across the more intimate folds of my being.

A gasp escapes me. "Please, Justin," I whisper, the words spilling forth unbidden.

He obliges, and the movements of his fingers are deliberate, rhythmic, circling and coaxing until the pleasure swells and crests within me. A delicious climax shatters through me, radiating out from the center he's meticulously focused on, washing away the remnants of the day's shadows.

In the aftermath, I lie breathless, every nerve ending softly buzzing. For these few moments, all the complexities of life fade. I'm truly cherished.

The heat of his body warms me as he spoons from behind, his breath on the nape of my neck. His heart beats a steady rhythm that echoes my own, and I tilt my hips back toward him, an invitation he answers with gentle urgency.

Justin enters me slowly, and we move together, a shared pulse in the quiet space of our room. I close my eyes, savoring the tender love we create, floating on the waves of intimacy that only seem to grow stronger with each shared breath. I'm in love with this man. There isn't a doubt in my mind.

Our crescendo builds at a leisurely pace, a counterpoint to the frenetic energy of the day. With each careful thrust, Justin anchors me to the here and now, to the truth of us. And I cling to him, lost in the intensity of sensation.

Afterward, we lie entwined, a tangle of limbs and contented sighs. The warmth of his chest against my back is comforting, grounding. Yet questions again churn in my mind, and I speak before I fully register the thought.

"Justin," I whisper, "have you and the guys thought about a share of the company for me? You know I've been here from the start. I understand that you don't have a lot of money right now, but I believe you're going to succeed in the end. Couldn't I have a small stake in that?"

There's a pause, a silent stretch that seems like hours. Justin shifts slightly, his hand tracing idle patterns on my arm.

"We haven't really figured out what we're going to do about that yet." He pauses again, seeming to search for the right words. "We don't want to confuse things, and we aren't sure we ever want to go public. Keeping EnergiFusion private means we're not forced to do things for stockholder gains. We can just do what's right for the company."

I turn to face him, trying to read his expression in the dim light. His eyes hold sincerity but also a hint of unease.

He continues, "Cameron has found an electrical engineer who might be able to help solve the charging issues. If he can, we'll probably have to give him a share of the company for his effort."

I chew on my lower lip, absorbing this information and trying to settle the anger that's rapidly taking shape. This was not even remotely the reassurance I was looking for. Is my value to SHN's future so uncertain? I can't solve the battery issue, but I solve a lot of other problems for them. This feels deeply unfair, but as I look at Justin, all the fight goes out of me. I can't add this burden to his shoulders. All I can do is ask, I suppose. Try to advocate for what's rightfully mine. Hopefully, they'll come around.

"Okay," I reply, nestling back against him. "Maybe if you cut him in, it won't seem so scary to cut me in eventually." I try to focus on the comfort of Justin's presence rather than the whirl of my thoughts. Staying in the moment, I let the security of Justin's arms shield me from the storm of doubts gathering on the horizon.

The next morning I sit on the edge of the bed, the light casting a soft glow across the room and onto the crumpled sheets. The warmth of Justin's arms has faded, and in its place is a knot of frustration sitting heavy in my stomach. It's not just about a share of the company; it's about being recognized as a member of the team and being valued for the countless problems I solve every day for EnergiFusion.

My phone buzzes with an email notification—a reminder of today's appointment with Dr. McKay. I swipe it away, my fingers lingering over the screen as if they could swipe away my discontent as easily.

"Underappreciated and underpaid," I murmur to myself, acknowledging the bitter truth. I pull on a pair of jeans and a comfortable sweater, my movements automatic as my mind races through yesterday's conversation with Justin. I know he didn't mean to downplay my role, but the sting still hurts.

Later that morning, ensconced in Dr. McKay's office, I unburden myself of all of this. My resolve not to share my secrets with her seems to dissipate in this space.

She sits across from me, her gaze steady. "Crystal, what are your options?" she asks.

I sigh. "I'm not sure anymore. I could look for another job, maybe go back to school?"

Dr. McKay nods encouragingly. "Going back to school could open doors for you. And perhaps finding a new job where you are more appreciated would be beneficial to your well-being."

Her words plant seeds of hope amidst the thorny tangle within me. Back at the office after the session, her advice echoes in my mind as I sit at my laptop, the cursor blinking expectantly on the search page for job listings and school applications.

I start with the course catalog I picked up from Berkeley, the one that sparked something within me yesterday. Technical writing courses, marketing classes—they seem to call to me, promising a future where I have more control.

Yet when I check the application deadlines, my heart sinks. I'm too late for the fall semester. Still, I press on, starting the transfer process, refusing to let this setback derail my newfound determination.

Turning my attention to job listings, I quickly realize the market isn't brimming with opportunities, even for someone with a year's worth of experience. My position has not changed much from when I first arrived here. My resume is thin, almost laughable, but I pore over it anyway, trying to add weight to my accomplishments at EnergiFusion.

"Maybe it's time to *show* them how much work I do," I whisper to myself, bolstered by Justin's suggestion. But I also need to show myself that I'm capable of more.

The office is silent. With each application I send, I feel a subtle shift within me. It's like I'm climbing out of a box they've put me in. When I've finished, I close my laptop, leaning back against the chair. I'm going to embrace the uncertainty, see it as the opportunity it is. I know things can be better than this.

seventeen

Crystal

The neon sign of Bar None sends a lazy hum into the night, tinting Teagan's mischievous smirk as we push through the door. We weave through the Tuesday-night crowd, regulars nodding at us as if we're part of some secret society, bound by cheap drinks and the clatter of darts.

"Your turf, huh?" I shout over classic rock hammering from the jukebox as Teagan leads me to the bar with the confidence of a local celebrity.

"Best watering hole in the Marina," she boasts, ordering two shots of tequila without even consulting me. "First round's on me."

The bartender slides two shots toward us, and I brace myself for the burn. We knock them back, and I wince as the liquid fire trails down my throat. Teagan laughs, her eyes glinting with a wildness that's both infectious and slightly intimidating.

"So," she says, leaning against the bar, "how are things

with Justin?"

I hesitate. "Things are great." The words flow more easily than I expect because they're true. Justin is great if you ignore everything else. "But work… It's a struggle."

"Those guys still treating you like their personal gopher?" Teagan's voice is heavy with concern, and that warms me more than the tequila did.

"More like their magic eight-ball," I sigh and then add a half-hearted chuckle. "Except I'm less 'outlook not so good' and more 'ask again later'."

The bartender offers another round, and I order a mojito. I don't want to get completely drunk. Teagan orders some martini thing.

"Crystal, you're too smart for that crap." She shakes her head. "You ever think about doing something else? Going back to school or something?"

"Every day." The admission hangs between us. I'm ready to stop pushing that suggestion aside. "I've been looking for a new job, but who wants someone with barely a year's experience? I'm like an idiot savant without the savant."

"Hey, don't say that." Teagan's hand finds my shoulder, squeezing gently. "You just need to find the right fit. I wish my startup was big enough to bring you on. You need someone who sees what I see."

"Thanks, Teag," I murmur. "I need to figure out what that right fit is."

"Exactly," she says, raising her glass for another toast. "To finding where you belong and kicking ass until you get there."

Our glasses clink, and I let myself believe anything is possible, that change is within reach, and that, with friends like Teagan, I might just have the courage to chase it.

"Girl, you need a vacation," Teagan declares, scanning her phone screen as she thumbs through an endless scroll of getaway deals.

"Tell me about it," I reply, but my voice trails off into the abyss of my bank account, the one that's locked down to support my dream of independence. "But it's not like I can afford to jet off to some tropical paradise."

"Ah, but that's where you're wrong." Teagan's finger comes to a halt, tapping triumphantly on the glass. She spins the phone to face me, revealing a deal too good to pass up. A cheap trip to Mexico splashes across the screen in bold promises of sun, sand, and escape.

I lean in, hesitant, as the numbers blur into the vision of a tiny studio apartment I've been coveting. Yet, the more I think about it, the more the idea grows on me. A chance to recharge… And maybe a way to show the guys I'm not just part of the office furniture.

"Okay," I say, feeling both resignation and excitement. "Let's do it. But we need a plan. They have to feel my absence, Teagan. Really notice it."

A conspiratorial grin spreads across Teagan's face, and together, we hatch a scheme to shake the very foundations of their complacency.

I can do this. The lab door is ajar. "Justin," I announce, pushing the door wide with more force than necessary. My heart thunders in my chest, each beat a drumroll for the words teetering on the edge of my lips.

He's there, buried in paperwork, his attention fused to whatever project has him and Theo hunched over the desk like two architects planning a city skyline. Neither of them looks up, not even a flicker of recognition. It's as if I'm invisible, and that sharpens my resolve.

"Guys," I manage to choke out, and now, I have their attention. Their faces tilt up in unison with brows knit in mild annoyance.

"Crystal, we're kind of in the middle of something," Justin says.

But I don't back down, not this time. "Actually, so am I," I counter, ignoring the tremor in my voice. "I'm giving my two weeks' notice." I slide a piece of paper across the table to prove

I'm serious.

Justin and Theo exchange glances, shock on their faces as if I'd slapped them.

"Two weeks," I repeat, the finality of it wrapping around me like a suit of armor. "I'll make sure everything's ready for whoever you hire to replace me."

Without waiting for a response, I turn on my heel and stride out, leaving behind the shell of who I used to be—a doormat—and stepping into the unknown with a newfound determination.

I feel better already. A weight lifts from my shoulders as sit down at my desk. Hands steady, I pick up the phone and dial Emerson Healy upstairs in SHN's offices. Today, I'm not asking for permission; I'm setting my own course.

"Emerson, it's Crystal. Do you have a minute?" I ask when she answers.

"Of course, Crystal. What can I do for you?" There's a warmth in her tone that belies the steel in her role.

"Can I meet with you? It's important."

"Of course. Come now," she says without hesitation.

Moments later, I'm standing in front of Emerson, her office a sanctuary of professionalism. She uncrosses her arms and leans forward, a silent cue for me to begin.

"It's been difficult working at EnergiFusion," I admit, my voice barely above a whisper. "They—they don't see what I contribute. And I… I need a break. I gave the guys my notice, but I'm for sure going to take a little time off."

Her expression softens. "Crystal, I'm sorry. We should have seen this. You're valued here, and I'm sure you do so much more than they realize."

"Thank you," I murmur, relief flooding through me. Emerson's acknowledgment soothes the rawness of feeling unappreciated.

"I can offer you several options," she continues, her gaze searching mine. "When you come back from your time off, we can find a place for you. A new beginning."

"Really?" I can hardly believe that might be true.

"Truly. You've been an exceptional part of EnergiFusion. There will be something for you at one of our other investments."

"Something better," I confirm, the phrase resonating deep within me.

She nods, and we hash out a few details. In the end, I leave her office with not just the promise of a vacation, but the assurance of a future, a future where I am seen, where my work matters. With each step, my mood lifts, and I haven't even been on vacation yet. *Why did I wait so long?* As I exit the building, for the first time in too long, I breathe freely.

After work, Teagan drags me out to go shopping for our trip. I trail behind her through Macy's, flipping through racks of vibrant swimwear.

"Look at this one." Teagan giggles, holding up a two-piece so minuscule it could pass for a doll's outfit.

"Seriously?" I laugh, taking the hanger from her. The fabric whispers between my fingers, and I hold it up against myself, skeptical. "I think you're mistaking me for someone who frequents the topless beaches of France."

"Crystal, you'd look amazing in it," she insists. "You'll have guys lined up for miles, trying to get your attention."

A flush creeps onto my cheeks as I imagine stepping out onto the sand, all eyes on too little fabric. "That's the last thing I need." My mind flickers to Justin, to his handsome face that's too often buried in work, to the way I know he'd smile at me if only he wasn't so caught up with Austin, Theo, and Rhys.

"Come on, live a little!" Teagan nudges me toward the fitting rooms.

In the cramped space of the dressing room, I slide the bikini on. The mirror reflects back a version of me that's daring, maybe even a little bold. It seems foreign, stepping beyond the comfort of my routine.

"Wow," escapes Teagan's lips as I show her the eye-patch-sized swimsuit clinging to my skin.

"Too much?" I ask, though part of me thrills at the thought of being seen like this—confident, carefree.

"Perfect amount," she asserts. "You are going to slay, girl."

I turn back to the mirror, considering the woman staring back at me. She's ready for something more, something better. And while Teagan's words about beating men off with a stick echo in my head, I realize I don't want just any man's gaze. I want someone who sees me fully, not just when it's convenient. I think I'll pick out a more conservative bikini that covers all my parts instead.

"Thanks, Teag," I say, still studying my reflection. "But the only eyes I'm interested in are Justin's, and I only want to influence him with his partners. If only he'd stand up for me like he does for EnergiFusion."

"Let's hope this little vacation gives him the jolt he needs," Teagan says, giving my shoulder a supportive squeeze.

Maybe it will. Maybe when I return, sun-kissed and self-assured, things will be different. I'll be different. Justin and I can make things work whether I'm working for him or not, right? Perhaps a little breathing room will make things better all the way around.

eighteen

Justin

I watch as Austin shuffles through the mountain of paperwork that now claims his desk. His expression is a mixture of confusion and annoyance, the reality of Crystal's absence settling on him like a thick fog. She hasn't even been gone two full days. I enjoy a twinge of satisfaction at seeing him this way. He was the first to raise a toast when she slammed the door on her way out last Friday afternoon.

"Can you believe this?" he mutters, shuffling another stack of receipts and invoices. "She actually kept track of all these expenses."

"Believe it," Rhys chimes in from the other side of the room, offering a respect that wasn't there before. He leans back in his chair, rubbing his temples as he eyes the financial chaos that has become his unforeseen burden. "Crystal did more than we realized, especially with the finances," he continues. Now our numbers guy, he looks lost without her meticulous work to guide him.

I nod silently. Not only did they underestimate her, we all did. And for Austin, the one who leaned on her the most in keeping the lab clean and full of supplies, this newfound grunt work is more than just inconvenient. It's a lesson in humility. If this wasn't such a crucial time, I'd be lifting a drink to toast Crystal for doing this. "Guess you'll have to start pulling your weight around here," I say, unable to suppress the edge in my voice.

Austin glares up at me, but I'm pretty sure there's a hint of guilt in his eyes. "Whatever," he grumbles, turning back to the disaster before him. "I'll figure it out."

Rhys sighs, pushing away from his desk to stand beside me, his gaze lingering on the mess that used to be Crystal's domain. "We took her for granted, didn't we?" he asks, though it's not really a question.

I nod. And as much as I relish seeing Austin knocked down a peg, it doesn't change the fact that we're in deep water without Crystal. We need her, no matter how hard that is to admit.

Theo enters and knocks the neatly piled sheets of paper from the desk corner. They cascade downward, each one catching air and tumbling into an unpredictable pile on the floor. He bends to pick them up, his movements stiff with irritation. "Can't believe you guys," he mutters under his breath, though loud enough for all of us to hear. "Crystal was the one keeping this circus in check." He shakes his head. "Fraser needs another set of those specs, and guess who's playing errand boy?" He thrusts a hand toward the door where Fraser Lamb, the electrical engineer we've brought on board, is tapping his foot impatiently.

"Crystal would've had all this stuff prepped and ready for him," he says, frustration clear in his voice. "She made sure everything ran smoothly so we could focus on actual problems."

"Like how we're going to manage without her," I add, unable to keep the bitterness out of my voice.

Before I can say more, Rhys's phone rings. He answers on speaker, and Crystal's voice fills the room, clear and calm as ever.

"Hey, Rhys," she greets, and there's a pause that tells me she's waiting for him to say something. When he doesn't, she continues. "I got your message, and it sounds like you've got a paper jam. Just open the back tray and—"

"Wait, Crystal—" Rhys starts, but she's already directing him with the ease of someone who's done it a thousand times. He scrambles to follow her instructions, and after a moment, the printer whirrs back to life.

"Thanks," Rhys says, a note of sheepish gratitude in his voice. "I'm also having trouble with the circuit-board orders."

"Check my notebook," Crystal instructs. "I detailed every vendor and their cost structures."

"Where are you, anyway?" Rhys asks.

"In Mexico," she replies, and it's impossible to miss the satisfaction in her tone.

"Good for you," Rhys says, but he's not fooling anyone. His shoulders slump, and I know he's kicking himself.

"Should have treated her better," I murmur, echoing Rhys's sentiment as he disconnects the call with wishes of fun and tequila. Theo nods in silent agreement. But maybe this was the right move for her. Rather than trying to get her back, what if we need to let her go?

"Maybe we should just look for someone who's more experienced and can help me with the financials," Rhys says, still staring at his phone.

"No way," Theo says. "It would take forever to get them up to speed in time, and for that amount of money, we're not going to find anyone else who cares about the company like she does. We need Crystal back."

The guys convinced me to hold off on replacing Crystal when she gave her notice. They were sure we could lean on Emerson's team and get by. But we're answering our own phones—or at least we're supposed to be—and things are falling apart. It's past time to hire someone. I'm hunched over my laptop and scouring the web for some semblance of hope—a life raft in the form of affordable help.

"Maybe we can find someone cheaper," Austin suggests,

but we just look at him. We all know that's wishful thinking. Minimum wage is as cheap as it gets.

But we can't exist like this anymore, so Emerson at SHN is my first call. Her voice is a beacon of professionalism that only highlights our current disarray. "You might want to consider a temp service," she advises after I explain our plight.

She isn't offering to help. I can only guess it's because she knows how things went down with Crystal, and she's in on this payback.

"Thanks, Emerson," I say, scribbling down the names of the services she rattles off. The phone is heavy in my hand as I dial each number, my hope dwindling with every quote that comes in. Turns out, just answering phones costs three times what we paid Crystal. My stomach drops with the realization. How did we not see her value?

A resigned sigh escapes me as I trudge down to Emerson's office. Once her assistant admits me, I slump into the chair opposite her desk. Her expression is sympathetic, yet it holds a knowing edge, as if she had foreseen this outcome.

"Any luck?" she asks, though her tone suggests she already knows the answer.

"Define *luck*," I reply with a dry chuckle. "Turns out, a good office manager earns about what we're being paid right now as officers of the company."

"Quality doesn't come cheap," Emerson remarks.

With no other options, when I go back downstairs, we bite the bullet. A temp it is. The words taste like ash in my mouth as I agree to the terms with an agency. They will send someone over in the morning. It's a stopgap, I tell myself, a patch over the gaping hole left by Crystal's absence. We definitely need to get her back. But it's something. For now, that will have to be enough. Help is coming at the price of a small car.

The temp arrived this morning, as planned, but then he went to lunch and didn't return. Is it really so terrible here? I don't think it is, but I do know it's been an incredibly long day, as a result, and yet we're still here, eating dinner at the office. We have so much to do, even more since we have to take on what Crystal would usually handle.

I push around the remnants of my takeout burger in its box, my appetite waning as I listen to Austin's latest gripe.

"You know, I thought the temp was supposed to make it better, but now that he bailed, everything just feels worse. It just reinforces all the extra crap we have to do." He shakes his head.

Theo snorts, tossing a napkin into his empty box. "I had to take out the trash this morning. Me! Since when did we become janitors?"

"Since Crystal left," Rhys says quietly.

A wave of guilt crashes over me, mixing with the frustration simmering since this morning's temp debacle. We gave him the notebook Crystal had left behind, and we asked him to do a coffee run. He told us in no uncertain terms that was not in his job description, and it went downhill from there.

"Guys, we need to talk about Crystal," I say, leaning forward, elbows braced against the cool surface of the table. "We didn't just lose an office manager; we lost the glue that held us together."

The table falls silent.

"Justin's right," Theo finally admits. "We treated her poorly, and now, we're paying the price—literally."

Austin sighs, running a hand through his hair. "So, what do we do? Beg her to come back?"

"More than beg," I assert, my resolve hardening. "We need to offer her a raise, and a share in the company. It's only fair. She's helping us get to success as much as Fraser is."

Rhys balks, his brow furrowing. "We can't just give away pieces of the company. If Fraser is successful, he's getting ten percent. We can't keep shrinking our shares…"

"Then what?" I challenge. "Keep losing money because we can't handle basic tasks? Watch the place fall apart because our pride won't let us admit we need her? If we don't succeed, we'll all end up with nothing. Then it won't matter what your share of it is."

They exchange uneasy glances. Nobody wants to lose their grip on the startup we've poured our souls into, but the reality is stark. We're floundering without Crystal.

"Fine," Austin concedes with a heavy exhale. "We offer her more money. But a piece of the company is off the table until we sort out the power dynamics with the new roles. If we give Crystal a part of the business now, she'll vote with you every time. You'll have more say than the rest of us."

I open my mouth to argue, but I suppose that's true, even though I don't think it's what Crystal wants. Once again, the dynamics of our intertwined relationships are making things more complicated.

"Agreed," Rhys chimes in, though I can tell he's not entirely comfortable with the decision.

"Are we sure she'll even want to come back after how things went down?" Theo asks.

"We have to try," I insist. "Crystal's too valuable to let go over some misplaced ego. She deserves better from us, and we're going to make it right."

There's a collective nod, and we return our focus to the remains of our meal. Crystal is worth it. Our company is worth it. And deep down, I know we all agree, even if none of us is ready to say it out loud yet.

My phone vibrates against the desk, and I snatch it up before the second ring, desperate for any hint of a lifeline.

"Crystal?" The word tumbles out.

"Hey, Justin." Her voice is a warm breeze.

Maybe I should be more strategic about this, but suddenly, I can't help myself. "Listen, Crystal, we—we need you back here. We're willing to offer more money, just please…" I trail off, my plea hanging awkwardly in the air between us.

The guys are all looking at me, eyes wide.

I can almost hear her weighing her next words. "I appreciate that, Justin, but it's not just about the money. I don't think I can live *and* work with the guys anymore. If I come back, I want us to move out. Get our own space."

I glance around at the guys, thinking about how personal boundaries have blurred with professional ones, and I can't blame her. But finances are tight, and dreams are even tighter.

"Crystal, I get it, I really do," I say. "Do you have a line on a place we can afford? Even with your raise, rents are so high in this city."

She sighs. "I know. But I just want to be alone with you."

"Trust me. I want that too. But right now, we can't swing it. As soon as we can afford it, I swear we'll move out, leave this college lifestyle behind."

"Okay, Justin. I hope that's true," she says softly before ending the call.

I'm left staring at the phone, wondering if I'm trying harder to convince her or myself that all this will be worth it someday.

"What did she say?" Theo asks.

"Uh, well, I think it was mostly positive…" I begin. But before I get any further, my phone blares again—Mason's name flashing. I swipe to answer.

"Justin!" he nearly shouts. "Where the hell are we with the Automotive Showcase application? You guys aren't answering the main line."

"Uh, we're working on it, Mason," I lie smoothly. Three days without Crystal, and we've lost the map to our own bathroom.

"Working on it isn't good enough! This Showcase is crucial, Justin. Don't screw this up!" he snaps before hanging up.

I stare at the scattered papers covering the table, none of which tells us where the damn application for the showcase is. Crystal would know. She would have had it filed, labeled, ready to go. According to SHN, this showcase is what we need to get the auto manufacturers interested in what we're doing. If we're lucky, we'll have orders to rely on for our next phase.

I slam the phone down, a pulse throbbing in my temple. "Guys…" I shake my head, looking up into their nervous faces. "We've got to figure this out, now."

They nod, but that doesn't change the fact that we're not

even remotely sure of what to do. I look online and finally find the blank application for the Automotive Showcase. *Holy shit,* this thing is worse than any college application I ever had to do. My heart races. I don't even know where to find some of this information. Cost analysis? I know Crystal was working on marketing materials with someone at SHN… There are pages and pages of questions. *How are we ever going to get this done in time?*

"Guys," I start, pacing before Austin, Rhys, and Theo, "we need to bend. Crystal's demands aren't outrageous. She deserves a piece of the company. This isn't about voting. It's about fairness."

My words hang like a challenge, yet they're met with nothing but more wide eyes. I can almost see the calculations running through their heads, numbers translating into percentages of ownership, slices of the dream we all baked together getting thinner.

"Come on," I press, hoping to stir them into action. "We have to—"

"Justin," Austin finally says, his voice tight as if he's physically restraining himself from saying more. His gaze is locked on his screen, away from confrontation, away from me.

Rhys rubs his temples, the lines of worry etched deep into his forehead, while Theo looks at me, his eyes flickering with something akin to betrayal. They don't say it, but the message is clear. No one wants their share of the company diluted any more than it has to be.

"Fine," I growl, the realization settling like lead in my stomach. *Then I'll give her some of mine.*

Without waiting for a response, I snatch my phone and go to the office to call Crystal again. My heart races at the thought of her actually picking up for a second time this evening. But I need to hear the voice that could bring us back from the brink.

"Crystal," I exhale when she answers, relief flooding my veins. "Listen, we'll pay you more. And we'll grant you a portion of the company. Please come back. Mason needs the application for the Automotive Showcase, and we don't know what to do."

A pause stretches across the line, and I fear she's about to reject my offer, but then she speaks, her voice calm and collected.

"Justin, check the binder I left behind. The application is all there, completed."

"Wait, really?" I blink at the simplicity of the solution, the lifeline she's thrown us.

"Yes," she replies, and I can almost hear the soft smile in her voice. "I'll see you in two days."

"Two days," I repeat, the words tasting like hope, like a promise of something better. Then I dial Mason's number, my fingers drumming anxiously on the cluttered desk.

The phone rings twice before he picks up, his voice brisk as always. "Justin? What's the update?"

"Hey, Mason. The application for the Automotive Showcase is all set. We're on track for the deadline."

"Good to hear," Mason replies. "And how are things with the new electrical engineer?"

I hesitate. The image of Fraser Lamb, our temporary savior, flickers in my mind—his furrowed brow, the way his hands shuffle through papers, searching for answers that used to be at Crystal's fingertips.

"Progress is slower than expected," I admit, rubbing the back of my neck. "Fraser's skilled, no doubt, but we've hit a few snags. So far, his ideas are things we've already done. But he's not giving up."

"He needs to be sure everything has been covered." There's no judgment in Mason's voice, just a matter-of-fact observation that stings because of its truth. "What's going on with Crystal?"

"She's on vacation in Mexico."

"Is she coming back?"

I know Crystal spoke with Emerson before giving notice, and I'm sure she told Mason. "We're working on that."

"Crystal is worth every penny you give her. I highly suggest you do what it takes to get her to continue in her position."

"We're realizing that. And I'm working on it—on getting

her to continue working for us."

"See that you do," Mason says, his words a command more than advice.

"Understood." I nod even though he can't see me.

"Keep me posted. And remember, time's ticking on that showcase. Be sure you're ready. It's a make-or-break moment for you guys."

"Got it, Mason. Thanks." I hang up and blow out a breath.

I look down at Crystal's binder, still clutched in my hands. With her meticulous notes guiding me, I know we have a fighting chance.

Two days. Just hold on for two more days.

nineteen

Crystal

I ride the escalator down to baggage claim, and my pulse quickens as I scan the sea of expectant faces until my eyes lock on Justin. He's looking the other direction, holding a bouquet of roses so red they look like they've been dipped in paint.

I break into a run. "Justin!" I call, and he turns, giving me the smile that always sends my heart somersaulting. In just a few strides, I'm in his arms, the scent of the roses mingling with his familiar cologne. I tilt my head back, and our lips meet in a kiss that makes me feel like I'm home.

"Get a room, you two," Teagan chides. We break apart, laughing, and she rolls her eyes in mock exasperation. She's got her bags slung over her shoulder, looking every bit the independent woman she is.

"Are you sure you don't want a ride?" I ask. I know she values her autonomy, but I feel strange just leaving her.

"I'm sure," Teagan replies firmly, waving a dismissive

hand. "My ride's already here. Go enjoy your evening." She gives me a quick hug, then heads off toward the exits, leaving me with Justin.

His eyes are alight with excitement, and I can tell he has something planned. "I'm so thrilled you're back," he says.

"Me too," I reply, my fingers tracing the soft petals of one of the roses. It's good to be back, even if part of me is still lingering on the sandy shores of Mexico.

"How about some dinner?" he suggests, taking my hand and leading me toward the parking garage.

"Sounds perfect," I agree, wondering where he might take me. Might this be a true wine and dine? Their calls of desperation while I was away couldn't have gone better. I'm so glad Teagan suggested the break.

We load my bag into the car, and Justin drives us farther down the peninsula, the evening sky painted in hues of orange and purple as the sun dips below the horizon. We weave through traffic until we reach Palo Alto, the city alive with tech entrepreneurs and Stanford students milling about.

"Welcome to Zola's," Justin announces as he pulls up in front of a French restaurant. The place is nestled in a busy open area, its warm lighting inviting passersby to step in and savor a slice of Parisian life.

"Wow, this looks incredible," I breathe, impressed by his choice. The atmosphere is both sophisticated and lively, a perfect blend for a welcome-back celebration.

We enter the restaurant, and the aroma of garlic, butter, and fresh bread teases my hungry stomach. It's clear that Zola's is a haven for those who appreciate good food and good company, and it seems to be a favored spot among the local tech crowd.

As we're shown to our table, I can't shake the anticipation bubbling up inside me. I scan the cocktail menu, skimming the descriptions until I land on something intriguing. "I'll have a Pensamientos," I say when the server appears, opting for a delicate balance of gin and blueberry with an undercurrent of floral jasmine—or so the menu says.

Justin gives a nod of approval before turning to our server. "A gin martini for me, please."

As we wait for our drinks, I fidget with the edge of the tablecloth, my mind racing with thoughts unvoiced. I have to play it cool, keep the upper hand my trip gave me, but I'd rather just get this over with. I need to know what he's thinking.

"Mexico must have been amazing," Justin says. "Besides soaking up the sun on the beach, what else did you get up to?"

"Mostly lounging by the pool," I say, forcing a smile. "And, well, some dancing."

His eyebrows rise slightly. "Dancing with other men?" There's a hint of tension in his voice now, veiled concern.

"Nothing serious, just dancing," I assure him. "It was fun, but that's all it was."

I catch a flicker of relief in his eyes as our drinks arrive, the Pensamientos a vibrant indigo hue, captivating and mysterious in its tall glass. Justin's martini is more austere, crystal clear with a single olive.

We toast to new beginnings, and the conversation flows more freely as the alcohol takes the edge off. Our server returns to take our order.

"Roasted chicken for me, please," I tell her, trying to sound nonchalant. My eyes drift to Justin as he orders steak frites, and when the server disappears, I find I can't wait for him to take the lead any longer.

"Justin," I begin, my voice low, "how did things go while I was gone?"

He sets down his napkin, giving me his full attention. "As you know, we missed you desperately. Nothing was the same without you." His sincerity warms me more than the alcohol could.

"Really? Because I want to come back, but I need to be clear." I meet his gaze, steeling myself for the negotiation ahead. "You mentioned it while I was away, but I want to make sure we're on the same page. I want equity in the business. It's only fair—I've put as much into this as anyone since we got here."

A moment of silence stretches between us as he seems to

wrestle within himself. "I know what I said, and I meant it. We'll do whatever it takes to get you back, Crystal. You're essential to us—equity included."

Relief washes over me, and I smile. I'm not sure why that had to be such a battle, but this feels good. Wait until I tell Teagan. Who knew a Mexican vacation could reap such benefits?

Our dinner arrives, and as we dine, Justin catches me up on what happened while I was gone. There seem to have been several near disasters, and he confesses that the guys have all agreed that I do much more for the company than they thought.

When we leave the restaurant, I'm practically floating, and Justin leans in. "I want you all to myself tonight, so I reserved a room close to here. Is that okay?"

My stomach flips with excitement. "Yes, of course." This could not get any better.

After that, our return to the car and trip to the modest hotel are a blur. I'm wrapped up in the experience of being with Justin, my senses heightened by the wave of joy that keeps crashing over me.

When we arrive, Justin strides past the sleek, modern front desk and swipes a plastic keycard over a sensor. The elevator doors open and then slide shut behind us, and he stands close enough for our bodies to touch. His lips meet mine in a soft, lingering kiss.

"God, I've missed you so much." He groans.

His hands find my breasts, sending jolts of electricity to my core. "Show me."

As the elevator dings to a stop on our floor, we step out into the hallway and make our way to his hotel room. The air crackles with anticipation. Justin closes the door behind us and pulls me into his arms, his touch setting my skin on fire.

We shed our clothes in a frenzy, scattering them across the floor as we come together with a desperate need.

His fingers circle my nub, and I let out a shivering moan, arching my back as sensations spread through my body. Justin's eyes lock onto mine, his expression hungry. I stare back at him, surrendering to the raw passion between us.

He gently caresses my breast, his fingers tracing delicate patterns before moving down to tease my sensitive nipple. My breaths come shallow and rapid. "I'm so glad you're here with me," he whispers, his gaze never leaving my eyes.

He pushes his fingers deep inside me, and he pivots them in and out. My heart races as he pushes me closer and closer to the edge. I groan loudly as my climax hits and my body shakes. Justin's eyes widen as he watches me surrender to the pleasure, thrusting harder and faster.

"That's it, baby," he growls, lifting me and carrying me to the bed. He lays me down gently, positioning himself between my legs.

He reaches for a condom and rolls it on his cock. "Are you ready?" he asks.

The corner of my mouth turns up. "Show me what you've got."

With a hard thrust, he's buried to the hilt, filling me. "You're so tight. I want everyone in the hotel to hear you."

I moan loudly. "Give it to me."

Justin's thrusts are deep and passionate, his hips swaying in rhythm with the beating of my heart. Each movement sends another wave of pleasure coursing through my veins. Right now, we are the only two people in the world. We move together as one, our bodies a single entity, lost in the heat of the moment.

My moans grow louder, filling the room as I reach for my peak. "I'm so close," I whisper.

Justin's expression morphs into pure lust as he watches me nearing my climax. "Come for me, baby," he growls, his voice hoarse with need. Our bodies slap together. "Show me how much you like this."

His words are my undoing, and I let out a loud cry as I reach my climax.

A little while later, we lie tangled in the sheets. Our breaths mingle in the quiet aftermath of our reunion, the world beyond these four walls forgotten for a few precious moments.

"Crystal," Justin whispers, his fingers tracing lazy circles on my arm, "you're so important to me." His words soothe the last of the silent fears that crept into my heart while I've been away.

I turn to face him. "Justin..." My voice trails off, but he understands, pulling me closer.

"I can't wait for us to finally live alone. I want us to feel this free all the time." He gently caresses my skin. "What do you desire?" he whispers.

"Only you," I answer without hesitation.

"One day, we'll have a beautiful home in Pacific Heights, and we can fill it with as many children as your heart desires. Our life will be everything we've always dreamed of." His kisses trace my jaw. "When the time is right," he murmurs, "I'll propose the right way. But know this—my future is with you, Crystal."

A wave of elation rushes through me, yet a moment later, there's a weight pressing down, the secret that nags my conscience begging to be set free. My bipolar disorder. But I can't tell him now, not when everything seems so perfect. The fear that he might change his mind about having children with me gnaws at my resolve.

His breathing evens out, and I listen to the steady rhythm, feeling him drift into sleep. In the room's silence, I hold on to the joy of his plans, pushing my worry to the darkest corners of my mind. This is a victory. I need to focus on that for now.

The first light of dawn is peeking through the curtains when my eyes flutter open. Justin stirs as soon as I do, and we dress quickly. We need to get going. It's Saturday, but it's also crunch time for EnergiFusion, so in to the office we go.

"Before we leave..." Justin pulls out a folder with a sheet of paper. "You need to sign this if you're going to have a share of the company."

My eyes grow wide. "Really?"

He nods, and I quickly sign the document. *Finally*. It feels good to be acknowledged for all I've contributed to EnergiFusion.

The traffic into San Francisco is slow, but I'm floating on air.

Austin, Rhys, and Theo greet me with an unexpected warmth, their expressions sheepish and apologetic as I enter the lab. "We're sorry, Crystal," they say almost in unison. "We took you for granted."

"Never again," Austin adds, handing me a green tea latte.

"Thank you," I reply. And I hope this is truly a new beginning, a promise from them that things will be different now. I own five percent of EnergiFusion, and that changes the game. Our success is truly bound together in a way it wasn't before.

Together, we dive into preparations for the Automotive Showcase, which is just an added burden on top of the perpetual battle to beat the charging issue once and for all. But based on what Justin has told me about the latest developments and progress, I'm confident that they will. So, I throw my energy into coordinating with Mason's team, ensuring the space at the Moscone Center is secured and orders have been placed for marketing materials. And in addition, I have something special up my sleeve. I reached out to Mason, and he thought my idea was good, so he helped me.

I'm working away on it, and the guys are busy in the lab when the office phone rings. I glance at the screen, and it's Turner Bishop. My heart leaps, as it does every time he calls, as I immediately picture him as the lead singer for Velvet Anomaly. But he's also quite the engineer, and these guys' friend since the good old Georgia Tech days. He calls periodically to check in on them, and we've gotten to know each other a little. It's still crazy to think that the guy I've watched sing his heart out so many times is now someone I chat with on the regular.

"Hey, Turner," I answer, pressing the phone to my ear as I lean back in my chair, taking a respite from the morning's work.

"Crystal! How's the brainiest girl I know?" His voice is like an electric guitar riff, vibrant and full of life.

"Brainy and buried. What's up?"

"I'm coming into town with Velvet Anomaly. We've got a gig in two weeks at The Fillmore. I'm setting aside tickets and backstage passes for you guys."

I feel myself smiling. "Awesome. We could use a break."

His laughter crackles through the phone. "Great! I've missed you all. Hey, how's EnergiFusion holding up?"

"We're gearing up for the Automotive Showcase. It's crunch time." I swivel in my chair. "We'll be presenting our EV battery to all the big names. It's a make-or-break opportunity, you know?"

"Damn, that sounds huge. You're gonna blow their minds!" I can almost see his grin, wide and encouraging. "Our tour is winding down, and the band's taking a breather, so I might come back and hang around a bit, get the lay of the land. We can celebrate EnergiFusion's success."

"Stay as long as you want, Turner. It'd be great to have you around." I'm sure the guys would love it.

"Keep a beer cold for me, Crystal."

"Always. Drive safe, rock star."

As I end the call, my attention shifts back to the list of calls I still need to make. Turner's faith in us is a welcome fuel. I'm determined to ensure that our vision for EnergiFusion is abundantly clear and tangible for the Automotive Showcase. But right now, I've got good news to share.

I grab a stack of photos from my desk and head down to the lab, where the familiar scent of solder and cold machinery hangs in the air. Until I was away for a while, I didn't realize how distinct that aroma is. In one corner, Theo's fingers dance over his keyboard like a pianist. He looks up as I approach, arching an eyebrow in silent question.

"Guess who's coming to The Fillmore?" I announce, unable to keep the grin from my face.

The guys swivel in their chairs. "Who?" Austin asks, leaning back in his chair.

"Turner," I say, and the room erupts. "Velvet Anomaly's going to blow the roof off that place in two weeks."

"Sweet!" Rhys punches the air.

"Tickets?" Theo asks, already reaching for his phone.

"Courtesy of the man himself. With backstage passes."

"Well, I'd better say thanks, then." Theo grins as his thumbs fly across the screen, tapping out a message to Turner.

It's good to bring some joy into the lab. These guys haven't just been to Mexico, so they could use a reminder that there's life beyond these walls filled with circuit boards and prototypes.

My gaze drifts to the corner where three tarps conceal our latest delivery of supplies. "And speaking of shows," I continue, flipping the photos in my hands to reveal a sleek American electric car. "Feast your eyes on this."

"Whoa," Theo murmurs, pocketing his phone. They gather around as I unveil the other two—a German model with a cutting-edge aesthetic and a Japanese compact renowned for its efficiency. Each one represents an opportunity, a challenge, and a promise.

"I've spoken with each of these companies, and they're ready for you to tailor prototype batteries for them," I say. "That way we're not just showcasing a product, we're demonstrating adaptability and innovation. This will show all the automakers that they won't have to redesign their engines to fit our batteries."

Austin nods, his gaze tracing the lines of the cars. "It's a bold move. We'll have to work nonstop to get them ready."

"Can we pull it off?" Rhys asks, skepticism and hope warring in his eyes.

"Of course we can," Justin affirms. "We've got the talent, the drive, and now, we've got the perfect stage. This Automotive Showcase will be our launching pad."

Their nods are hesitant but determined. We all know what's at stake, and as I look at the faces of the team, I see the reflection of my own resolve. They'll make this happen, for EnergiFusion, for all of us and the future we're trying to build.

I hover at the edge of Lamb's workspace, my gaze fixed on the cluster of battery cells spread across the bench. In that moment, he returns to the lab, appearing as if out of nowhere and seeming barely aware that the rest of us are here. "More sodium should have done it," he mutters to himself, his fingers rearranging the components like a conductor coaxing harmony from an orchestra. His brow is furrowed, lined with countless equations and failed experiments.

"Could there be an issue with the conductivity?" Austin ventures, stepping closer.

Fraser shakes his head, frustration evident. "I've triple-checked the calculations. The conductivity is fine. It's something else."

Every cell, every wire, is like a personal taunt. Justin's restless shadow flits at the periphery of my vision. His usual confident demeanor is undercut by the quick, clipped way he paces behind us.

"Justin," I say softly, reaching out to still him with a touch. His hand is clammy, betraying the cool front he presents. "We'll figure this out."

His nod is automatic, but his eyes are stormy. If EnergiFusion can't solve the charging issue, the battery will be dead on arrival, no matter how many cars they can tailor it for. EnergiFusion's dreams will deflate like a punctured balloon.

"Maybe it's the balance between the sodium and aluminum," Justin muses. "Have we considered shifting the ratio incrementally instead?"

Fraser pauses, a glint of interest cutting through his exasperation. "Incremental… Yes, small steps might show us where the imbalance lies."

"Exactly," Rhys chimes in, latching onto the lifeline of hope. "We find the tipping point and then recalibrate."

"Let's get to it, then," Theo declares, rolling up his sleeves. "We don't have time to waste."

Fraser nods, already lost in thought, his fingers dancing anew over the battery cells. Justin gives my hand a quick squeeze before letting go, a silent thank you for the support I know he needed.

This is what we do, what we have to do. We fight, we innovate, we solve. We keep moving forward. Failure is not an option.

twenty

Justin

I'm slumped over a circuit diagram when Mason and Cameron stride into the EnergiFusion lab. Their arrival is like an alarm clock, jolting us all into a more upright position. Dark circles hang under everyone's eyes, as it's been weeks of burning the midnight oil. For every step forward we take, we take a step back. The incremental approach to adjusting the ratio of sodium to aluminum did help us home in on the balance that's most effective, but it did not eliminate the charging problem entirely. The batteries are still not holding a charge for as long as they should, and our time with Lamb is running out.

Crystal's return has been a booster shot of energy to the team, but even she can't stave off the weariness that permeates the room.

"Guys," Mason begins, "the Automotive Showcase is just around the corner."

I nod. He doesn't need to elaborate. We're all painfully

aware of the ticking clock.

"Seven weeks," Cameron adds, folding his arms across his chest. His gaze sweeps over the cluttered lab—wires sprawling like vines, screens flickering with lines of code, tools scattered across workbenches.

"Seven weeks," I echo, the words tasting like lead on my tongue.

We exchange looks, a silent conversation passing between partners. We're exhausted, running on fumes and fading hope. Then there's the issue of Fraser Lamb. The guy was supposed to be our ace in the hole, our electrical engineering maestro. We took a risk on him, but it turns out, even maestros hit wrong notes.

"Fraser's contract ends today," Mason informs us, and I can't decide if it's relief or dread that floods me. Not having to share a portion of the company with Fraser means more profit stays in our pockets, but that's assuming there's ever anything to pocket at all.

"Unfortunately," Cameron continues, a grimace shadowing his features, "he couldn't solve the battery-charging issue."

The air in the room thickens, heavy with implication. Without a functional battery, there's no product. Without a product, there's no Showcase. And without the Showcase… I shove the thought aside. Can't go down that road, not yet.

"Any backup plans?" Theo asks, the hopeful lilt in his voice sounding more like desperation.

Mason and Cameron share a glance. They don't have an answer, and their silence speaks volumes. Have they decided this whole investment was a mistake?

"Tonight, we're taking a break. We'll regroup tomorrow," Austin says suddenly. "We'll find a way through this. We always do."

"Right," Rhys agrees, though the slump of his shoulders tells a different story.

I nod along, trying to believe it myself. We've been in tough spots before, but this is different, and the breakthrough we need has proved stubbornly elusive. Now, it feels like the future of EnergiFusion rests on a knife's edge, teetering between breakthrough and breakdown.

"If we don't have a functional product to secure orders from the Showcase…" Mason trails off, but he doesn't need to finish. We all know what's left unsaid. EnergiFusion is on its last breath.

"Guys," Cameron adds, trying to smile, "we believe in this project, in all of you. You've made progress since arriving here a year ago, and you've got seven weeks to figure the last of this out."

With a final nod, the door clicks shut behind them, leaving us in a silence that's anything but peaceful. Rhys runs a hand through his hair, a tell that he's beyond stressed. Theo's eyes, usually alight with ideas, are dull and defeated. Austin turns to stare at the schematics on the wall, as if willing them to reveal some hidden solution.

"We can't let this be the end," I whisper.

"Justin's right," Austin says, his gaze snapping from the blueprints to meet ours. "We've hit walls before. This is just… It's a bigger wall."

"Feels more like a damn fortress this time," Rhys mutters, kicking at a loose cable on the floor.

The door opens again, and Crystal steps into the lab. She must have seen Mason and Cameron heading back down the hall. She doesn't say anything, just leans against the wall near the door.

"We must be missing something," Theo suggests, but his doubt is a tangible thing, filling the room and squeezing our throats.

I shake my head. "Fraser Lamb couldn't figure it out, and he's one of the best." Despair has crept into every corner of the lab.

It's Crystal who breaks the desolation, her presence like a breeze through stale air. "Hey, tonight we're going to let loose and have fun at the Velvet Anomaly show," she reminds us. "It's the perfect chance to reset and recharge."

"Is Turner stopping by?" Austin asks.

"He'd better," I say. "Austin's right. We'll take tonight off, focus on something other than the battery, and maybe we'll come up with a solution. But meanwhile, he did say he would stop by this afternoon to see our digs."

"Great. We can show him our revolutionary battery that doesn't work," Rhys scoffs, though I catch the faintest glimmer of amusement in his tone.

"Come on, it'll be good to see him," I counter. "And shaking things up has to give us a fresh perspective."

"Or at least a good story for when we're famous inventors. We'll look back on this sad time when we were down on our luck. This could be the turning point," Theo jokes, and it pulls a genuine laugh from me.

"Down, but not out," I correct, pushing away from my workstation. "Let's clean up a bit before Turner gets here. No need to seem like a complete disaster."

"Right," Austin agrees, clapping his hands together. "Impress the rock star with our…organized chaos?"

"Exactly." I nod, grateful for even this small respite from the weight of impending failure. Maybe Turner's visit is exactly what we need—a reminder that there's a world outside these walls, full of possibility and life still waiting for us, no matter what happens with EnergiFusion.

I busy myself with organizing all the spare parts we've left lying around, and Crystal goes back to the office. The clink of metal-on-metal echoes in the lab as I watch Austin and Theo prod at the stubborn power cells. They're so absorbed in their work, faces tense with focus, that they barely register the door swinging open. It's Turner, hair longer than I remember, but with that same easy grin that lights up the gloomiest of spaces.

"Hey, guys!" he calls as he strides in, followed by Crystal.

"Turner!" Austin exclaims, dropping his tools and wiping his hands on his jeans before going in for a bro-hug.

Theo follows suit, leaving the power cells momentarily forgotten. "Been too long, man," he says, shaking his head with a laugh.

"Way too long," Turner agrees, glancing around the lab

with interest. "Place looks…intense."

"Intense is one word for it," I say dryly, pushing aside a pile of schematics to clear a spot on the workbench. I grab a couple of Scofflaw IPAs from the mini fridge we stocked for occasions just like this—or when the burnout hits hard—and pass them out.

"Hey. The hometown brew," Turner says, tapping his can against ours.

"Cheers!" We all raise our beers high before taking a drink.

"So, how's the rock star life treating you?" Rhys asks, leaning back against a cluttered desk.

"Great, great." Turner nods, taking a swig of his beer. "The girls are plentiful; concerts are insane." But then his shoulders drop ever so slightly, and he lets out a sigh. "Honestly, though? It gets old, living on the bus, crashing in hotels night after night."

"Really?" Theo looks surprised.

"Yeah, I'm thinking about making San Francisco my home base for a while," Turner says, and something like relief flashes across his face at the confession.

"San Francisco? That'd be awesome, man." My spirits lift at the thought of having Turner close by again.

"Would definitely make things more interesting around here," Austin agrees.

"After this West Coast swing is over, the band's taking a break before we dive into the next album," Turner continues. "And if we play our cards right, we might snag the opening act for Coldplay's northern hemisphere tour in two years."

"Whoa, that's huge!" Rhys whistles.

"Speaking of tours…" Crystal cuts in, her eyes alight with mischief. "I volunteer to join you on the road."

"Absolutely not," I say immediately. The thought of Crystal surrounded by the mess of touring life sends an uneasy twinge through me. "We've got too much to do here, and we need all hands on deck."

"Party pooper," she teases, but I can see in her eyes that she was only kidding.

"Anyway…" Turner sets his beer down on the bench. "Let's see what you geniuses have been up to."

The moment hangs in the air, charged with potential. Maybe Turner's presence is the catalyst we need. Maybe, just maybe, we can turn this impending disaster around.

We huddle around the battery prototype, and Theo fiddles with the components. I hit the highlights of our frustrating journey for Turner, indicating how we've made some progress with getting the charge to last longer, but we still don't have a reliable solution or a sense of what's actually causing the problem. I even tell him about Fraser Lamb and our most recent attempt to try gradually adjusting the concentrations of sodium ion and aluminum. The math works, but the ratio is still not working in our experiments.

Turner nods thoughtfully but doesn't speak.

"We've been tweaking the concentrations of sodium ion and aluminum. But what if it's about reducing them?" Austin asks after a moment, his voice slicing through our frustrated silence. His face is thoughtful as he works through the idea in his head.

"What if you're not directing the flow efficiently?" Turner asks.

"Like a bottleneck?" Rhys asks, brows furrowed.

"Exactly." Austin's hands are a blur as he reconfigures wires, and something akin to hope flutters in my chest, though it comes with a healthy dose of fear. I'm afraid to put too much stock in anything right now.

"Try now," Austin commands, and Theo hits the switch.

I hold my breath as the hum of electricity grows louder than before. The gauges spike, and then the numbers even out. We wait and watch the battery for deterioration—fifteen minutes, all good. Thirty minutes and it seems to be holding. I pass out a second round of beers. Forty-five minutes, still strong. When we hit the hour mark, nobody moves. Then the room explodes in cheers.

"Damn, Austin!" I clap him on the back, grinning wide. "You're a genius."

"Team effort," he deflects, but his smile betrays his pride.

"I think you guys might just pull this off," Turner says. "Glad I could get your juices flowing." With a wink, he checks his watch, which reminds me again that there's other life waiting outside these walls. "Time for me to get to The Fillmore. Sound check calls." He pulls backstage passes from his jacket pocket, handing them over with a flourish. "Don't say I never gave you anything."

"Thanks, man," Rhys says, tucking the pass into his shirt pocket. "Wouldn't miss it for the world."

"Seriously, Turner, you're the best," Crystal adds, her eyes lighting up as she takes her pass.

"Enjoy the show," Turner says with a wink. "And keep up the good work. Maybe our next tour will have an EnergiFusion-powered bus."

"From your lips to God's ears," I mutter. But now, with the power cells buzzing around us like a swarm of bees and the promise of music and camaraderie tonight, everything seems possible.

When it's time to head out, a few hours later, the batteries are still cranking out power. The charge has never lasted this long before, and it feels like this could be the breakthrough we've wanted. We set gauges to monitor their progress overnight, and we're on a real high when we head out for dinner before the show.

The scent of miso and pork broth greets us as we push open the door to House of Ramen, a dimly lit box with walls plastered in band posters, the air thick with steam and chatter. My stomach growls, but there's electricity in my veins that has nothing to do with hunger. Crystal points out the chicken and vegetable ramen bowl before excusing herself to the ladies room.

"Check this out," Austin says, already at a corner table with his phone out, scanning the QR code stuck to the varnished wood. I follow suit, thumbing through the digital menu. Noodles or rice bowl? Spicy or mild? The choices are a welcome distraction from the usual grind.

"Go for the extra chashu pork," Rhys advises over my

shoulder. "You'll need the protein after today."

"Good call." I tap the screen and add it to my cart, then add Crystal's chicken ramen before sending the order through.

Crystal returns, and I drape my arm over her shoulder and pull her in for a kiss. I feel a little giddy right now.

"Can you believe how much juice we got?" Austin's face is lit up like he's just discovered fire. "And it was still going when we left…" This surge is more than data on a screen. It's hope. It's potential. It's the future.

"Man, if this works…" Theo trails off.

"Let's not jinx it," I say, but I'm smiling too. When the food arrives, we slurp noodles and share laughs, letting ourselves believe, just for now, that everything's on the upswing.

"What song are you hoping they'll play tonight?" Crystal asks, and we spend the remainder of dinner talking about our old friend and all the good times listening to our favorite band.

After dinner, we head over for the end of the sound check and stand around backstage. I recognize a few of the roadies from our days at Georgia Tech, and it seems like they're eyeing Crystal. I pull her a little closer.

Turner has barely finished with sound check before he has two girls hanging on him, and he has to break free to greet us. "This place is sublime," he gushes. "I mean, we've had more than fifty shows on this tour, and this is still fucking amazing. I'm so glad you're here tonight."

We share hugs and wish him well, then make our way out front to watch. The opening band starts, their melodic tunes echoing through the crowded concert hall, but I hardly notice. My attention is focused on reconnecting with old friends from school, because, of course, Velvet Anomaly doesn't travel alone. I spot Crystal chatting with the guitarist's girlfriend, and there are lots of other familiar faces from Atlanta as well. *Does no one have a job?* As I make my way around the room, I'm surprised by the different paths my classmates have taken since graduation. We exchange stories and updates, and I field many questions about EnergiFusion. This is the cherry on the ice cream sundae of today, but then things really get going when Velvet Anomaly finally takes the stage. The bass thumps against my chest as we turn our attention forward and merge into the sea of bodies at The Fillmore. Velvet Anomaly positively owns this place, and Turner is a silhouette against the strobes, his voice a rallying cry that pulls the audience together into a pulsing, screaming being.

Crystal's hand finds mine, and she turns to me, her eyes reflecting the stage lights. In that moment, I see the girl I met at a show just like this one. Her smile is wide, unrestrained, and all the weight we've been carrying seems to lift.

"It's like coming full circle, isn't it?" she shouts over the music, leaning close so I can hear.

"Only better," I yell back, and I mean it. With her by my side, we have a viable path for our battery, and with the band tearing it up, I feel nothing but joy.

The set rolls on, each song an anthem, an escape. When the crowd roars for an encore, I look around at my friends, at Crystal, and everything clicks into place. This is going to happen. We're exactly where we're meant to be.

twenty-one

Crystal

"What did SHN tell you?" Teagan asks as we hang under the trees in the little park by the office on a beautiful summer afternoon.

"The solution the guys have developed for the battery could change all batteries. SHN has put the paperwork in for a patent, and not just for the automotive industry. They believe any battery-operated product will want to use our technology, and they'll have to pay us for the usage."

"That is huge."

I let out a sigh and nod. I still can't quite believe it. "The Automotive Showcase will be a test. We'll see if SHN is reading the market right."

We're down to the last week before the showcase. The videographer is finally done filming, and they're editing the video for our booth now. The guys from SHN are down here at least once a day, and their excitement is obvious. They've been a huge help in reaching out to automotive companies to make sure they come by the booth. Everything's coming together, but I don't think the guys are sleeping a wink right now.

Teagan shakes her head. "Absolutely amazing. Just remember me when you're living the high life in Pacific Heights and I'm still struggling with Intellithread."

"You have people who are interested," I remind her. "Your life is going to change here very soon. We'll be neighbors in Pacific Heights."

"I like that!"

I glance at the silver watch clasped around my wrist, and there's a familiar tug of urgency. "Sorry, Teagan, I need to get going, and I need to stop back in at the office." She knows I have an appointment with Dr. McKay to get to this afternoon.

"No problem. Thanks again for the tickets to Velvet Anomaly up in Portland. It was a blast." She gives me a hug and stands to gather her things. "I know you're slammed right now with the Showcase, but if you need a break, promise to call me."

"I promise."

We say goodbye again when we get back to the building, and we each head for our own spaces. I stop in at the office just long enough to snatch my worn leather bag from the back of my chair, then I make a beeline for the door.

"Hey, where you headed?" Justin's voice comes from down the hallway, where he's just stepped out of the lab.

"Quick errand," I say, a half-truth that sits uneasy in my chest. "Back in a little over an hour."

"Can you grab me some Swedish Fish on your way back?" He rubs his temples, eyes bloodshot from days tethered to his computer. "I need sugar and caffeine to survive the homestretch."

"Sure thing." I nod, guilt nipping at my heels as I slip out of the office. Swedish Fish—the gummy sweetness he craves. But my mind is elsewhere, wrapped in thoughts of Dr. McKay's office, where I'll soon unravel pieces of myself I prefer to keep hidden away. I started this for the meds, but Dr. McKay has us doing cognitive behavioral therapy, which has me talking about my feelings, thoughts, and behavior. It's actually been useful, and she's great at showing me how they influence each other and how to find patterns I might want to change. I have a long way to go, but I look forward to our appointments. If only she'd lay off on me talking to Justin about my mental health.

I navigate the streets filled with the bustle of city life. It's a short walk to Dr. McKay's, one that gives me space to breathe and prepare.

"Crystal, come in," Dr. McKay greets me with her usual warm smile, though today it seems like a lifeline.

I sink into the plush chair opposite her, the fabric cool against my skin. "Work's been…intense," I begin, not even waiting for her to prompt me, and it's like opening the floodgates. My words spill out, recounting the progress we've made, the relentless pace, the fatigue on the faces of my team. "Austin had this idea, and it's making a real difference. We're pushing forward with a product that actually functions as intended, and we have batteries for three EV models ready for the Automotive Showcase. Everyone's poured their soul into this."

"Sounds promising," Dr. McKay says, her pen poised over the notepad she always keeps close.

"Promising and exhausting," I agree. "But we're a good team. We're getting there." Pride swells within me, mingled with exhaustion—our shared currency as we race against time.

Dr. McKay nods, her gaze both kind and piercing. "And you, Crystal? How are you holding up in all this?"

"Me?" I pause, feeling suddenly under the spotlight. "I'm…managing." The truth is complicated and something I'm content to let go unspoken.

"Good," she replies, a note of encouragement in her voice that buoys me just enough. "Remember, self-care is crucial, especially when the stakes are high."

"Of course," I promise. I know well the delicate dance of pushing my limits while guarding the fragile balance of my well-being.

"Keep that in mind," she advises again before our time

runs out and I'm ushered back into the chaos of the world beyond her door. At least, this time, she didn't push me about telling Justin my health history. We both know I need to, but this isn't a good time. Not when there's so much at stake.

With a renewed sense of purpose, I stop at a local bodega, gathering Swedish Fish and an assortment of chocolate bars—a small token of appreciation for the guys on this final climb. As I pay for the sugary contraband, I realize that if what SHN is telling us comes even half true, our lives are going to shift drastically. I hope the success doesn't change us too much.

Armed with candy, I retrace my steps to the office, ready to face whatever awaits. I find the team in the lab, much as I left them, leaning into white boards and screens, their concentration palpable. "Got your sugar," I announce, holding up the bags like trophies. They emerge from their technical reveries, faces lighting up with childlike delight.

"Crystal, you're a lifesaver," Justin says, grinning as he snags his Swedish Fish. The others echo his thanks, tearing into the chocolate with fervor. It's the small victories that keep us going, and right now, candy is king.

Shoving a bite into his mouth, Austin hands me a list—on a piece of paper this time—wires, components, and more sodium chloride. "For the prototype EV batteries," he explains. "Thank you."

"Consider it done," I reply, pocketing the list and waving as I return to my computer in the office to place the orders. In these moments, I feel most connected to our success. Each item checked off brings us one step closer to standing out at the Automotive Showcase.

Order confirmed, I find myself with a sliver of time—a rare commodity these days—so I slip away to a quiet conference room, closing the door behind me. I don't talk to my parents very often, but I promised Dr. McKay I would reach out. If I don't do it now, I'll never get it done before my next appointment. The sunlight slants through the blinds, casting long shadows across the table, a reminder that the day is waning here but still at its height in Florida.

My hand shakes slightly as I dial the familiar number, the sequence embedded deep in muscle memory. It rings, a sound that at one time would have filled me with warmth, but now brings anxiety. The call connects, and the moment of truth awaits.

"Hey, honey!" Mom's voice crackles through the phone. "I'm so glad you're calling. We miss you so much."

Dad's baritone rumbles in the background, a sure sign he's listening in.

"Everything's fine," I assure them, my fingers tracing the cool surface of the conference table. "I'm seeing Dr. McKay regularly, and I'm stable." The words make me proud, a small declaration in my ongoing battle for normalcy.

"Stable? That's good, sweetheart," Dad says. "But what about school?" I can imagine him leaning closer to the phone.

"Actually," I interject before they can spiral into their well-worn lecture, "I've enrolled in a class at UC Berkeley for the fall."

There's a pause, and then Dad chuckles. "What are you, becoming a hippie?"

"Compared to you, probably," I quip.

Their relief is almost tangible. "We're just glad you're continuing your education." Mom sighs, her worry momentarily assuaged.

"Also…" Dad chimes in, "when do you plan on bringing that boy, Justin, home to meet us?"

I press my lips together, thinking of Justin's chaotic schedule and the tangled web of our lives. "With everything going on, it won't be soon," I tell them.

"That's unfortunate." Mom sighs again, and I can practically see Dad's frown.

"Y'know, you could always come visit out here," I suggest, though the words seem futile even as they leave my mouth. They've never ventured west of the Mississippi, and I doubt they'll start now.

"Maybe one day," Mom says. That's the noncommittal response I've come to expect after growing up in their house.

"Sure, one day," I echo, letting the conversation and my expectations drift away into silence.

The phone's weight grows in my hand as silence stretches across the line.

"Have you told Justin about your bipolar disorder?" Mom's voice is sharp with concern.

A lump forms in my throat, and the words come out more quietly than I intend. "I haven't brought it up." I clutch the phone tighter, bracing for impact.

"Crystal," she starts, her tone tightening, "if he truly loves you, he will accept you as you are."

Her words sting, mixing guilt with the fear already simmering inside me. "It's not that simple, Mom. He's under a lot of pressure with work…" I trail off, knowing my excuses sound hollow.

"Pressure or not," she persists, "you should be honest with him. And if he can't handle it, then—"

"Then what?" I cut in, frustration mounting. "You want me to just pack up and crawl back to Georgia Tech or Florida?"

"You being closer to home would put our minds at ease," Dad interjects, his voice stern.

"But what about me? About my mind?" I mutter. "I'm here because I'm part of something and because of Justin. We have something special." My words are a plea for understanding, but they fall on deaf ears.

"It doesn't seem so special if you're afraid telling him the truth will make him leave," Dad says flatly.

His words hit like a punch, leaving me reeling. My heart races, and the familiar feeling of being trapped creeps up. I need to escape. "Look, I have to go," I say abruptly, fumbling for an excuse to end the call.

"Crystal, we only want what's best—"

"I understand. I've got to go. Bye, Mom. Bye, Dad." I don't wait for their response. I just press *end* and drop the phone onto the table like it's on fire.

Staring at the silent device, I take a deep breath, trying to shake off their words. It won't do any good to let their doubts infect me now. I need to focus on something else.

A ping and a message on the screen rescues me—a

notification. The order I placed for Austin has arrived. That's quick, even for me. I zip out to the front desk to grab the package and hurry to the lab.

"Hey, guys!" I call as I approach.

Austin and the others are huddled near the German car. Their faces light up when they see me.

"Wow, Crystal, that was fast!" Austin exclaims, grinning as he takes the package from my hands.

"Fast and efficient, just how I like it," I quip, forcing a smile.

"Oh, that's why you're with Justin," Rhys teases.

I shake my head and offer him an eye roll. Then I cross my arms and shrug. "That's life, living with all of you."

"Thanks for this," Justin says, coming to my rescue, or his own. I'm not sure which. "You're a lifesaver." They all nod in agreement.

"Anytime," I reply, and this time my smile is real. Their appreciation drowns out the frustration left by my call with my parents.

twenty-two

Justin

The pulse of excitement is palpable as I step into the sprawling convention center, the air electric with innovation and ambition. The Automotive Showcase has finally arrived—a four-day carnival of technology with an array of pitches and dreams, each display more dazzling than the last. Cutting-edge everything—from car seats to halogen lights to carpets and fabrics to batteries and computer systems—is available for car manufacturers' perusal as they decide how to outfit their next-generation vehicles.

I weave through the throng, my partners close behind as we find our designated spot. As we begin our setup, we realize it's not just us here in the EV battery arena. There's another player, another electric vehicle battery that might just rival our creation. My stomach tightens. Of course, there's always competition, but I hope this will be our time to shine.

Then, amidst the flurry of activity, Turner appears like a

familiar ghost, slipping into our booth, unnoticed by the crowd. No one recognizes the lead singer of Velvet Anomaly—at least not until he sings—so here, in this different context, he's just one of us, a tech enthusiast getting his fix.

"Love this, man," he murmurs, fingering a component of our prototype battery. "It's like being back at school, using both the left and right sides of my brain."

I smile. Here's a rock star, incognito, nerding out over circuitry and energy densities.

Just as we'd hoped, soon our booth becomes a beacon, drawing in curious souls with a looping video that showcases our battery's potential. Crystal is running point behind the scenes, keeping everything going and preparing for the big demonstration we'll have in a bit. Austin, Rhys, Theo, and I are bombarded with inquiries, which is thrilling. I count it as proof that we have something that matters and can truly make a difference.

"Can it handle extreme temperatures?" a bespectacled woman asks, peering at the specs displayed on the screen.

"Absolutely," I reply, my voice steady despite the rapid drumbeat of my heart. "We've tested it in conditions ranging from the frigid to the scorching—"

"Efficiency during long-term use?" interrupts another, a notebook clutched in his hand.

"Minimal degradation," Rhys chimes in.

"Recharging times?" A skeptical brow arches from a potential investor.

"Still improving," Theo admits with a charming grin. "Obviously, it depends on the charging station, and the emptier the battery, the longer it takes to recharge. But our latest model cuts significant minutes off the standard. EV can recharge in eighteen minutes, and EV1 is typically done overnight because it's the slowest."

Question after question, our answers volley back, each one a testament to sleepless nights and relentless trials. And Turner's enthusiasm never wanes as he stands beside us. This is our moment. We've waited so long, and *damn*, it feels good to be here.

The conversation swells around me, a slurry of deals and dreams bartered over glossy displays. Then Mason's voice cuts through. "Cost projections look solid," he says, his eyes flicking between the charts on Crystal's tablet and the automaker representatives encircling us.

"Market penetration by Q3 next year could be realistic," Cameron adds, tapping a finger against his chin.

I marvel at the way Dillon weaves through the crowds to join them. They are the trinity of SHN, the founders. Their presence at our booth is a fortress against uncertainty. The crowd is three people deep now, and we have SHN to thank—well, and Crystal. But SHN is behind so much of our buzz at the show. In this moment, I realize the depth of their belief in us, not just in our technology, but in our vision. The difficult conversations, the unwavering support despite the turbulence—it's all led to now, to these discussions that could anchor our future.

Gratitude tightens my throat. They've done so much more than invest; they've believed, and that belief has been our bedrock. Crystal steps up beside me and slips her hand in mine. I'm so grateful she's here and for everything she's done to get us to this place. I squeeze her hand as a ripple of laughter draws my attention to Theo leaning casually against the edge of eBattery's sleek display. Stephanie Green, the brain behind the battery that's our friendly rival today, tosses her hair back, her smile wide. Theo's charm is a live wire, sparking as he leans in, murmuring something that makes her laugh again.

"Your charge time is enviable," he concedes, respect and a dash of mischief in his tone. "Our power output is neck and neck, but you've got us beat there."

Stephanie tilts her head, an eyebrow quirking. "Perhaps a collaboration could benefit both parties?" She's teasing, or maybe she's serious; it's hard to tell.

"Or perhaps a friendly competition will push us both to greater heights," Theo counters.

Their banter is a dance of intellects, and I admire the way Theo navigates these waters—flirting not just with a person, but with possibility.

"Justin?" Crystal's voice snaps me back, and I turn to find her nodding toward the crowd headed into the theater. "They're waiting for you."

"Right," I breathe, stepping forward to collect the guys. We've got to get set up for our mainstage presentation.

"You've got this! Go break a leg! Or blow it out of the water?" She giggles. We're all a little giddy right now.

A few minutes later, I step onto the stage, microphone in hand. I glance at Crystal, and the world plunges into semi-darkness, save for the spotlights that cut like beacons through the gloom. My heart races, not with nerves, but with a kinetic energy that propels me forward.

"Good afternoon." My voice booms over the speakers, clear and confident. "We're EnergiFusion, and we're here to ignite your imagination and drive innovation straight into the future."

On cue, the first vehicle rolls in, Austin behind the wheel of a sleek electric Japanese sedan, its lines cutting a sharp silhouette against the backdrop of pulsing lights. Rhys follows in an avant-garde German sports model, low and predatory, the crowd's awe audible as it prowls into view. Lastly, Theo rolls up in a luxury American SUV, the kind that speaks of power without uttering a single word.

The music swells, a soundtrack to revolution, every beat a promise of progress, all orchestrated by Crystal, the unseen conductor of our electric dreams.

Out of the corner of my eye, I catch Turner slipping away, his wave a silent goodbye. He's off to another stage, another crowd in another city.

I launch into our presentation, and everything flows smoothly. Eventually, we shift gears into Q and A.

"Have you considered production scale?" one potential buyer asks.

"Where will these be manufactured?" another probes.

I exchange a look with Austin. We're on the brink, teetering on the edge of the next monumental leap. Our technology has captured their imaginations; now, we must make them a reality.

"Manufacturing is our horizon," I admit to the sea of faces. "We're exploring several potential sites for our plant, as we want to ensure that we can meet demand and maintain the quality that defines us."

Nods of understanding greet my words, and when our time is up, the crisp feeling of impending success follows us out of the convention center and into the warm embrace of Quince's dining room. Mason leads our merry band to a private space.

Once everyone has a seat and something to drink, Mason rises to address the room. "Tonight," he says, raising a glass of amber liquid, "we're not just celebrating a successful showcase. We've secured an advance deposit from all five major car manufacturers and have piqued the interest of several smaller ones. Car makers are ready to use EnergiFusion batteries as soon as they become available. This level of interest is beyond our wildest dreams. Your financial outlook is about to have a huge shift. There will be nothing you can't afford. Gentlemen and Crystal—" He nods at her with a smile. "The fruits of your labor are about to set seed."

Dillon nods in agreement and Cameron's eyes dance as we burst into applause. A grin stretches across my face, feeling wider than the span of the Golden Gate Bridge. This is it. The moment we've been gearing up for, turning every hypothetical into a solid plan.

"I know the Valley is all about stock options," Mason continues when the room has settled again. "But going public means playing a different game, one that doesn't guarantee the kind of control or return we want. SHN's goal has always been to make our money back, and then some. These deals secure that promise."

I let out a breath I didn't realize I was holding. Mason's perspective echoes my own desires. SHN has been an invaluable ally, but I don't want anyone else calling the shots around here.

"Besides," Mason adds with a sly smile, "who says you can't make a ton of money and keep your souls intact?"

Laughter ripples around the table, and the weight of

unspoken questions lifts. We raise our glasses, the clinking sound merging with a shared sense of accomplishment and relief.

Then a server in a crisp uniform approaches, balancing a tray of effervescent champagne in flutes.

I hand a glass to Crystal as I take one for myself. She grins at me as if I hung the moon. "Thank you."

"Everyone," Mason calls. "I've been in this game a long time." He pauses, letting the anticipation build. "But never—*never* have I seen a team achieve what you have at such a breathtaking pace." Pride swells in my chest, warmth spreading through me that isn't just from the alcohol. "Though you did save the exciting part for right at the end."

Everyone laughs at that, though thinking of our longstanding charging issues still makes me want to throw up.

Mason raises his glass again. "To the fastest billionaires I've ever had the privilege of working with!"

"Here, here!" Dillon echoes and Cameron nods.

We all stand, a seamless motion, clinking our glasses together. Laughter and congratulations mingle, and I look around at the faces of my partners—my friends. Their smiles are as bright as the future we're stepping into.

Theo, as always, has that mischievous twinkle in his eye as he lifts his flute again after the rest of us have settled. "And let's not forget the one who orchestrated much of today's spectacle." He nods to Crystal, who blushes slightly. "To Crystal, whose vision and flair gave us the edge we needed. You turned a showcase into a showstopper."

"Cheers to Crystal!" Rhys chimes in, and the rest follow suit, another round of clinks resonating around the table.

My gaze lingers on Theo a moment longer than the others, noting the ease of his charm, his deliberate choice of words. Crystal's laughter is genuine, but I sense something more, an undercurrent that perhaps only I'm attuned to. I file the thought away for later; now, isn't the time for conjecture.

I slip my hand into Crystal's and give it a squeeze. I always knew she and the guys would figure out a way to get along. "Thank you for everything you do for EnergiFusion and for us."

She turns to me and smiles.

Now, it's about the celebration, the shared triumph. Champagne flows, dinner is delicious, and lively tales of the day's events spill over each other. We bask in the glow of achievement, the camaraderie that comes from having weathered storms and ridden waves to the shore of success. Our financial outlook is now totally different than it was just a few hours ago. I can't even grasp how that's possible. Tonight, we are more than a company; we are conquerors who have claimed the future as our own.

twenty-three

Crystal

Since the Automotive Showcase, things around the office have shifted gears. We're past strictly problem solving now, and we're strategizing for the next phase: production. Mason and Dillon met with us last week, and we've been inundated with lists of tasks to get through as we prepare for manufacturing. SHN is helping us see the leaves in the forest we've been immersed in.

Meanwhile, Justin and Rhys are traveling to different parts of the country with Dillon, checking out factory options. The initial money SHN offered will go to cover the facilities. The cash we received after the Showcase from manufacturers eager to secure the right to buy our batteries will go toward materials, and companies will be able to buy at a discount when production gets up and running and they finalize their orders. Best of all, the cash infusion from the Automotive Showcase triggered a significant payout to all of us, and we're now collecting monster salaries—even me!

Mason put me in touch with Lori Neilson, a real estate agent, and strongly suggested that we each invest in something. It thrills me to think of Justin and I finally having our own place, not just somewhere to shove our stuff, but an investment, a stake in the ground.

The guys on the team all agreed, and since there are fewer demands day to day in the office now, I've been put in charge of this task for them. I'll look through the different options on the market and whittle it down to two or three suggestions they can each view in an afternoon and make a decision. The responsibility here both thrills and terrifies me. And it's led to a lot of conversations I never imagined having with these men.

"Crystal," Theo informs me one afternoon when we all happen to be in the office together, "I want something that touches the sky, a space in a high rise where the pulse of the city strums beneath me." His hands slice through the air, mimicking the sharp lines of the buildings he covets.

Austin leans back in his chair. "Not me," he declares. "I'm thinking charm, you know? A gingerbread house, something quaint and intricate."

Rhys nods as he takes in their requests. "I'd like a view of the Golden Gate and the ability to enjoy the waterfront. Maybe a small yard for a dog."

"Got it," I reply, already cataloging their wishes. When I look over, Justin gives me a supportive smile; he's always had faith in my ability to deliver.

Lately, we've spent our evenings dreaming of homes, of places that could be ours, where the echoes of our footsteps would tell a story. Justin is pretty easy going. He'd like a view, but he's not even particular about that. He just wants me with him, and he's insisting on buying our house.

With so many options suddenly available, it's easy to get carried away. But right now, I need to focus on translating their visions into tangible addresses.

"Let's do this," Lori says with an assertive nod when we finally find a time to get together. I've shared everyone's wish lists with her, and she's armed with listings and a determination that matches my own. We spend days touring San Francisco, from the polished floors of penthouses to the creaky steps of historical havens. We pore over Victorian trims and analyze green space and water access. And then together, over coffee-stained maps and endless property specs, we curate a list—three potential winners for each guy, each choice a reflection of their personalities.

Then, one by one, I send them off with Lori on their own.

"Which one's speaking to you?" I ask each of them after their tours, my heart racing with anticipation. I'm nervous they won't like my choices, but in the end, they all found something that fits. Theo put an offer on a place in a high rise in the financial district, where all the action is. Austin ended up choosing one of San Francisco's most famous Victorian homes on Alamo Square Park. It has a stunning bridge-to-bridge view and also looks out on downtown San Francisco. Rhys picked out a home at the San Francisco Marina, right off the docks and with a view of the Golden Gate Bridge.

Justin is still perusing his choices, but if he makes a decision soon, we'll all be homeowners in the next month or so.

Then finally, one afternoon I stand on the sidewalk of Lyon Street, a crisp San Francisco breeze ruffling the papers in my hand. I steal another glance over at the smallest house on Billionaires' Row. Just over three thousand square feet, it's more than enough for us and nestled in the nicest neighborhood in the city. It's perfect.

Justin saunters up beside me, hands in the pockets of his jeans, an easy smile on his face. "So, this is it, huh? The last one on my list?"

"Yep, the very last," I reply, struggling to keep my voice neutral, not wanting to sway him with my own bias.

He surveys the property, his gaze thoughtful. "You've got a good eye, Crystal. But you know I'm not much for picking houses."

"Still, I want this to be your decision too." My insistence surprises even me. All three houses we've seen hold a charm that's undeniable, but my heart clings to this one. "I love them all, Justin. Choose the one that seems right."

"Even if it's this one?" He nudges me gently with his elbow, a teasing glint in his eyes.

"Especially if it's this one."

Silence sits between us like a welcome friend as we take in the quiet prestige of the neighborhood. Then he nods, decisively, a choice made without fanfare. "Let's do it, then. This one. It feels like…us."

A surge of joy floods through me, and I laugh, a sound of relief, of celebration. "Really?" I ask, needing to hear it again.

"Really," he confirms.

We step closer to the house, and I'm already imagining it as our future home. This seems like stepping into a new chapter. The plans we'll make here, the life we'll build—everything seems possible.

"Then let's make an offer," I say, the words a vow, a promise of beginnings.

"Let's make an offer," he echoes, wrapping an arm around my shoulders. And just like that, we're no longer just looking at a house. We're envisioning a home.

The plush leather of Dr. McKay's couch envelops me, a stark contrast to the clinical coolness of her office. The hum of San Francisco fades beyond these walls, leaving room for the truths I've come to share. My fingers trace the smooth material, seeking solace before I confide in her.

"Dr. McKay," I begin, swallowing the lump of apprehension lodged in my throat. She's going to bug me about talking to Justin, and I just don't have the energy today.

"Did you get the house?" she asks.

I relax into my seat and nod. "We did. Well, we're in escrow, but they accepted our offer."

"That's wonderful news. How are you feeling about it?"

"I'm excited. Justin is putting down the money, but he

wants to put me on the title. He says he wants it to be our place. Though I don't know how we're going to fill it. We don't even have a bed."

"Have you talked to Justin about your bipolar disorder?"

"Well, uh, I tried, but we've been so caught up in getting the business going and now the house…"

She leans forward slightly, her eyes locking onto mine with an intensity that beckons honesty. "Why is it that you're still holding back from telling him?"

I take a deep breath, and the air struggles against the tightness in my chest. "It feels like a shadow would scare him away."

"Even though he's moving forward with plans for you to live together?" Dr. McKay looks at me a moment and then nods with an understanding that seems to reach beyond her professional demeanor. "Your mother said something to you about this, didn't she?" Her voice is a gentle nudge, urging me toward reflection.

"Nothing you haven't said to me… If he isn't interested in me because of my disorder, then he doesn't truly love me."

"Your mother is a wise woman," Dr. McKay says, her tone soft yet firm. "You must trust that Justin's feelings for you are based on who you are, not on the challenges you've helped him navigate."

I nod. "I suppose that's true, but the challenges keep coming, so it's hard to totally separate the two."

"Can you say more about that?" she asks.

"We're living in undisclosed places to stay out of the media spotlight until we close on our new homes," I explain. "Justin and I are staying at Mason and Caroline Sullivans' place. Mason's company is EnergiFusion's investor. It's temporary, but privacy has become precious."

"And the others?" she probes.

"Austin, Theo, and Rhys are just up the street at one of the Sullivans' friend's guest house. Having secure accommodations has been crucial with all the attention we're receiving. And no one has closed on their new property just yet."

"Security is important," she agrees. "Especially now, when so much is changing for you all."

I chuckle, shaking my head at the absurdity of it all. "You wouldn't believe the attention they're getting now. The female population has certainly taken notice."

"Oh?" Dr. McKay prompts.

"Justin's had four marriage proposals this week. And an up-and-coming rock star sent her people to set up a date with him," I say, trying to keep my voice light, amused.

"How does that make you feel?" she asks.

I hesitate for a moment, my smile fading. "It bothers me, to be honest. More than I thought it would."

"Understandable." She nods, encouraging me to continue.

With a deep breath, I lean back. "SHN's PR team—they've been amazing. We're everywhere in the financial press. Austin, Rhys, Theo, and Justin are these media darlings now." I pause, gathering the strands of my thoughts. "There's a feature on them in *Vanity Fair*."

"Sounds impressive."

"It is, but…" I fidget with the hem of my sweater, betraying my inner turmoil. "We decided to keep my relationship with Justin out of the spotlight. To keep my profile low, you know?"

"Protection and privacy can be valuable," she acknowledges.

"Right, but now, he's this eligible bachelor in the public eye. It's…it's getting to me."

She doesn't rush to fill the silence that follows, allowing the complexity of my emotions to unfurl in the quiet space between us. There's a part of me that knows it was the right decision at the time, but another part—the part that's sitting here now—feels exposed and uneasy about where I fit into Justin's new, glossy narrative.

I tap my foot nervously on the plush carpet.

"Your financial situation," she begins, "how has it changed with the company's success?"

The question pulls me from my reverie, snapping the

world back into focus. "It's…good. Really good. I got a raise—a six-figure raise." The words are too good to be true, even as they spill from my lips, a stark contrast to the uncertainties swirling inside me.

"Congratulations, Crystal. That's quite significant." Her smile is genuine, but her eyes probe deeper. "Have you thought about what you want to do with this newfound financial independence? Perhaps move out on your own instead of moving in with Justin?"

My gaze drops to my hands, knotted together in my lap. I have thought about it countless times, but there's a tug-of-war within me. "Part of me wants my own space," I confess, the truth tasting bittersweet. "But another part wants to experience more alone time with Justin, to keep things as they are for as long as possible. And I do like that he wants me there with him."

"Change can be daunting," Dr. McKay acknowledges, leaning forward slightly. "But holding on to someone isn't just about proximity; it's also about connection and honesty."

Her words send shivers down my spine. Honesty—the thing that seems most vulnerable to offer, especially when it means exposing the rawest parts of myself.

"Justin needs to know all of you, Crystal. The only way to truly hold on to him—or anyone—is by being authentic and open. I suspect you won't feel fully secure in your relationship until you tell him about your bipolar disorder."

My throat tightens, and I nod. I know she's right. The fear of losing him battles against the need for him to love all of me, not just the parts I've polished for public viewing. "I know I need to. It just never seems like the right time. I'm so afraid…"

"Being honest doesn't guarantee an outcome," she continues, her voice a grounding force. "But it does give you both a chance at something real, something lasting. And whatever his response, you'll know it's based on the full picture of who you are."

This is nothing new, of course, but I find it hits me a little differently today, and I'm still pondering it as I walk back to the office. I fill my lungs with air before releasing it slowly, as if I could also expel the tangled fears binding me. Dr. McKay's words are a guide through the darkness of my apprehensions. If I want to hold on to Justin, to us, it won't be through silence or half-truths. It will be through the courage to show him the real me.

As I step back into the EnergiFusion office, the contrast between Dr. McKay's calm sanctuary to this vibrant hub of activity is like stepping onto a moving train. The guys are sprawled across various couches and beanbags, interacting with the casual ease of people who've ridden a rollercoaster together and come out laughing on the other side.

"Hey, Crystal," Mason calls. "You're just in time for the great debate."

"Headquarters," Austin announces, not looking up from his tablet. "San Francisco versus…everywhere else."

"SHN gave us the boot," Theo adds, his tone light but his eyes serious. "Says it's time we left the nest."

"More like they need the space for fresh blood," Justin quips, tossing a crumpled paper ball at Theo, who bats it away.

"Seriously, though," Rhys says. "We've all agreed—headquarters here, in San Francisco. You did wonders with the housing, Crystal. We're hoping you'll wave your magic wand again for our office space. Think you can find us something with a decent lab and space for a production line?"

I nod, already mentally cataloging agents I know and spaces that might fit the bill. "Of course. I'll start reaching out first thing tomorrow."

"Good, because we need somewhere that screams 'innovation'," Austin pipes up, finally tearing his gaze from the screen to offer me an appreciative smile.

"About production, though…" Justin starts, and unease settles over the group. "We've got options. Utah's got the salt, but the Bay Area's got…well, everything else. And the big five auto manufacturers are in Detroit."

"Costs are higher here," Rhys points out. "But the back-and-forth would be a killer if we set up shop in Utah. And I'm not crazy about Michigan winters."

"Let's not forget talent acquisition," Theo interjects. "The Bay Area draws a certain crowd, one that can fuel our growth."

"Right. So, we should stay local," Theo summarizes.

"Local, it is then," I say, looking around for confirmation. "I'll include potential production spaces in my search. Proximity will be key."

"Crystal's got it under control," Justin says, smiling at me with a confidence I wish I could bottle and drink before each daunting task. His faith in me… It's more than just reassuring. It's a lifeline. I hear Dr. McKay's voice in my head. *He deserves to know.*

I jot down bullet points in my notebook, and the guys' voices blend into the background as I prepare for the task at hand—scouting locations for both our new headquarters and production facilities. Yet my mind continues to return to my session with Dr. McKay. *Be honest. Be direct. Changes need to happen.*

"Hey, Crystal, you with us?" Theo's voice cuts through my concentration, and I lift my head to meet his questioning gaze.

"Absolutely," I reply, forcing myself back into the moment. "Just making sure I've got all the details right."

"Great because we're counting on you." Austin gives me an encouraging grin, but Rhys who narrows his eyes thoughtfully, as if sensing there's more to my distraction than the task at hand.

twenty-four

Justin

These days, Crystal and I are pinching ourselves with disbelief. Just a year ago, we were struggling to make ends meet and living with three other roommates. We worked unending hours to make an electric vehicle battery that is more environmentally friendly. But then we did, and the automotive industry took notice in a big way. Since then, we've become billionaires practically overnight. And SHN has helped us find a home for our battery technology in several additional industries, beyond just electric vehicles. I know for certain now that EnergiFusion is going to have an impact on the world and revolutionize the battery industry.

Thankfully, despite all we still have to do as we move toward production, we're able to afford a day off here and there and a real weekend most of the time. So, after a Saturday spent wrapped in the luxury of the fancy shops we wandered when we first arrived in San Francisco—this time buying Crystal a new wardrobe and a few baubles—Seven Hills restaurant looms before us, promising still more elegance. We're greeted with warm smiles and led to a cozy table by the window, where the last traces of dusk paint the sky in hues of purple and orange.

Once we're seated, Crystal studies the menu, her eyes sparkling in the soft candlelight. She decides on the tagliolini, the word rolling off her tongue as if she's been ordering dishes like this all her life. The server nods approvingly and turns to me.

"I'll have the market fish," I say, trying not to sound too eager. I'm mostly in it for the risotto and artichokes that accompany it.

"An excellent choice, sir," the server responds.

Once he departs, we toast with glasses of Chianti. I watch Crystal as she savors each sip, her eyes closed. It's still strange, this ability to simply enjoy life and make choices without the shadow of financial constraint looming over us. I look forward to enjoying it for the rest of my days.

"Here's to new experiences," I say, lifting my glass.

"And not forgetting the old ones," Crystal adds with a wink.

"Never," I agree, and our glasses chime together, the sound as clear and promising as our future.

As the first course arrives, I lean back into the plush embrace of my chair. I'm struck by how far we've come, how different this is from our usual haunts.

"You know," I begin, twirling my fork in the air, "we don't have to slum it at the House of Ramen anymore." Even as I speak, though, I feel a small pang at the thought of leaving behind a piece of our past.

Crystal looks up from her plate, a gentle frown knitting her brows. "I hope we don't change too much, though. I still want takeout from there. Their ramen has seen us through some tough times."

I nod, understanding the sentiment and not surprised that we feel the same way about this rapid change in circumstances. "Of course. We keep what matters, always."

After a few minutes, the server sets down our entrees with

a flourish, and the aroma is intoxicating. But food suddenly seems less important as I notice the hesitancy in Crystal's eyes, a seriousness that wasn't there before.

"Justin," she begins, pausing as if searching for the right words. "There's something I need to tell you." Her hand trembles slightly as she sets down her fork.

"Hey, whatever it is, we can handle it," I assure her. "You can tell me anything, remember?" I reach across the table, offering my hand for support, even as I wonder what this could possibly be about.

She takes a deep breath, steadying herself. "I have bipolar disorder," she confesses, her voice barely above a whisper. "I didn't tell you sooner because… Well, there never seemed to be a good time. And I understand if you want someone without complications like mine."

I sit there for a moment, taking in her words, watching as the weight of her secret lifts and uncertainty takes its place. It's clear how hard this confession has been for her. It must have been equally difficult to carry this knowledge alone for so long.

"Crystal," I say, squeezing her hand, "we do whatever we want, remember? And that includes facing challenges, together. Your disorder doesn't change how I feel about you. Nothing could."

She blinks, eyes glistening, and I hope my words are enough to reassure her. Because in this new world of ours, where dreams are now within our grasp, it's not just the success of EnergiFusion that matters. It's the journey we share and the promise to weather any storm, side by side.

I move my chair closer and slide my arm around her. The warmth of her body seeps into mine as I kiss her softly, a gentle brush of lips. For a moment, we are cocooned in a bubble of intimacy, the murmur of the restaurant fading into insignificance around us.

"Crystal," I whisper against her cheek, "I've known for a while." Her body stiffens in my embrace, so I hold her tighter. "Back when we were driving out from Georgia Tech, I saw the pills in your makeup bag."

The confession hangs between us—my acknowledgment of her fight, the secret she's guarded so closely. The tension remains coiled within her, waiting for rejection or shock, but there's none to give.

"I understand why you didn't tell me sooner," I continue. "But it doesn't change anything. I love you, and I'm here for you. Always."

Her eyes widen, surprise on her features as if she's seeing me for the first time. She lets out a breathy laugh, laced with disbelief and relief. "You were rummaging through my makeup bag?" she teases, a playful accusation that dances in her still-watery eyes.

"Nope," I reply, shaking my head. "I did no such thing. You left it open one morning. I zipped it up and packed it." It's good to see the hint of a smile tugging at the corners of her mouth. The lightness returning to her gaze tells me she believes me—believes in us.

As Crystal's laughter fades, it's as if the world has slowed down, allowing me to take it all in—the success of EnergiFusion, the pride that swells in my chest, and more than anything, my gratitude for the woman sitting with me, her eyes sparkling like stars in an evening sky.

It's strange how life can pivot on a dime. One day you're scrambling for funds, and the next, you're part owner of a game-changing company. I turn my wine glass slowly between my fingers, watching the deep red liquid swirl, thinking about the four of us—me, Austin, Rhys, Theo—owning eighty-five percent of what we've built. The rest is in SHN's hands now, a necessary partnership that comes with its own set of golden handcuffs.

I have my own secret I've been keeping from Crystal. She doesn't actually have a stake in the company. The guys wouldn't budge, so I drew up paperwork to give her a portion of my shares. I couldn't let her dedication, her sacrifices, go unrecognized. Not by me. But since then, I've learned that no matter what the paperwork says, I can't change the ownership of the company without everyone agreeing. So, I'm back to square one. I can't bring myself to go through it all again with the guys, and I don't have any idea how to explain what happened to Crystal, so I'm stuck. Paralyzed, actually. Part of me hopes I can just ride this out and marry Crystal eventually. Then she'll own half of what I own anyway, and it won't matter what the guys think…

"Justin?" Crystal reaches across the table, searching for my hand.

"Sorry," I tell her. "Just got lost in my thoughts for a second there."

"Good thoughts, I hope?" There's a hint of concern in her question.

"Great thoughts," I assure her, and it's the truth. Because no matter the success, the money, or the share of the company, it's her presence in my life that pays the highest dividend.

twenty-five

Crystal

I rub the diamond pendant Justin bought me this weekend and smile as I sort through the papers in front of me. It's one of those rare moments when everything just seems right. Justin and I are solid. He's been nothing but supportive, seeming to understanding the ebbs and flows of my bipolar disorder with a grace that even Dr. McKay commends.

I flip open my technical writing textbook and skim back through the pages of notes I've taken. They're meticulous and detailed, a reflection of how much I'm thriving in this class. In fact, I've enrolled in four classes for the spring semester. I can't wait to dive further into this new career possibility.

With a contented sigh, I stand, stretching my arms above my head. There's a slight shift on the horizon for my responsibilities here at the office, a decision I've mulled over for weeks now. EnergiFusion is going to see a little less of me. I've decided to step back from some of the day to day, but I can't cut ties completely. Being a minority shareholder comes with a sense of duty, and there's no way I'm leaving our accounting in Rhys's unreliable hands. The guy doesn't know the first thing about a profit-and-loss statement. He really drew the short straw when they divided up responsibilities. The only way I sleep at night is knowing that the accountant looks over our books and does all our taxes. The thought of Rhys on his own sends a shudder down my spine.

My phone buzzes with message from Justin—a simple heart emoji, but it's enough to quicken my pulse. He doesn't have to say much; his love is a constant. I type back a smiley face, my digital shorthand for *everything is wonderful*, because, at this moment of time, it genuinely is.

I should make sure the conference room is ready for today's meeting, so I step down the hall to the room I've been setting up. I've laid out the carefully organized packets on the table for each of us and two of SHN's founders. Pride tingles within me as I look at them; these are more than just papers. They represent growth and potential.

I reach out, running a finger along the smooth edges of the presentations, ensuring not a single page is out of place. The list of manufacturing locations is comprehensive, though South San Francisco and San Jose stand out as frontrunners, each with their own set of advantages. It's crucial that we make the right choice, and I'm confident in the groundwork I've prepared.

A soft chime signals Mason and Dillon's arrival from SHN. Their voices precede them, a low murmur of conversation that grows louder as they approach the conference room. This is it, the moment to discuss the future, to share visions and align strategies.

With a deep breath, I scoop up my notepad and step into the hallway to greet them, anticipation coursing through me. I'm ready to dive into the details, to negotiate and articulate the vision I have so clearly in my mind.

But before I can even see them, Rhys's hand lands gently on my shoulder. "We've got this," he says, and there's an apologetic tilt to his smile.

"Excuse me?" My heart skips, and confusion prickles at the back of my neck.

"This meeting's for stakeholders, Crystal. We need to present a united front, and…" His voice trails off, but his meaning is clear.

The color drains from my face. This is supposed to be my meeting too, my input valued, my efforts recognized. He's going to take credit for all the work I did. I take a step back. "But I have a share," I remind him. "When I came back from Mexico, I signed paperwork."

Rhys's expression shifts from polite dismissal to something resembling pity, mingled with confusion. He opens his mouth to speak, but before he can articulate whatever defense he's mustered, Justin appears at the end of the hallway with the guys from SHN.

The sight of him sends a jolt through me as he approaches; his face is ashen, drawn tight in a way that signals bad news. "Crystal," he says, his voice low and urgent. He doesn't wait for a response before gently grasping my arm and guiding me away from the conference room, away from the doorway that separates me from decisions being made about my own future.

The others file into the room, and once we're out of earshot, tucked into the alcove by the water cooler, he hesitates. His eyes search mine, and I see his inner turmoil, though I don't yet understand it. Finally, he exhales sharply, his words coming out in a rush. "I gave you some of my shares," he admits. "I couldn't get the others to agree."

My mouth falls open.

"Because what's mine is yours, Crystal. That's how it should be." He reaches out, as if to offer comfort, but I step back, stung by the revelation.

Betrayal and anger swirl within me as I piece together the implications. The guys… They never saw me as one of them. Not truly. They don't trust me enough to give me a stake in EnergiFusion. Instead, they let Justin carve out a piece of his own claim to keep the peace, to keep me appeased.

"Justin..." My voice cracks, betraying the hurt I'm trying so hard to swallow. "Do they dislike me so much? Was I just...what? Charity to you?"

His face crumples. "No, never charity," he insists, reaching for me again. This time, I don't move away, but I don't lean into his touch either. "You are everything. They just... They can't see past their own egos. I'm sorry, Crystal. I wanted things to be right, so I tried to make sure you had a share the only way I could."

"Wait—what do you mean you tried?" Can it be possible that there's more bad news to come? I wrap my arms around myself, a self-imposed barrier to hold back the onslaught of emotions. "Am I an owner of this company or not?"

Justin looks at the floor. "It turns out what I did isn't legal without the signatures of the others... I'm sorry. I want to fix it, but I still haven't figured out how."

My mouth falls open, and my vision tunnels, going black around the edges.

"Everything will be okay," Justin murmurs, sounding more like he's trying to convince himself. "We'll talk about it tonight, once I get home, all right? We'll figure it out together." His voice is steady, but his eyes plead in a way that suggests he knows the gravity of what he's asking of me—trust, patience, forgiveness where it may not be deserved.

But there's a storm brewing inside me. I turn on my heel and head down the hallway. If I stay, I'll say something I'll regret. Justin just watches as I scoop up my things and leave.

Downstairs, the rideshare app blinks at me, a glaring reminder that I'm retreating. My finger hovers over the *confirm* button, and with a press, my escape is in motion.

As the car rolls away from what once felt like a joint venture, the rideshare will deliver me to the Sullivans', our current home. But it's not *ours* even temporarily, not really. It's *his*, and I'm just a guest cloaked in the illusion of something more that isn't there. The thought stings, so I shift my focus to the screen of my phone, scrolling through listings for Berkeley apartments.

"Somewhere sunny," I whisper to myself, craving light to chase away the shadows. A studio near campus catches my eye. It's smaller, humbler than the apartment we were all sharing, but it will just be me living there, and maybe that's what I need, a space untouched by compromise or false promises.

I ask the car to drop me off as we sit in traffic. Exiting, I'm met with the familiar whoosh and clatter of the BART station. I swipe my transit card at the turnstile. Each click of the rotating bars marks a step away from the life I knew.

The train jostles rhythmically, soothing in its predictability, unlike the upheaval in my head. I ride it to the university, like I've done for months. And I walk into one rental property after another. I survey each apartment with a critical eye, but it's no use. They're all lacking, each one a stark contrast to the comfortable nest Justin and I were planning for our house together. One doesn't have a dishwasher, another doesn't have a washer/dryer, and several have showers so small that my elbows would hit the wall when I washed my hair. These things seem trivial until you've had them. Now, I don't want to live without them.

Finally, I let out a breath and find a bench in the California sun. It offers warmth but no solace. I sit amidst students and street musicians, tears betraying the turmoil within. How did I end up here, trapped between indignation and heartbreak?

"Stupid," I mutter, chastising myself for the anger boiling in my veins. Justin lied, yes, but his pale face flashes in my mind, that tremor in his voice. He was trying to do the right thing, desperate to keep me close, keep me involved, yet keep the peace among his partners. But love shouldn't have to dress up as deceit.

The sun dips lower, and my phone remains silent in my lap. No rescuing calls, no messages of apology, just the feeling of being pushed out echoing in my memory.

Finally, my phone pings.

Teagan: I'm having a shit day. Bubbles for happy hour?

Me: Sure. I'm in Berkeley. I'll be there in 40.

The golden hue of the setting sun reflects off the glass façade of Bubbles by the time I approach. I push open the door, the chill from the air conditioning brushing against my skin like an unexpected shiver. Teagan's already perched elegantly on a high stool at the bar, her posture relaxed but her eyes sharp. She's always been an anchor in the storm, the kind of friend who sees through my brave face.

"Hey," I greet her, feigning a smile.

"Crystal!" She slides off the stool and gives me a quick hug. "You look like you've been through the wringer. Tough day at school?"

"Have you heard?" My throat tightens as I climb onto the stool beside her. "About EnergiFusion, I mean."

"Heard what? That all your hard work is finally paying off?" Teagan waves it off, her tone breezy, yet there's a hint of something more behind her casual demeanor. "I've missed you, you know. You all don't spend any time at the incubator these days. It's been too long since we caught up."

I let out a halfhearted laugh. "Yeah, it's been crazy."

"Best part?" Teagan raises her eyebrows and signals the bartender for two champagne cocktails. "You don't have to deal with greedy shareholders prioritizing money over good business sense."

I nod. Her words are meant to be comforting, a toast to our efforts. But they land heavily in my chest, a reminder of the stake in the company that was never really mine. I accept the flute filled with bubbling liquid gold.

"Cheers," Teagan says, lifting her glass.

"Cheers," I echo, the clink a reminder of my world falling apart.

Her eyes narrow. "What is it?"

The chill of the glass is a stark contrast to the heat rising in my cheeks. My fingers tighten around the stem, anchoring me to the present as I force the words out. "Justin…he said they'd agreed to cut me in, make me part owner. That was the deal when I came back to EnergiFusion after our trip to Mexico." My voice trembles. "But today…I found out that's not true at all. The paperwork I signed… It was a transfer. He tried to give some of his share to me. The other guys didn't agree, didn't know anything about it, and it turns out, without their consent, the transfer wasn't legal. But he never told me."

Teagan's eyes darken, her lips pressed into a thin line. "Crystal, that's just— How could they? After everything you've done? The late nights, the strategies, your brilliant work? It's because of you that they got such great deals from the showcase."

I nod, feeling the sting of tears. "I feel so betrayed, Teagan. Justin says he wants to fix it, but how? It's like I'm not worth being a real part of it at all."

She reaches over to squeeze my hand. "You are worth it, Crystal. More than they'll ever realize. Clearly, Justin knows that."

We sit there, two flutes of champagne between us, and I let myself lean on her strength.

"Look at it this way," she continues, lifting her glass with a determined glint in her eye. "You're in a good position, regardless of their nonsense. You have a fantastic salary now, and you have a man willing to go to great lengths because he loves you."

I take a sip, the bubbles dancing on my tongue as I consider her words. It's hard to see any angle where I come out on top, but Teagan wouldn't say it if she didn't believe it.

"Make them grovel, Crystal," she insists. "They need to realize your worth. And as for Justin…" She pauses, her gaze softening. "Try to see it from his side too. He needed you there, and he wasn't going to let the guys' attitude interfere with that. He's trying to keep the peace, keep everyone working together."

Her advice is the slap in the face I need. Of course. Justin knew I wouldn't come back without a raise and a stake in the company.

"Okay," I whisper. "Okay, I'll try."

"Good," Teagan nods, raising her glass once more. "Now, let's enjoy these cocktails and plot our next move. Because no matter what, Crystal, we're going to come out of this shining."

"Shining," I repeat, clinking glasses with her, a semblance of determination taking root within the chaos of my heart.

twenty-six

Justin

For a long time after the meeting, I trudge down San Francisco streets, the weight of the day's confrontations dragging my steps. The boardroom fiasco plays on loop in my mind; I stood at the center of a storm, defending my decision to the team—Austin, Rhys, Theo, along with Mason and Dillon. Their faces, contorted in frustration, accuse me silently even now. I gave Crystal something that legally I couldn't without their approval. And at the worst possible moment, that left her with nothing. I tried to keep everything together, yet now everyone feels betrayed.

I'm determined to keep pushing on this, though. They have to acknowledge all the work Crystal did that contributed to our success. We wouldn't be here without her. No one has fought for us like Crystal. No one has put in the hours or brought the dedication she has, all for a paycheck that only since the

Automotive Showcase has become respectable. She deserves more than recognition; she deserves a stake. And yes, there's the unspoken truth that she'll own half of everything that's mine soon enough when we marry. California law makes sure of that. But it's more than legal eventualities. It's about respect, about acknowledging her worth as an independent person.

A cold gust sweeps up from the Bay, chilling me, but it's nothing compared to the chill that settled over the conference room when Theo dropped the next bombshell. Turner might leave Velvet Anomaly. And he wants in with EnergiFusion. He has grand plans for us to work together the way we did at Georgia Tech. It's true that he built the first engine powered by our battery, but he sold that concept. So, what does he have to add now? No one seems exactly clear. And Turner is a bit of a wildcard, caught at a crossroads between music and engineering. How long will he stay interested? And what exactly does he want? I'm certainly not giving him a share of the ownership before we agree to give one to Crystal.

I pause at a street corner, waiting for the light to change, battling the twin tides of loyalty and leadership. I love Turner. His support has been unwavering. Yes, he said the right thing that helped us fix our problem that day in the lab, but does that mean we're obligated to bring him in? The light turns green, and I cross, my decision just as uncertain as the flickering street lamps overhead.

Our temporary home awaits, a sanctuary that seems less welcoming tonight. Crystal will be waiting, another confrontation I'm not eager to face. But I have to, and I'll need to beg her to forgive me.

When I arrive, the door shuts behind me, even as Mason's words still ring in my ears. *"Turner wants to build cars, but you're about building batteries."* I shake my head. He's right. Turner's dreams are grand, but they're his own. He can't just waltz into EnergiFusion and expect the red carpet. He needs to understand that he's one among many automakers lining up for our tech. It's not personal; it's business. With that sorted, I feel slightly more settled.

But then Crystal appears as I move through the entryway, her form outlined by the living room lamp. She's wearing a tank top and sleep shorts, but her stance—hands on hips and a scowl on her face—tells me sleep is the last thing on her mind.

"Justin," she says, her voice brimming with hurt and anger, "how could you lie to me?"

I'm already defeated, weighed down by the day's battles, and now this. She's upset, understandably so. The lies sit heavy on my conscience. "Crystal, I…" I trail off, unsure where to start.

"Did you think that would make everything better? That giving me part of your share would suddenly make me feel appreciated?" Her eyes are wells of disappointment.

That's exactly what happened, but it doesn't seem wise to point that out at this moment. "I hate how they've treated you," I tell her, my throat tight. "You should have had their support from the start."

"Because I'm your girlfriend?" There's an edge to her words, a challenge.

"Because you're incredible at what you do," I counter, taking a step closer. "I knew I wanted to marry you the moment you said you'd come to San Francisco with us. Giving you part of my share…it wasn't a ploy. It was because I love you, Crystal."

She scoffs, crossing her arms, but I see something flicker in her eyes. "Marry me? When were you going to tell me I didn't really have any share in the business? I was honest with you. Why didn't you use that as an opportunity to be honest with me?"

"I thought the transfer was going to work, and then once we were married, it wouldn't matter anyway. It was dumb. I see that now, and it was especially dumb since it wasn't even legal. I should have done things differently, but it doesn't change how I feel or what I want to accomplish for you," I say, standing my ground. "I'm not going to let this go with the guys."

"I just want to be seen, Justin. Not as your plus-one, but as me. As Crystal. I may not be an engineer, but EnergiFusion is successful in part because of my contribution."

I nod. Her words sting because they're true, and I have no

idea what's blocking the others from seeing this. We bicker back and forth, the tension between us taut but not unloving. It's the kind of argument that clears the air, where even through the heat of disagreement, there's an undercurrent of care and commitment.

"Look, I didn't do any of this to deceive you, Crystal," I insist, holding her gaze. "I wanted to share what I have with you because I love you, and because I see that you deserve it, even if the others are stubborn in a way I can't understand. As far as I could control things, I wanted to make them right."

Her posture softens for a moment, and I recognize the shift toward resolution. But she's still working through a lot of energy, I can tell. Her anger is a live wire, sparking with every word that clashes between us. And it's not just the fury that catches my attention. It's the passion behind it, a fierce determination I've always admired in her. "You're incredible when you're fired up," I admit, my voice thick with an emotion that isn't frustration.

"Am I?" Her eyes flash, but the edge in her voice smooths as she steps closer, narrowing the chasm between us. "Because I love that you're the one person who's always got my back."

She's right. I do. It's a pull stronger than gravity, this need to support her, to be her unwavering ally. I close the remaining distance, pulling her fiercely against me. Our lips collide in a messy, fierce kiss, teeth nipping and tongues tracing familiar paths with a hunger that's insatiable.

In a sudden surge of energy, I hoist her over my shoulder like she's nothing more than a feather. Her laugh, light and surprised, is music to my ears as I carry her to the solitude of our bedroom. There, I gently lay her on the bed, the anger from before dissipating like mist under the sun.

Crystal peels off her tank top, her movements a dance of defiance and invitation. She shimmies out of her shorts, revealing herself to me in a way that still sets my heart racing, though I've seen her like this countless times. My own clothes fall away as I hurry to join her and have the warmth of her skin against mine.

I lower myself, starting at her feet, my lips tracing a path upwards, worshiping her with every kiss. My hands glide over her, fingertips playing across her skin until they find her breasts. The weight of them fills my palms perfectly, and I knead her nipples, coaxing moans that resonate deep within me.

Beneath me, Crystal moves with a restless energy. Her hips arching to meet my touch, her body speaking volumes in the silent language of desire. The heat between us builds, a tangible thing that threatens to consume us both.

"God, Crystal, you make these sounds…" I murmur against her skin, my voice husky with want. "They go straight through me."

She writhes, and the sight of her like this—unguarded, raw, completely in the moment—ignites something primal within me. "I'm yours, heart and soul," I whisper, seeking her gaze, needing her to understand the depth of my commitment. "Tell me what you want."

Crystal's eyes, dark and urgent, lock onto mine. "I want you," she breathes, her voice heavy with desire. "Now, Justin. Please."

Without further words, I position myself above her, my body responding to the command in her voice. With a gentle but insistent nudge, she slides her legs behind me, an invitation that pulls at every fiber of my being. I ease into her, enveloped by the warmth and softness that is uniquely hers. My breath hitches as sensation floods through me, grounding me in this moment, in this profound intimacy.

"Crystal," I gasp out her name like a prayer, a recognition of everything she represents to me. Home isn't a place; it's right here, within her embrace.

We move together in rhythm, each push and pull knitting us closer, weaving our souls into one tapestry. The night stretches on, a canvas for our passion. As we explore and claim, love becomes an act of defiance against the world outside our sanctuary.

Hours pass until the fervor gives way to tender exhaustion. Her breaths are even and soft, the aftermath of our connection still lingering in the air.

"Justin," she murmurs, pulling me from the edge of sleep.

"I'll stay on at EnergiFusion… But I'm doing it for me. I don't want to rely only on you."

I tighten my hold around her, pressing a kiss to the back of her neck. "I know," I assure her. "And I love that about you."

In the quiet that follows, I recognize that true partnership isn't about possession or dependence. It's about supporting each other's strengths and ambitions. And as sleep claims us, I drift off secure in the knowledge that together, we're unstoppable.

twenty-seven

Crystal

I drag myself across the freshly polished concrete floor of the manufacturing space, the weight of last week's confrontation sitting like lead in my stomach. The guys—Justin, Austin, Rhys, and Theo—are already here, their backs to me as they huddle over a blueprint sprawled across a makeshift table. It's been seven days since our blow up, and even though we've managed to keep things professional, the air still crackles with unspoken tension.

"Good morning," I murmur as I approach, my voice barely a whisper, unsure if I want to shatter the fragile peace that hangs between us.

"Morning, Crystal," they reply in an oddly synchronized chorus, their eyes flicking to mine just long enough to acknowledge my presence before darting away, as if afraid of what might be said in a lingering gaze.

We've pored over leases and plans to bring this new space

to life, a cathedral of innovation where the batteries will soon come into existence. The skeleton of the manufacturing area looms around us, steel beams and dangling wires promising our future.

And then there's the office space. I'm still striving for a shared vision of equality. I've designed five offices, identical in square footage and each with a view. I've spent hours with the blueprints, ensuring that not even a sliver of difference could be detected between the spaces. It's the only way to keep us all on equal footing.

While the ghost of our manufacturing dream is taking shape around us, the reality is that neither it nor the offices will be ready for months. We're moving forward, nonetheless. Fueled by the cash influx from the automakers, we've hired engineers—their résumés stacked neatly in my outbox—and placed orders for robots that will serve as the backbone of our operation. They'll arrive soon, ready to assemble the power sources of tomorrow.

In the meantime, we continue to tinker with the battery's formula, chasing the few elusive percentage points that separate our prototypes from the efficiency of standard lithium and copper batteries powering today's electric vehicles—and that will one day power anything with a battery. It's a gap we're determined to close, a puzzle we're bent on solving. Every day is another step, another chance to push past the frustration of not being there yet.

"Crystal, the order for the robots… Have you confirmed delivery dates?" Justin asks.

"Confirmed and double-checked," I assure him, pulling out the tablet that houses my schedules and charts. "They'll be here as planned."

"Perfect," he says with a nod, and I catch a glimmer of appreciation in his eyes before he refocuses on the task at hand.

We may not have everything figured out, and last week's scars are still fresh, but for now, at least, we stand united in the face of the monumental task ahead. At Justin's urging, Theo, Austin, and Rhys have agreed to allow SHN to mediate our disagreement about company ownership, and I'm hopeful that will help them all see reason. I truly hope we can work something out because as I watch them now—heads bent, minds churning—I know that despite everything, this is where I belong.

A little while later, we assemble in the conference room, and I step up to the front, clutching my summaries like a shield. Justin nods to me, signaling that it's time to bring everyone up to speed on our progress. The walls, still stark and unadorned in our unfinished office space, echo back the sound of shuffling papers and the restless shifting of chairs.

"Okay, let's start with where we are on the buildout," I begin. I scan their faces—Justin's earnest gaze, Austin's impassive scrutiny, Rhys's impatient frown, and Theo's encouraging smile—all waiting for me to lay out the future of our work environment.

As I delve into the details, pointing to the projected images of the new office layout, Rhys interrupts with a question that slices through my carefully laid plans. "Crystal, why are there five offices? And who belongs in each one?" His tone isn't accusatory, but it needles at me all the same.

I pause, taking a deep breath before addressing his query. "There are five offices because there are five of us on staff right now, and as for who sits where, that's something we'll have to figure out together," I say, attempting to keep my response diplomatic. "I've ensured that all the offices are identical in size, and each view is unique. We're partners in this venture, and the space should reflect that."

There's a rustling as the guys shift, exchanging glances. I sense the tension, the unspoken hierarchy they're determined to force on me. But before anyone can press further, Justin starts to speak, likely aiming to smooth things over.

I cut him off, my patience wearing thin. "Justin, I know you don't like to rock the boat," I assert, locking eyes with him. "But I've been here from the start. Just as much as any of you." My fingers grip the edge of the podium, the hard surface grounding me.

I might not have been there when they dreamed up the schematics of our future batteries, but without me, those dreams would be ashes. "I might not be engineering the battery, but I'm the one making it possible for you to do that work. I make sure bills are paid on time and you have the supplies you need. And without me, the Automotive Showcase wouldn't have been nearly as successful." My voice rises, firm and clear, as if volume can underscore my value to them. "Maybe that's taken for granted, but it shouldn't be." I stand taller, with a surge of defiance. "I'm part of this, and it's high time that's recognized."

The room falls silent, save for the faint buzz of fluorescent lights overhead. I meet each of their gazes, challenging them to refute my claim, daring them to overlook my contributions any longer.

I press on, the momentum of my conviction bolstering my courage. "While you guys were buried in your work, I'm the one who found the homes you bought and are moving into now. Who made sure you weren't sleeping on the floor? Who made sure you were fed? Who did the legwork and negotiating for the Automotive Showcase demos? Who handles the logistics that you all conveniently never have time for?"

A collective discomfort settles over them, and only Justin meets my gaze. The rest of their eyes shift as if they're searching for excuses in the corners of the room.

"I'm not here to point fingers, but it's time for some appreciation. Respect." I lock eyes with each of them, ensuring my message finds its mark. "Recognition."

Before anyone can respond, Theo clears his throat, drawing our attention. He stands, his expression serious. "Crystal…" he begins, and I brace myself for more platitudes or empty promises. But what comes next is neither.

"We've talked it over with SHN—Mason and Dillon," he says. "We've all agreed that it's only right…" He pauses, and something like anticipation flickers in his eyes. "The four of us will each give up two percent of our ownership in the company. To you."

The air is electric. I blink, trying to process what he's just offered.

"That will make you a minority owner with just under

seven percent," Justin adds. "And, officially, a founder of this company."

A surge of emotions cascades through me—vindication, shock, pride. I nod, unable to find words just yet.

Austin's jaw clenches, his eyes scanning the faces around him as if searching for an ally in dissent. But there's only Rhys, whose shoulders rise and fall with a resigned sigh.

"It's the right move," Theo says.

He nods at me, but it's Justin who holds my focus. "Long overdue," he echoes.

"Thank you," I say, my voice filling with emotion. "For standing by me."

Justin's smile is small but genuine, a shared secret that speaks of late nights and early mornings, of plans sketched on napkins and dreams spun from the thinnest air. It's proof that love can be woven into the very foundations of ambition and success.

We're not just building offices or manufacturing batteries. We're crafting a legacy. And now, officially, I am a cornerstone of that legacy.

twenty-eight

Justin

The streets are lined with twinkling lights and festive decorations. Two months after we finally made Crystal a stakeholder in EnergiFusion, the holiday season in San Francisco is in full swing. Inside the EnergiFusion factory, workers scurry to put the finishing touches on the new battery-production setup. We're so close to seeing our batteries come off the assembly line. Despite the guys' lengthy holdout, the power-sharing deal SHN outlined for us has taken the pressure off of everyone. The guys now seem to acknowledge how valuable Crystal is, and where they once doubted her abilities, they now look to her for guidance and respect her opinions. With Christmas only ten days away, there's a newfound harmony at work, and I couldn't be more glad.

I pull in at the valet for Van Clef and Arpels on this Friday afternoon, my heart racing with anticipation. Other than our house, I've never spent this much money on anything before, but it's worth it for Crystal. I step out of the car and head inside, excitement and nervousness washing over me.

As I approach the counter, my palms feel sweaty. The sales associate greets me with a smile, and I explain that I'm here to pick up an engagement ring. She nods and asks for my name, then disappears into the back room.

A moment later, she emerges with a small box in her hand. My heart skips a beat as she opens it up, revealing the most beautiful ring I've ever seen. The oval diamond sparkles in the light, flanked by two smaller diamonds on either side.

"Wow," I breathe, reaching out to take it from her. It's heavy and solid in my hand, like my commitment to Crystal.

As I leave the store to pick Crystal up from the office, I'm grateful for Caroline Sullivan's advice. Without her guidance, I might never have found the right ring.

Now, all that's left is to surprise Crystal and ask her to spend the rest of her life with me. I can't wait to see the look on her face. Tonight is going to be very special. And she's not expecting a thing!

I make my way through the heavy traffic, back to the office, and when I arrive, I send her a quick message to let her know I'm waiting downstairs for her. A few minutes later, Crystal settles into the passenger seat of the Suburban, looking exhausted after a long week of work. Her eyes close, and she takes a deep breath as she relaxes into the seat. She's been working hard lately, getting everything ready for the company's move, plus taking a class at Berkeley, and I want to give her a break.

"Hey, babe," I say, reaching over for her hand. "How about we take a little trip this weekend?"

She opens one eye and looks at me skeptically. "What kind of trip?"

"It's a surprise," I say, grinning.

Her eyes widen, and she sits up. "Really? You're serious?"

"Absolutely," I say. "I even packed a bag for you, so you don't have to worry about anything."

"Wow," she says, shaking her head. "Twist my arm. I love

that you knew I needed a break. Thank you." She kisses me on the cheek, lacing our fingers together.

As we drive out of San Francisco, my phone rings, and I answer it without thinking. It's one of the intellectual property lawyers working on the patent for the battery, and I listen carefully as she explains some new developments. The rhythmic thump of the car going over the bridge has Crystal sitting up and looking around, curious about where we're going.

"Thank you. I'll look for that on Monday morning," I say, ending the call and turning to look at Crystal. "Just some work stuff. But we're almost there."

She smiles at me, and warmth spreads through my chest. No matter how busy or stressful things get, she always makes me feel better. And soon, I'll be able to show her just how much she means to me. This weekend is going to be perfect.

When we arrive at the bed and breakfast in Yountville, which is up in Napa Valley, about an hour from San Francisco, Crystal is practically glowing. She spins with her arms open wide as she exits the car. "Thank you for the surprise. This looks lovely."

We go inside to our room, and while she's arranging her things in the bathroom, I put the ring in the safe and pray no one breaks in and takes it. I can't wait to propose tomorrow and spend the rest of my life figuring her out.

Ready for dinner, we walk hand in hand down the block to the restaurant. The night air is crisp and cool. I direct her to enter French Laundry, and we're seated right away. From there, a wonderful evening unfolds. The tasting menu is a slow and relaxing parade of delights, and it allows us to fully enjoy the wine pairings as we dine.

"Is this how it's always going to be?" Crystal asks.

The corners of my mouth turn up. "I hope so."

We eat oysters and caviar, grilled Pacific Shima, and risotto with truffle shavings. From time to time, the need to tell her all about our plans for tomorrow almost overwhelms me, but I hold myself back. I don't want to ruin the surprise.

When we've finished every delicious morsel they've

brought us, we walk back to the bed and breakfast.

"I now understand why people speak so highly of French Laundry," Crystal says. "Dinner was fantastic, and each course was just enough to leave you wanting more, but I'm full."

I agree, but I fall speechless as I turn and take in her beauty. Everything about her captivates me. My heart races as I search for something clever to say, but my mind is drawing a blank. "I love you."

She stops and steps toward me. "I love you too."

Her lips touch mine in a gentle caress, sending a rush of warmth through my body. The world seems to fade away. I hustle us the rest of the way back to our room.

Once the door closes behind us, she reaches for my belt buckle and deftly pulls it open. My cock is immediately hard as my pants drop to the floor at my ankles.

She kneels before me and licks her lips as she stares up.

"God, you're even more beautiful now," I whisper, my voice trembling with desire.

She smiles, her eyes filled with lust and love. Taking me in her mouth, she swirls her tongue around my shaft. I moan softly, unable to control the sensations coursing through me. Her skilled hands work in tandem with her mouth, stroking and squeezing as she pleasures me.

With a low growl, I pull her up and lift her onto the couch, our bodies colliding in a frenzied embrace. Kissing her passionately, I strip off her clothes, desperate to be inside her. Her breath hitches as I slide in, our bodies melding together.

This is my forever home.

I thrust into her, our hearts pounding in sync. She moans softly, her legs wrapping around me, pulling me deeper. The familiar rush of ecstasy builds within me as I look into her eyes. With one final thrust, I explode inside her, our bodies trembling beneath the waves of pleasure.

Afterward, panting and entwined, I pull her close and whisper, "I never want to leave this place."

She kisses me gently, her breath warm on my skin. "Neither do I."

twenty-nine

Crystal

Justin wakes me in the morning when it's still dark, and I stretch my limbs, feeling a pleasant soreness in all the right places. This is a little early to get out of bed on vacation, but he assures me it will be worth it. I have no reason to doubt him. It's been an incredible trip so far, exactly what I needed to get away from the stresses of daily life. Justin has been amazing, anticipating my needs without me even having to ask.

After taking a quick shower, I find him already dressed and sipping coffee. He looks so stylish in his dark blue roll-collar sweater, jeans, and Chelsea boots. I grab my favorite red sweater from my bag and slip on some jeans before we head out. On the way, Justin announces that my next surprise is a hot air balloon ride to watch the sunrise.

When we arrive, people are bustling about with balloons laid out and fans blowing to inflate them. I've never seen anything like it. I can't wait to take flight and watch the sun break the horizon from high up in the sky.

"Isn't this incredible?" Justin says, taking my hand in his.

I nod. We follow the signs to a sectioned-off area where our balloon is waiting. A friendly pilot greets us and gives us some brief instructions.

"Are you ready to fly?" he asks, grinning from ear to ear.

I swallow nervously but nod. I trust Justin, and I know he wouldn't put me in any danger. As we climb into the basket, I realize it's just the two of us and the pilot. Butterflies launch in my stomach.

The burner fires and roars as we lift off slowly from the ground. And then we're floating. In no time, we're hundreds of feet in the air, and the view takes my breath away. The colors of the sunrise are so vibrant, and the acres of vineyards below us are breathtaking. This perspective is different than anything I've experienced before.

"Crystal," Justin says softly, pulling me close. "I need to tell you something."

I turn to look at him, my heart racing. What could he possibly want to say?

"I love you," he whispers. "You mean everything to me. You've been there for me through thick and thin, and I can't imagine my life without you by my side."

Tears prick at the corners of my eyes as he pulls a small box from his pocket. My heart is about to burst.

"Will you make it official and marry me?" he asks, opening the box to reveal a brilliant diamond ring.

Without hesitation, I say yes, throwing my arms around him as we kiss passionately in the basket of the hot air balloon. When the pilot offers his congratulations, I can feel myself blushing. I'd completely forgotten he was there.

For the rest of the trip, Justin and I enjoy the quiet solitude of floating, wrapped in each other's arms. This is a memory I'll store away for the days he leaves his clothes on the bathroom floor. As we begin to descend, we take pictures and send them off to our closest friends and family. The text messages come flooding back with congratulations and well wishes.

When the ride is over, I remain overwhelmed with gratitude for this incredible experience and for Justin, who has shown me what it means to truly love someone. I cannot wait for all that lies ahead for us.

sneak peak

Austin

With a shaving brush, I cover the whiskers on my face in a thick foam. While Mom tells me all about the cherry blossoms blanketing the mall in Washington, D.C., I draw the razor down my cheek, the sound of stubble yielding to the blade harmonizing with Mom's excited chatter over speakerphone. She's detailing her plans for a week packed with social engagements.

"I'm having lunch today with Mitzi Murray. You remember her? She has that adorable daughter who graduated from Yale Law. She's single."

"Where does she live?" I'm guessing either Boston or New York. That's always my Get Out of Jail Free card. I draw the razor down again, focusing on not cutting myself.

"New York, but you could make it work," she counters. "You have a private plane."

"But I work most weekends." I rinse the razor clean.

"I'm also having dinner with Kitty Pittman and her

husband this evening. He's bringing one of the partners in his firm for me to meet." I stop and look down at the phone. "That sounds interesting."

"He's been divorced three times. Nope. But I promise to play nice."

I rid myself of my impending mustache as she goes on to tell me about a carousel of meals, shopping sprees, and drinks near the chic comfort of her Georgetown condo.

"Sounds like you've got a full calendar, Mom," I say, wiping the remnants of shaving cream away.

"Life's too short to waste, honey," she replies. "And these old bones need to keep moving. Besides, those new boutiques aren't going to browse themselves."

Old bones? She's not even sixty. She has more energy than I do. She's not old. I shake my head. We are a country apart, yet in moments like these, she's right here with me. Our bond is woven from years of it being just the two of us.

I look up to assess the outcome of my shave in the mirror. Satisfied, I ask about her health, the weather, anything to keep her talking. Her laughter is a melody, this conversation a wonderful counterpoint to the frenetic pace of EnergiFusion, the startup I'm shepherding toward success with three of my buddies from school—well, and one of their girlfriends now as well. It's not always easy, but in Mom's world, I can do no wrong. Sometimes, we all need a person who sees us that way.

"And how are things at EnergiFusion?" she eventually asks, her tone shifting to one of gentle inquiry, tinged with pride.

"Busy. We're running behind on orders," I admit. It's the truth, and it hangs between us for a moment, a cloud shadowing her sunny disposition.

"Is everything okay, Austin? You know you can tell me anything," she probes, her internal mama bear kicking in, always attuned to the subtlest note of strain in my voice.

"Everything's fine, Mom. Just the usual challenges. You know how it is." I force a lightness into my response, not wanting to pile any worry on her plans. She's been through enough, and my struggles at work are just another set of problems to solve, not burdens for her to shoulder.

"Remember, you got that brilliance from somewhere," she teases, her confidence in me never wavering. "You'll figure it out. You always do."

"Thanks, Mom. I appreciate it." Her belief is a fuel, one that powers me more than she realizes. With a final glance at my reflection, now clean-shaven and ready to face the day, I feel bolstered by her words. Whatever today brings, I'll meet it head on.

"And I believe it. You were the one who figured out the problem with the battery. They had that big, fancy man come in for an exorbitant amount of money, and he did nothing. It was you who figured it out."

"It was the group and your support. You don't give yourself enough credit." I smile, picking the phone up and taking it off speakerphone. "You raised me on your own, and we grew up together. You're the success story here."

Her laughter trickles through the phone, the soundtrack to my life. "I just did what I had to do. And look at you now. You're one of the youngest billionaires on the list."

The pride in her tone is a familiar refrain. She spins tales of our early days with the same enthusiasm she'd recount a blockbuster movie plot—a young single mother, an infant son, the world against them. I've heard this story a thousand times, yet each retelling adds a layer of lore to our family saga. The truth is, she was young. My biological father was young. She wanted to keep me. He didn't. Her parents kicked her out. So she worked hard to provide for both of us. She's the rock star here.

As I exit the bathroom, a sudden percussive banging on the front door jolts me out of nostalgia. Sandrine, my guest last night, is already stretching into Pilates poses at her gym by now, so it can't be her.

"Mom, can you hold on for a second? Someone's at the door." I set the phone on the counter, my mind racing. It has to be someone from the building; the doors all require a key fob to get in. They wouldn't let just anyone up without calling first.

"Be right back, Mom," I call.

I stride toward the door. Who could need me urgently enough to hammer on my door like the police in a drug raid? My bare feet pad against the cool hardwood floor of the loft, my heart keeping time with the knocking. Whoever it is has a message that can't wait.

I look down at myself as I reach the door. My sweatpants hang loose, slung low on my hips in a way that's comfortable but hardly presentable. No matter. It's too early for decorum anyway. Without a shirt, the cool air of the condo raises goose bumps on my skin.

The door swings open, and there she stands—strawberry blonde hair ablaze in the corridor lighting, hand frozen mid-knock. Her eyes travel over me, from my tousled hair down to the edge of my sweats, lingering just a moment too long on the semi I hadn't noticed was pushing against the fabric.

Her cheeks bloom with a fiery shade of crimson, but not for the reasons I initially guess. She doesn't seem embarrassed, not in the slightest. She's downright furious. Words spill from her like water from a burst pipe, fast and relentless, each one sharp enough to cut.

"My parking space!" Her voice is at an octave only dogs can hear, and I'm catching maybe every other syllable. "The noise! And the woman you had over last night—" The accusations fly at me, punctuated by rage. "Parking tickets piling up like it's a game to you! Who do you think you are?"

She pauses long enough for me to respond, but I have no clue what she's talking about.

When I have nothing to offer, she caps her tirade with a final pointed jab. "And for heaven's sake, put on some clothes when you answer your door!"

I blink, taken aback by the ferocity in her petite frame. *Who is she?* A neighbor? I've never seen her before, and I'd remember someone who carries such fire in their voice, someone who can make me feel so defensive without knowing anything about her. "Hey, I—"

But she's not having any of it. My words dissolve into space as she disappears down the hall. The slamming of the stairwell door is her final punctuation, leaving me in a silent hallway with my thoughts scattered like the accusations she's just flung at me. *Crazy*, that's the only word for it. I shake my head, trying to dislodge the bewildering encounter from my mind as I stride back inside.

"Sorry about that, Mom," I say into the phone, the device cool against my flushed skin as I resume our conversation. "Some neighbor with a short fuse."

"Everything okay?" she asks.

"Nothing I can't handle." I return to the bedroom and pull on my designer jeans and a crisp, white shirt. When I catch a glimpse of myself in the mirror, I find myself every inch the executive now, no trace of the morning's chaos visible. "Have a great lunch and don't be too hard on your dinner date. I'll call you tomorrow, okay? Love you."

"Love you too, Austin. Take care of yourself."

I slide my phone into my jeans' back pocket and grab my messenger bag, pausing for a second before I step out the door. The corridor is empty, the only sign of life being the soft hum of the city seeping through the walls. My neighbor Anna's condo remains as still as ever. She's out of town for a while and is the only other person who lives on this floor. Now, there's no evidence of the fiery sprite who visited me earlier. I'd wonder if she was a hallucination if not for the lingering sting of her words.

I lock the door behind me and descend to the garage where my car awaits, a Lamborghini Revuelto, which is a plug-in hybrid with a 6.5L V12 engine. Eventually, I'd like to outfit it with one of our batteries, of course. But it's a sleek machine that was the first thing I bought after EnergiFusion took off. Well, after I bought Mom the condo in Georgetown.

As I navigate through the crowded streets of downtown San Francisco on my way to our offices in South San Francisco, my mind returns to the angry pixie ranting about her parking space. There are four condos in my building, and eight parking spaces. What did she mean? And Sandrine was pretty loud last night. But how would that woman know that? *Where did she come from?* It's just strange.

As I draw closer to the office, I shift my focus to all the things I need to accomplish today. A list begins to form—emails to answer, calls to make, reports to review. They stack one on top of the other. I need space, time to breathe and strategize without interruption. And most of all, I need to shake off whatever that was this morning.

"Please let today be smooth," I mutter to myself, a half-hearted plea to the universe. The traffic inches forward, a sluggish river of metal and exhaust, my only calm before the storm of the day ahead.

After parking my car, I make my way into the building. The revolving doors of EnergiFusion's lobby offer no resistance as I push through, but the usual buzz of the office is missing. Instead, there's a palpable tension that tugs at my nerves. I follow the silence to its source—Justin's office—where a cluster of colleagues is rooted in place.

Their eyes are fixed on the television mounted on the wall, where a column of smoke billows from an electric vehicle engulfed in flames. The ticker on the screen confirms my dread: "EnergiFusion battery implicated in interstate blaze."

The talking head reports the morning's events, and I piece together that the flaming car is in Detroit. Based on the view on the television, it's at an interstate change. It's like watching a nightmare in high-definition. This is the fourth battery fire in the last twelve months, and my stomach tightens into a knot. The onset of a headache pulses behind my eyes.

"Where's Justin?" I ask. Justin Capriotti, Rhys Smalls, Theo Reed, and I founded EnergiFusion at Georgia Tech with our invention of an environmentally friendly electric vehicle battery five years ago. These days Justin is our CEO.

Rhys turns to me, looking worried. "No idea," he says, shaking his head. "But the board wants us—all of us, Justin, Theo, you, and me—to meet later today."

The news settles heavy in my chest. A board meeting without notice can only mean trouble. I rub my temples, trying to quell the throb. Whatever peace I sought earlier this morning has vanished, burned away like the wreckage on the TV screen.

I navigate through the crowd and out to my office. Justin's absence gnaws at me, the void he's left feels ominous after the accusations we exchanged on Friday.

"Hey, Austin," Rhys calls, breaking into my thoughts. "Got a minute later today?"

I hesitate, an excuse perched on my lips. But Rhys looks earnest, his eyes searching. I nod. "Sure, I can make some time."

"Great," he says. "After the board meeting? We could grab drinks, talk things over?"

"Sounds good." I agree, though my mind reels with the list of tasks ahead. The lab beckons, a sanctuary where I might find answers. But first, there's the smoldering aftermath on the screen and the board's impending inquisition.

"Thanks, man." Rhys turns back to the television.

My gaze lingers on the door to our offices, feeling the pull of responsibilities beyond this room. Justin is out there somewhere, probably nursing the sting of our last confrontation last Friday. Scattered—that's what he's been lately, like a jigsaw puzzle with pieces missing. And now, with the board's sudden interest, it feels like we're on the edge of a precipice.

Swallowing hard against the building pressure in my skull, I continue toward my office. I need to prepare for whatever's coming next.

books by ainsley st claire

Venture Capitalist Series
Forbidden (Emerson & Dillon)
Promise (Sara & Trey)
Desire (Hadlee & Cameron)
Temptation (Greer & Andy)
Obsession (Cynthia & Todd)
Flawless (Constance & Parker)
Longing (Isabella & Christopher)
Enchanted (Quinn & William)
Fascination (Caroline & Mason)

Tech Billionaires Series
House of Cards (Maggie & Jonnie)
Royally Flushed (Corrine & Jackson)
Sleight of Hand (Tinsley & Landon)
Running Hot (Marci & Walker)
Showdown (Lilly & Nate)

Stiletto Sisters
Bubbles with Brunch (Mia & Axel)
Martini Lunch (Elena & Josh)
Happy Hour (Ryder & Logan)
After Dinner Drinks (Claire & Morgan)

Clear Security Holidays
Gifted (Kate & Jim)
Unwrapped (Fiona & Bash)
Merry and Bright (Grace & Vincent)
Naughty and Nice (Anna & Clay)
Secret Santa (Cora & Beckett)

Paper Billionaires
The Set Up (Scarlett & Grayson)
Indebted (Harper & Jaxson)

Vanquished (Shay & Nick)

Billionaire Secrets

Rival CEO (Crystal & Justin)

Bossy CEO (Danica & Austin)

Printed in Great Britain
by Amazon

46188860R00129